Juniper Cottage

Juniper Cottage

and other stories

Moosa Raza

Vitasta

Published by
Renu Kaul Verma
Vitasta Publishing Pvt Ltd
2/15, Ansari Road, Daryaganj
New Delhi - 110 002
info@vitastapublishing.com

ISBN: 978-93-90961-51-1

First Edition 2022
MRP ₹395

This novel is entirely a work of fiction. Names, characters, events and incidents are entirely imaginary. Reference to real places, actual regions, institutions or community practices has been made in a fictitious manner. Any resemblance to actual persons, living or dead or actual events is purely coincidental.

Edited by Veena Batra
Typeset & Cover Design by Somesh Kumar Mishra
Printed by Vikas Computer and Printers, New Delhi

This book is dedicated
to my children

contents

Acknowledgement

This book would not have seen the light of day but for the efforts of my son Jafar, who repeatedly went through every story, especially every non-English word and the translatations. A large part of the credit goes to my editor, Veena Batra, who went through every sentence, every comma and every full stop "to give to airy nothing a local habitation and a name" (Shakespeare). My daughters Shahla, Gazala and Maliha read my writings as they came off the home printer. They made many suggestions "some helpful and some otherwise".

One Measure of Rice

It took seven days for Karim's body to be discovered. He had been hanged with a strong pleated jute rope from one of the thick branches of the malgova tree. Zain was very fond of that luscious variety of mangoes, large, juicy and sweet. Green outside but ripe inside. But for long after he had seen Karim's body swinging from the tree, Zain could not bring himself to touch the fruit. For years, he continued to detect a faint putrid smell in every malgova mango. In fact, it was the strong repelling odour of rotting flesh that led to the discovery of Karim's body, that and the vultures. Otherwise, Karim would have continued to swing amongst the dense foliage of the mango tree for God knows how much longer, perhaps until the fruits had ripened and were ready to be taken down. When they took down the body, or whatever was left of it, it was well on its way to falling apart. They had to carry a gunny sack up into the high branches, bag the body in it and then lower it to the ground gently. Zain was there, watching the *padials* (labourers) climb up and hearing their excited shouts and raucous cries as they tried to fend off the iridescent cloud of blue bottles that buzzed around the decaying body. The stench had hit the nostrils of the assembled curious like a blast as the remains were laid on the ground, even though enclosed in the bag. Zain attempted to get closer, impelled by his strong curiosity but the horrible sight of Karim, with most of his flesh missing, and the strong putrid odour drove him away to a respectable distance. He hovered there, balanced between curiosity, sadness and repulsion.

Zain had gone to the mango grove to play. The cool shade of the grove and the attraction of the green fruits in season with the sweet and sour taste had made it a favourite haunt of the under-tens. Zain was not immune to the atavistic urge of all children, the instinct to stoop and pick up a stone the moment the eye spotted a fruit on the tree. The watchman had, of course, removed all bricks and stones from the vicinity of the orchard, but Zain and his friends brought their own supply of missiles. Generally, the orchard would be deserted, except in the mango season when the watchman and lessees, if any, would make an occasional surprise visit. This time, however, he saw a crowd in the grove and caution with curiosity had made him creep up to them. There was a motley group of his respectable elders staring up into the branches of the malgova tree. Zain followed their gaze. Some of his friends bold enough to accompany him had come, but kept their distance. The stench acted as an invisible barrier. Up in the branches, Zain noticed several *padials*, most of them holding their noses, gathered around some shapeless form hanging from one of the larger branches. He came to know that it was Karim only when a *padial* had shouted down the name from the top of the tree. For a moment, he did not believe he had heard right. He could not believe that this thing which had been brought down in a gunny sack was Karim.

Zain had known Karim as a 22 or 23 years old jovial, lively and active youth, full of the joy of life. To believe that Karim had died, that too in such a gruesome way was too much for his young mind. How could a man like Karim, so good, so kind, so helpful die like this and hang from the branches of a mango tree? No! No! There must be some mistake, Zain thought.

As he stood staring at the gunny sack, nobody, of course, thought of summoning the police. The police were not a great favourite in the village of Minambur. Moreover, the nearest police station was roughly three miles away. Nobody was willing to volunteer to go to

Gingee, the nearest town with a police station, and get involved in a police matter. Zain learnt much later in life that the police were never favoured by anyone anywhere in the world. Moreover, Karim was after all only a servant employed by Masood, the village leper. Servants in Minambur, especially of lepers, hardly ever came to the attention of the gentry. Masood himself was not held in high regard in the village. With his caved-in nose, caved-in sunken eyes, swollen lips and missing eyebrows, he was quite a frightening phantom to the children. When he spoke, his voice came out as a loud hoarse whisper. The sound made him appear even more sinister. Every time Zain passed him on the street, he gave Masood a wide berth. "Don't ever go near him," Nanajan, his grandfather, had warned him several times. "He is a *jazami* (leper) and *jazam* is a most horrible contagious disease. When Allah wanted to test the Prophet Ayyub, he afflicted him with *jazam.* His friends and even his wife and sons abandoned him. But Masood has brought it on himself. It comes from eating beef. Masood ate nothing but beef. Beef generates too much heat in the body. It then erupts into *jazam."*

Along with the rest of the navayatas of Minambur, Nanajan held the strong belief that eating beef caused leprosy. While, therefore, mutton was priced at two rupees a seer, beef could be had, if at all a cow was occasionally slaughtered clandestinely, at a quarter that price. The

Palliampetans, of course, ate beef without inhibition. Occurrence of leprosy among them was not much more than in the rest of the village but it was an added reason for the navayatas to avoid close contact with them.

Zain was not alone in avoiding Masood. Most people in the village did. Nobody would ever touch anything that Masood had touched. It was well known that leprosy was a highly contagious disease. If you even so much as tasted anything touched by a leper, you would see your fingers curling up the next day. Some believed that even touching a *jazami*, or his clothes or anything touched by him would immediately result in infecting you. Masood himself knew where he stood in this regard. He rarely touched anything, for he had no fingers. He had only stumps for hands which he always held close to his chest He rarely came into close contact with anyone except his wife and his grown-up sons. He knew how people felt about him and so kept his distance. Masood, however, could not be totally ostracised. He was, after all, a navayata. Had he not been a member of that elite village clan, he would have been unceremoniously drummed out of Minambur long ago. Masood had too many relatives in the village to be subjected to that treatment. Moreover, he owned land and a couple of houses in the village. Also, he had obliged many of his clan whenever any dirty chores had to be performed so people did maintain limited social contact with him.

He was reluctantly invited to all marriages and other feasts; that could not be avoided without endangering tribal traditions. The lukewarm invitation was extended at the last minute with the unvoiced hope that he would take the hint and not attend. On occasions when he refused to take the hint he would come to the marriage in his check-patterned dhoti and old shirt open at the neck showing his dirty undervest. His rolled up sleeves would reveal the large nodules of leprosy on his wrists. He flaunted his misshapen body perhaps in defiance of a society which ostracised him. A separate plate and glass were kept aside for him which would be quietly thrown away after he had eaten from it. He was rarely invited to a friendly meal at any home. While he could sometimes call on friends and relatives in their houses, the mosque was off-limits to him. For in the mosque, he would have had to perform his ritual ablutions in the open *hauz*, washing his hands, feet and face there. That would have polluted the entire water body of the tank. The whole body of water would have had to be emptied, the large tank cleaned and refilled.

Masood's sons, too, because of their association with him, were not very popular with the other villagers. Living in the same house, it was as though they too carried the taint of leprosy. Someday, people said, sooner or later, they too would fall victim to the disease. And quite probably, they already carried the contamination in their bodies which would erupt anytime.

Living an insulated life had affected Masood's character. He looked at the world with a warped eye. Since the villagers did not like him, he felt no obligation to be pleasant to them. He was gruff with his equals and harsh with those below him. Leprosy had affected his vocal chords. He always spoke in a hoarse voice, as though he was suffering from a perpetual cold. Even his sons had developed this warped mindset. Like their father, they too remained aloof from the navayata society. Their acerbic tongue and uncivil language did not endear them to their already unsympathetic clansmen. Any servant of Masood's too attracted little attention from the villagers. Did he not belong to Masood's household? Who knew what corruption he had acquired from Masood?

So, when Karim's body was discovered, nobody thought of informing the far away police. A leper's menial did not deserve such official attention, the village elders believed. Informing the police also meant inviting a pack of hungry wolves to dinner. They had voracious appetites, those policemen, and sharper claws. The prowling police would certainly rope in the innocent informant also as a prime witness. That meant repeated visits to Gingee at one's own cost. The police never compensated either the travel cost or the wasted day in the court. It was safer to inform the Village Munsif; then the assembly could wash their hands of it. It was the VM's headache to summon the police, if he suspected any foul play. But in the case of Karim's death, there was no breath of suspicion; at least no one voiced any. It was clearly a suicide, most said. It *could* be suicide, some averred.

"But if it is suicide, how come he chose the highest branch and the thickest foliage to hang himself from," Bashirjan asked.

Bashirjan was the Doubting Thomas of the village and was endowed with a mind that suspected everyone and everything. By asking inconvenient questions at most inappropriate times, he planted doubts in the minds of otherwise simple folks. "Of course, he would choose that," said Hujjat al Kekdi. "What else would he do? Would he commit suicide at the *khoot* (village crossroads)? "

Hujjat al Kekdi always took the contrary view on principle. It gave him an opportunity to argue and demonstrate his forensic skills. "Moreover, he was merely a servant of Masood. So, why are we discussing his death so seriously standing here in the sun?" That was the clinching argument as far as the Quibbling Crab was concerned. He was named the quibbling crab because of his habit of arguing on any or every question whether the issue warranted it or not. And like a crab, once his argumentative claws pierced some issue, they would never come off. So, in the end, the group of senior citizens that had assembled around Karim's dead body decided to summon Masood the employer and leave it to his discretion to decide what to do next. After all, Karim was *his* servant and it was for the master to take responsibility for his servitors.

Masood lumbered in half an hour later huffing and puffing. Even walking a short distance, he always huffed and puffed. He was in his dirty checked lungi and unwashed undervest as usual. The loss of his toes made him walk with a rolling gait. He reminded Zain of the brown bears in the Accharpakkam forest coming down the hillside. As soon as he was noticed wobbling towards the mango grove and before he could reach close enough, the crowd melted away in ones and twos. He smelled horribly of rancid sweat. Only Bashirjan, Hujjat and a couple of other intrepid souls stayed back, braving the sun and the stench, to watch Masood's reactions. Even they drew back to give Masood a wide passage. "The fellow is dead, is he?" Masood said in his hoarse whisper glancing indifferently at the gunny sack. He peered near-sightedly at the remains, as though he suspected Karim would get up any moment to reclaim his life. "He was a good for nothing *kamchor*," Masood spat out the expletive like a wad of chewed tobacco. He believed that all his servants were malingerers and never worked a day's worth of wages. Karim must have heard Masood calling him a malingerer many times in his life, but perhaps he had never expected to be accused posthumously.

Masood enjoyed the not too uncommon reputation of being a harsh and cruel master to his servants. In fact, he revelled in it. "My servants tremble when they hear my voice," he was wont to boast. There were many landlords who agreed with him about the right way to treat servants. "*The footwear should be kept on the feet*", was a popular saying in the village. "*It should never be borne on the head*". It was known that Masood would flog his serfs mercilessly at the slightest provocation. He had no fingers to hold a whip so his sons would do the thrashing at his behest. Several servants who laboured on his paddy fields never returned for work after a sound thrashing. They simply disappeared. It was rumoured that they had run away to Penang across the seas. In the days before India became independent, the rubber plantations of Malaya required labourers. So, the British encouraged the farm workers from South India to migrate to Penang and Rangoon. Since these labourers were not from the Brahmin caste, they never lost their caste by going overseas. Considering that Burma and Malaya did attract many labourers, it was not unlikely that Masood's disgruntled *padials* too went there.

Many a *Padial* had gone abroad abandoning his wife and children. Some had gone to improve their fortunes; others because they could not stand the wrath of their vindictive masters. But only a few had ever returned. Their families cowering in their miserable huts in Kavarai and Shittanpoondi always lived in hope. They ultimately approached the very landlords who had driven away the farm-workers. If the absconder had left a nubile daughter behind, the landlord would employ the family for household work. The young woman, of course, would service the landlord whenever he desired, much to the consternation and jealous anger of the noble lady of the house. This was the first time a servant had hanged himself in the village, leaving no wife and children behind him.

"When did you miss Karim?" Bashirjan asked waving his hand in the air questioningly. It was rather forward of Bashirjan to ask such a question of Masood. Masood could have replied that it was none of his business, of course. In Minambur, however, everyone's business was everybody else's too. The expectant expression on the faces of the onlookers especially on the face of the quibbling crab to hear Masood's response was proof of that. It *was* a bit strange that while Karim had not reported for work for three days, Masood had made no enquiries about his missing servant. "I never missed that *haramzada,*" Masood said looking down at the gunny sack. "I thought the bastard had run away to Penang. Good riddance too." That seemed a reasonable explanation and it satisfied the curiosity of the listeners. Even if some still had lurking doubts about Karim's suicide, they remained silent, not wanting to establish uncomfortable precedents by asking masters to explain the whereabouts of their servants.

"What do you want to do with the body?" Samad Sab asked, coming to the main issue. The body was developing a higher and higher level of putrefaction and needed to be buried as early as possible. And who could take up that responsibility but the former employer. "Do with it? Why would I have anything to do with it? It should be given to his mother. She would do whatever needs to be done." After all, what were mothers for his tone seemed to imply, if not to take care of their dead sons? As far as Masood was concerned, he was not Karim's keeper. Had he had any hands, he would have washed them there and then.

As soon as Masood walked away from the gruesome scene, the Quibbling Crab sidled back into the situation and sent someone to inform the Village Munsif. Zain continued to hover a little upwind of the dead Karim and watched the situation avidly. So far nobody had noticed his lurking presence. If they had noticed him, some officious elder would have shooed him away, on the pretext that children should not loiter near dead bodies, especially of suspected suicides. There were a number of superstitions surrounding suicides. Often, the Qazi Saheb was hard put to ensure that such bodies were given the proper ritual bath and buried with due ceremony and prayers in the village cemetery. Under pressure from the superstitious village elders, the body was often buried in a far corner of the graveyard, away from other graves, nor was the spot regularly visited by any relatives or mourners. As soon as Zain heard that the Village Munsif was to be summoned, he knew the game was up. If his grandpa saw him anywhere in the vicinity of mango garden, he was sure to be in trouble. It was well known that the souls of those who committed suicide hovered over their dead bodies for long, reluctant to leave the habitations from which they had been so violently parted prematurely. If they found any child nearby, they then *shadowed* the child, perhaps in the hope of taking over his body. Zain knew that as his grandmother had told him many tales of the children whose bodies were taken over by ghosts of suicides and who had spoken of strange things in adult voices, and others who had died violently.

"You would not remember, Zain, that Mukaddam had committed suicide by hanging himself in his own bedroom from the beam. You were only two years old at that time," Nanijan had told Zain.

"Why did he commit suicide?" Zain had asked. Nanijan had remained silent for quite some time debating whether a seven-year-old should be told the facts of life. Perhaps, she thought, being a curious brat who read all those large Urdu books of his grandfather, he would eventually learn the harshness of the world he lived in.

"He hanged himself because Fatma, his wife, had run away to Cuddalore with Hakim Khan," she had said.

"Then what happened?"

"His ghost haunted the village for a long time in search of a young body. Finally, he caught the young son of Shajan, I forget his name. That poor boy went mad. He would get up in the middle of the night shouting 'Fatma, Fatma'. His father took him to the Mustafa Shah Qadri's mausoleum. Your grandfather gave him permission to stay in the *mandap*. He had to be given a daily dip in the tank behind the mausoleum. Shajan had to feed the poor boy for forty days before the ghost left him."

So, Zain decided to retreat, rather reluctantly. Even though he had liked Karim in life, he had no desire to let Karim's ghost take over his body.

While returning home he saw several people making a beeline for the mango orchard. Many of the octogenarians who hung around the street corner to discuss such weighty and exciting matters as the enormous price that Waheed paid for his buffalo, or Amirjan got for his black jaggery, found something even more exciting in dissecting Karim's death. Zain was very unhappy at having to leave the scene at such a crucial juncture. The moment he entered the courtyard of his house, he was spotted by his aunt. "Where are you coming from? I have been searching for you all morning," his aunt who had no children of her own complained mildly. Poor dear, she was too fond of Zain to ever rebuke him, and Zain took full advantage of it to play truant.

"I had gone to the Khan Sab's mango garden where

Karim was found hanging." Zain rarely revealed where he had been loafing around but his candour this time was for effect. He wanted to show off his knowledge and shock Amanna in the bargain. He thought he was bringing news of great import.

"Oh yes, I heard about the suicide. Dadabhoy has gone there," his aunt said, robbing Zain of his glory. She called her father, the Village Munsif, Dadabhoy and that is what everyone in the village called him

"If you ask me, it's that *jazami* who did it." Grandma made the weighty pronouncement from the veranda. "Suicide, my foot! I don't believe a word of it. Masood was always beating up his servants. May Allah consign him to hell. Karim was such a nice boy, so young and so full of life, why would he go and commit suicide? Of course he was poor. Masood paid him so little, he was starving half the time, he and his mother." Nanijan's swing was creaking agitatedly. Grandma had the habit of leaping to conclusions on the flimsiest evidence. This time, her dislike of 'that leper' Masood was evidence enough to accuse him of murder.

"But no one kills himself just because he doesn't have enough to eat," murmured Amanna.

"You take my word for it, it's Masood who has done it," Nanijan asserted as though she had been an eye-witness to the murder.

"Why would he kill the boy?" Amanna asked in a tone

that had a sceptic note. "He usually beats his servants and throws them out. He has never killed anyone before; at least there was never any scandal."

"Maybe he lost control this time," speculated Bajijan.

"Or maybe Karim had been bitten by one of the cobras which Masood was always making him catch in the fields," Bapu surmised without realising that cobra victims didn't go about climbing trees and hanging themselves for a cure. Cooked cobra meat was believed to be one of the cures for leprosy and being bitten by a cobra was known to be an even more efficacious remedy. But even a cobra refused to bite a leper however much it was provoked. Stories abounded that Masood had handled many a cobra without ever being bitten by one. Of course, Karim caught cobras for Masood, but Bapu's surmise about Karim's suicide did not appeal to Zain.

Zain recalled that it was a cobra which had brought him and Karim together. On one of their picnics to Mustafa Roza in Shittanpoondi, Zain had gone wandering off, away from the stone *mandapam* where the family bivouacked into the vast palmyra grove owned by his grandpa a little distance away, beyond the water pond.

There were several clumps of palmyra trees scattered around the periphery of the land that formed part of his grandfather's *jagir*. The dilapidated mausoleum with its white painted dome was perched ten feet above the ground with eight or ten weathered stone steps leading up to the plinth and to the narrow entrance of the grave of the saint. It was the central attraction of the land. Every time the family visited the saint's tomb, they would carry some flowers and some incense sticks up into the vault where the saint lay at repose, light the incense sticks and spread the flowers, and then invoke his protection for themselves and for the village as a whole.

Zain had been forbidden from wandering off too far from the adjacent ancient stone pavilion, and especially prohibited from entering any palmyra grove, for it was known that such groves were infested by snakes of various kinds—cobras, both black and brown, king cobras, kraits, vipers, green tree snakes etc. Moreover, the *nandetars,* the large sandal scorpions, black, with claws the size of large crab claws and tails with bulbous black stings, lurked behind the bark of the palmyra tree. Many an unwary *padial* who had climbed up the palm, without first making sure that the peeling bark harboured no *nandetars*, had been bitten by these monsters. Luckily, they were not as poisonous as the smaller red variety. So, the *padials* survived the sting, but suffered deep painful pangs.

It was the taboo put on the palmyra groves that always attracted Zain to enter them. He could no more resist the lure of the forbidden tree than his first ancestor. And like her, having entered the grove he found himself regretting the act. The floor was strewn with large dead palmyra leaves and decaying smelly fruits, which were exuding a sweetish-sour acidic odour. He had advanced cautiously crunching the dry leaves underfoot. Suddenly, someone from behind him gripped his shoulder. He was pulled back with a violent jerk. He had looked up to see a fair-complexioned young man, tall and well-proportioned, who was carrying a long staff in his left hand, his right gripping Zain's shoulder. He was wearing a frayed shirt and a check lungi, its hem turned up and tied below his waist. "Ssh...ssh," said the young man, before the surprised Zain could utter a word. "Look there, right in front of you," said the youth. Zain's eyes turned involuntarily to where the young man was pointing with his staff. At first, he had seen nothing but a heap of dried fan-shaped palmyra leaves, shed by the trees long ago, covered by brown matted bark, but then, he observed something moving amongst the leaves. It was the swaying movement that betrayed the presence of a large cobra, its hood fully extended, half its body off the ground, which was watching them intently with black beady eyes from among the leaves. Zain had drawn a sharp breath. Had he advanced a few steps more, he would have certainly trodden on the snake.

Zain was not afraid of snakes, having had passing acquaintance with many species that lived in his own backyard, but he had no desire to be bitten by one, especially a cobra as large as this one. Before reaching all of seven years, he had seen death by bullets, drowning, house collapses, etc. but death by snakebite was something else. Anyone who died by snakebite, he was convinced, died a little more certainly than by other means. So, the sight of the gently swaying cobra, hardly six feet away, did raise goose bumps on him. "Get back, get back," whispered the young man, his hand exerting a gentle pressure on Zain's shoulder. Zain did not require any further urgings and he drew back a dozen steps keeping a wary eye on the swaying snake. He stopped there to watch where the snake would go. With the staff extended, his saviour had advanced boldly on the serpent. The audacity of the advance had surprised Zain no end. Obviously, it was no less of a surprise for the cobra. It had not expected any such aggressive behaviour on the part of a human. Zain was sure that in nine out of ten such encounters, the humans had slunk away ignominiously from the encounter, leaving the cobra the master of the field. The snake, realising that this time he had met his match, conceded victory and drew back.

Quietly, it lowered its hood and tried to slither away in the undergrowth, but the young man would have none of it. With an agile leap he placed one end of the staff on the neck of the cobra, just where its head joined the long undulating shiny body. The cobra was effectively pinned down. Its body writhed this way and that, attempting to extricate itself from the stranglehold. It wrapped itself round the staff, using its leverage to struggle free. Before it could accomplish any part of its purpose, the young man had stooped down and gripped the snake expertly at the spot where the staff had held it pinned, and picked it up. Zain saw that it was more than six feet long. He had never seen such a large cobra, though even larger rat snakes were often found in his backyard. It was still struggling, now wrapping itself around its captor's arm, its gaping fangs dripping with venom. Then the young man unslung a jute bag from his shoulder and gently pushed first the body, and then the head of the cobra into it. With a sharp jerk, he withdrew his hand before the angry, hissing snake could strike back. Tying the neck with a string, he slung the bulging bag, which was clearly showing the struggles of the angry snake inside, onto his shoulders. Then he turned to Zain. "Now let us go back. I have already caught three cobras today. That should last Masood for a week."

"Who are you?" Zain had asked him, the young man who went about catching and bagging live cobras with such dexterity.

"My name is Karim," the young man had replied. "You don't know me but I know you. You are Zain, Dadabhoy's grandson." Zain was not surprised. Being the grandson of the village munsif did bring a certain amount of recognition. Sometimes it was useful, but most times it invited envious comments.

"What do you catch snakes for?" Zain's curiosity at this strange pastime of the young man had not abated.

"Because I work for Masood. You know he suffers from leprosy. The *hakims* have told him that he should eat cobra meat three times a week. So, I have to catch three cobras every week for him."

"Isn't it dangerous? What if you get bitten?" Zain had asked apprehensively. Karim smiled ruefully. "In the beginning it was risky. Once or twice I almost got bitten, and to save myself I had to kill the snake. A dead snake was no good for Masood. So, I had to throw it away."

Karim's matter of fact tone had impressed Zain. "Then I watched the Irulas catch snakes and learnt the technique from them." The Irulas were the native tribals who made a living catching snakes from the suburban houses and farms to make them safe for living. Later, the Irulas learnt that there was a demand for poisonous snakes as the laboratory manufactured antidote out of the poison. They sold the snakes to the laboratories and made some money out of the hazardous job.

As they were walking back to the *mandapam,* Zain had discovered that Karim was a lively young man unfazed by the hazardous labour he had to put in for Masood, even risking his life for him.

"That is all nonsense," Nanajan had told him later. "Neither the cobra's flesh nor the cobra's poison cures leprosy. There is no cure for leprosy. Some village quack has told that to Masood and in his desperation, he risks the life of his servants to catch cobras!"

Often, Karim had told Zain that Masood had got him thrashed by his sons for some minor mistake or for not getting more snakes. He could not even change masters, for Masood would never let go a *padial* of his. A *padial* was almost a slave. Moreover, who would employ him, having worked for a leper? Would not they suspect that he too carried the germs around with him? So, Karim had never minded the occasional beatings he got. He had no relatives except for an old mother with whom he lived in a thatched hut on the outskirts of the village.

Listening to the woes of Karim, they had reached the *mandapam* where the rest of the family had been camping. Zain's long absence had created a commotion. *Padials* had been sent hither and thither to search for him. His aunt had even convinced herself that he must have fallen into the deep pond by the side of the mausoleum and drowned. Some p*adials* were already churning the muddy waters, searching for his body. So, when he walked in nonchalantly with Karim by his side, everybody was too relieved to rebuke him.

"This is Karim," Zain told Amanna. "He saved my life from a cobra. It was more than six feet long." If Zain hadn't been conscious of the wriggling evidence in the bag slung across Karim's shoulder, he would have made it twelve feet. Everybody thanked Karim. The impression that he had practically pulled Zain out of the jaws of a dragon cobra had endeared Karim to everybody in the family. Thereafter, Karim became a welcome visitor to the house. Sometimes, he brought his old mother along. Whenever they came, Amanna would feed them with whatever was available in the house. He also became a supplier of the various leaves, roots and berries that Amanna needed to make simple, traditional Unani remedies for the various illnesses the villagers and their children suffered. Karim, in the course of his search for snakes, came across such botanical wealth—the fragrant *hulayd* leaf, so effective in the treatment of headaches, Dog's Tongue Leaf, Cow's tongue, Long Leaf, Broad Leaf, Sweet stick, etc. He had learnt under Amanna's guidance to recognise these medicinal plants which grew wild in the forests. Zain and Karim became good friends. Karim took Zain on many of his forays into the forest, though Zain kept a safe distance whenever Karim spotted a cobra and went to catch it. These outings were kept hidden from his aunt and grandma. They would have gone into a frenzy had they learnt of his wanderings and would have broken up his friendship with Karim. However, Karim's visits were not as frequent as Zain would have liked for Masood allowed him little leisure to indulge in the luxury of playing with children.

Zain recalled all this as he sat and grieved with his aunt and grandmother at Karim's untimely death. They were all deeply affected. Zain believed his grandma was right about who had killed Karim. He was convinced that Masood had got him killed. He hoped Nanajan, with all his wisdom would discover the truth. He waited for his grandpa's return impatiently.

Nanajan came home a couple of hours later. His red face was proof that he had been standing in the sun for a long time. He went straight to the water pot in the corner, drew out a gurgling pail full and splashed his shaven pate and face with the cool water. Everyone waited with bated breath for him to settle down, holding in check their bubbling curiosity to know more about Karim's death.

"It seems to be suicide," Nanajan announced in an unsure voice, sensing the expectant silence of his family members.

"There you go," burst out Nanijan, accusingly. "I knew it. I knew that is what you would say. I tell you it is Masood who has killed that poor boy but you would support that good-for-nothing leper just because he is a navayata." Nanijan never missed an opportunity to refer tauntingly to what she believed was her husband's misplaced loyalty to his clan though she herself belonged to it. But since her family came from another village, the navayatas of her husband's village were fair game. "You know very well who killed Karim but you refuse to believe it. Why don't you call the police? Why are you afraid of calling the police?"

"Keep quiet, woman," said Nanajan, exasperated at this unwarranted accusation. Even though he took pride in being a navayata, he resented any allegation that he would favour someone on that score alone. "There is no proof that Karim was murdered. If he was hanged, it would have taken several strong men to have carried him up that tall mango tree. Masood himself couldn't do it, you know he has no hands," said Nanajan.

"Allah took away his hands knowingly. He would have done even more evil if he had them, but his sons and his *padials* have enough strong hands to do his dirty work," persisted Nanijan. "Those rascals are all as cruel as he is," she continued, adding "*Baap par poot, zaat par ghoda, bahut nahin to thoda thoda*". Nanajan ignored the saying. He was least interested at the moment in being reminded that sons inherited their fathers' traits and horses demonstrated their breed even if not fully, at least in some respects.

"Just because they are all rascals, I cannot charge them with murder," Nanajan protested. "There has to be proof before even making any such accusation."

"You could at least call the police," she repeated helpfully. "They would come and make enquiries. Then the truth will be known."

"Enquiry about what?" Nanajan wanted to know. "This boy goes and hangs himself. There is no prima facie evidence of a crime. What is there to enquire about it? Why can't you let him rest in peace? You want to go on a wild goose chase. You want me to call in the police just because you don't like Masood. I am not going to do anything like that just to oblige your prejudices." Having said that, Nanajan shook his scarf, wrapped it around his head in lieu of the elaborate turban and walked out. His gesture made it clear that he had no desire to stay and debate with his wife on the suspected guilt of Masood, much less to call the police.

Karim's death would have been forgotten in time, but for the wild rumours that continued to fly around in the village in the aftermath. Though his body was buried in the far corner of the cemetery, the memory of Karim's suicide often intruded into the gossip at Pyare's tea shop. No one who had died a violent death in the village had ever been allowed to sleep peacefully in his grave.

"Karim's ghost has started haunting the mango grove," Bapu announced one morning, as he returned from the mosque after his morning prayers. Bapu was given to wild flights of fancy. Many a time Zain had sat by his side and heard many ghost stories. He created a stir amongst the assembled family members. Zain gasped. The mango grove was one of his favourite playgrounds. If that gets haunted, where will he go with his friends?

"You always bring such tales, frightening the poor child," Amanna rebuked her husband. "It's all your stories that keep the poor mite from visiting even the toilet after dark."

That wasn't true, of course. It was not Bapu's tales alone that kept Zain away from the toilet. There were other more weighty reasons for that. The toilet was an open-to-sky enclosure located in the far corner of the backyard, shadowed by a tall wood-apple tree. Often, when the wind blew, the hard-rinded wood-apples would fall into the enclosure. Also, weeds grew around and all kinds of insects lurked among them! Each wood-apple must have weighed half-a-seer. At least that was Zain's surmise.

"Who has seen the ghost?" Nanijan asked from her swing. She, of course, believed in ghosts, ghouls, jinns and other miscellaneous evil spirits.

"Last evening, Bashirjan was visiting his farmland and had to pass by the mango grove. He heard the voice of a man crying in an eerie tone something in Tamil. At first he thought it was someone wounded or in pain lying in the grove. So he went closer. He saw a white shrouded body hanging from the tree. It was Karim. The voice was coming from Karim's body. He was crying "*Oru padi arsi, usir wangachee.*"

"*One measure of rice, took away a life,*" Nanijan translated into Urdu, wonderingly, though everyone understood Tamil perfectly. Zain noted that it sounded like a line of poetry. Even the ghosts in Minambur cried in rhymed verse, he thought. Everyone who heard this was intrigued. What could the tortured ghost of Karim mean by that? Was there some significance to that cry, or was it just a meaningless rhyme? Could it be true? Or was Bashirjan, a nondescript navayata seeking attention? Or had it sprung from the active imagination of Bapu's fertile brain? Bapu was known to embellish a tale, now and then. Was it one such tale from his repertoire? But then he was only quoting Bashirjan and so Bapu's story was verifiable.

"It only proves what I have been saying all along," Nanijan said sitting up with a jerk on her swing. All the four rusty chains squealed in unison. Nanijan generally tended to discount the gossip brought in by her son-in-law but this time she chose to believe Bapu as it accorded with her own convictions. "No one believed me when I said it. Now Karim himself has come back from the grave. The great Village Munsif will have to do something about it; he cannot escape his responsibility now. Call the old man, Zain. I want to know from him what he thinks now," she concluded triumphantly. Zain did not stir. Trembling with part excitement and part fright he wanted to hear more. He could clearly fancy Karim's shrouded ghost pacing the mango orchard. Zain always liked to hear a good ghost story, especially in the winter nights ensconced in a blanket and hugging his aunt.

"What are the people at the khoot saying?" Amanna wanted to know the gossip of the street corner. "How do they interpret Karim's cry? *Zaban-e-khalq, naqqare-*

e-khuda," she added quoting another proverb (the voice of the people is the drum of God). The ladies of his household had a propensity to quote proverbs and verses of poetry at the least provocation, Zain knew.

"What do the people at the *khoot* know?" Nanijan interrupted, waving her hands. "The meaning is quite clear. That leper hardly paid any wages to Karim. That poor boy and his old mother were starving. That *jahannami*, that dweller in hell, hoards his grains to last for ten lifetimes. Karim must have taken some rice from his store. The miser must have found out (may he suffer from cholera and may the pox rot his body). It is he who has killed the poor boy. That's what Karim is revealing," Nanijan spoke with absolute assurance as though she was privy to Karim's ghostly claims. Zain recalled the Friday preacher's confident voice in the mosque giving his interpretation of the Quran in assured tones from the pulpit as though he was privy to God Himself! She sounded as assured.

Nanajan, of course, would have none of it when he returned from the *khoot* in the evening. "That Bashir is a liar, and he has got a fertile brain. He goes about inventing tales just to attract customers to his shop and make himself important," Nanajan dismissed the story perfunctorily. In fact, since Bashir's claim, the business at his shop had increased. The forlorn cry of a ghost even if true was no proof, Nanajan said. Everyone in the family though tried to convince him. For them, the evidence of the haunting ghost was clinching.

Nanajan was an exception. Everyone, practically everyone in Minambur believed in ghosts, just as they believed in the angels, the jinns, the evil eye, *khabees arwah* (an evil spirit) and assorted other supernatural beings. They also believed that everyone who died a violent death by murder, drowning, snakebite or a tiger attack, his soul lingered on after his body was consigned to the earth. Hasina's young spirit is believed to be haunting the Karai jungle even to this day. She had been accidentally shot by her uncle when she had followed him without his knowledge into the forest on a hunt. Many a shikari who had gone to hunt there in the night had sighted a white shrouded figure flitting from shrub to shrub where she was shot.

Kankiyan, who was shot by the customs police, was still seen on the *chabootra* of his house crying "*badla, badla*", so said Ghud ki Khatun who lived by the manure heap, though her credibility was often questioned by her own children. Kankiyan was too much of a wimp in life to demand revenge after death. That is why perhaps the village had named him Broken Rice. So Khatun's listeners could be forgiven for being a wee bit sceptical. Besides Khatun no one else had seen Kankiyan and his ghost.

"But several other people too have seen Karim's ghost," pleaded Amanna, after Karim and his ghost had become the talk of the village. She now believed that the time had come to stand by her mother. "And all of them have heard Karim's cry. Biyanjoo told me only this morning that her husband too had seen Karim's ghost and had heard the cry about the measure of rice."

Biyanjoo lived across the wall and Amanna usually gossiped with her in the evenings, standing against the dilapidated wall on a large upturned water pot. Zain always wondered how she managed to balance herself for long hours of gossip standing on that curved pot. The mention of Biyanjoo's husband had raised Nanajan's hackles. "That crazy fellow made his living capturing wild animals and selling them to circuses." He had been badly bitten by a jackal, hence his name, Narikarchan. He carried his macho tendencies into his house. When he was not engaged in caging wild animals, he spent his time confining his wife and children in the single room of his house and tormenting them. Nanajan did not like husbands who beat their wives, particularly when their cries could be heard through the house walls.

Though as Village Munsif, Nanajan put up a show of indifference and unconcern, internally he could not remain unaffected. The spreading gossip in the village was disturbing him. He was worried that it would reach the police station in Gingee. Who knows, even the British sub-collector in Tindivanam may come to hear of it. "So call the police," advised Nanijan.

"And you think that when I summon the police and tell them of the ghost, they will all pat me on the back and say 'Zakir Hussain Shakir, landlord and village munsif, you have done well in believing all these good for nothing loafers, these jackal-bitten scoundrels who go about beating their wives and in their spare time see ghosts under mango trees. We are grateful to you for having summoned us on such flimsy evidence all the way from Gingee. Now that you have taken the trouble to summon us, we might as well exhume the stinking, rotting dead body in your presence and ask you to make all the necessary arrangements to transport it intact to Tindivanam for a postmortem. As you know, we do not have forensic experts in Gingee to determine the cause of death. You will also kindly round up enough willing and living witnesses against Masood, since it is unlikely that Karim's ghost would oblige us by coming forward to depose in the court. While you are going about these pleasant chores, we will camp in the village and make ourselves comfortable in the school building for the next few weeks and partake of your nice biryani, your chicken korma and kebabs. You may throw in some *ande ki mithai* and khoya nan khatai. Since your idle womenfolk whose only pastime is to gossip across walls have persuaded you to call us, they should all be happy to cook and wash our dirty linen for us. You will kindly make the school available for our stay by declaring a holiday for the children, unless your old woman is kind enough to put us up in your own house for that duration." Nanajan concluded his scathing harangue, his voice dripping with bitter sarcasm. Then he turned to Nanijan. "Make up your mind woman, quickly. Is that what you want me do?"

There was no answer from the swing. The picture Nanajan painted was so horrendous that Nanijan was for once effectively silenced. But the villagers could not be. Many of them had long-standing disputes with Masood. And the safest way to settle a score with your opponent was to get him entangled in a criminal process. There was a saying in the village—a man should avoid the proximity of three dangers—*police ke bohtaan see, phoos ke makaan se, randi jawan se* (entangled in false police accusation, a house with a thatched roof and a young concubine). Sometimes the wheels of justice move faster when private motives oil them. There was also a group of angry young men who sincerely believed that Masood should be made to pay for his alleged crime. Pyare of the tea shop was foremost amongst them. He was one among those along with Bashirjan who had the first encounter with the Karim's ghost, and since all the others had been merely confirmatory sightings of the obliging spirit, so to speak, the mantle of leadership naturally fell on his shoulders. In this, he was ably assisted by *Lathpakru* Azimullah who had a long-standing grudge against Masood. He had been given a sound thrashing by Masood's sons sometime before Karim's death.

Azimullah was a short, stockily built man with a squint in one eye. His pock-marked face with a scar from his left ear to his mouth and greying stubble gave him a sinister look. Though he lived close to the bathing well, he was rarely seen to take a dip. As a result he always stank of rancid sweat. People maintained a safe distance when conversing with him.

Azimullah was known to be the village paedophile; that is why he had never married, it was said. He lived by himself with two low-caste mistresses in a large house with a tiled roof that stood on an isolated plot of land beyond the tank bund. No one visited him there and he held little contact with the elders of the village. Few villagers ever came to know of what went on in that lonely house. Whether it was Azimullah who had built that house in that location, or had inherited it, no one knew or cared. Its isolation, however, came in handy for Azimullah. Zain had often seen half-a-dozen young boys hanging around at the *chabootra* of the house, sometimes by themselves and sometimes in the company of Azimullah. Once or twice while returning from his bath, Zain had been invited by some of them to come and play with them but he was too scared of Azimullah to accept the invitation.

"Never go near that house," Bapu had warned him.

"Why?" Zain had asked, curious as ever to know the reason behind every command. "Never mind why. Just don't go there."

Such peremptory responses from adults always irked Zain. Why did they assume that Zain could be fobbed off with a brusque reply simply because he was not as tall as or as fat as they were? Zain was not to be put off so easily even though he had no intention of ever approaching Azimullah's house. When he taxed Amanna with his eqnuiry, she had come out with greater candour. "Azimullah is a bad man and all the boys that hang around there are bad fellows. He captures young boys, kills them and cooks them into a *momai,"* she explained. "What! Azimullah does that?" asked Zain shocked out of his wits but without an inkling of what a *momai* was. It sounded something like a delicious stew. Bajijan later clarified that it was a kind of sticky glue. He had certainly no desire to be cooked into stew, however delicious it sounded, or a glue, sticky or otherwise. He had, therefore, avoided the house.

It was only much later that Zain learnt that Azimullah and the boys did some kind of a bad thing together, a thing so mysterious or so unspeakable that no one in his family would ever explain its nature. "You know Azimullah was caught with Fakhru in the vegetable patch by Fakhru's father?" Fazlu had once told Zain. "Fakhru's father and his friends took Azimullah to the mango orchard and gave him a sound thrashing."

"But what was Azimullah doing with Fakhru?" Zain had asked in all innocence.

"Oh, something very bad. You remember for one

week Fakhru did not come to school after that. They said he was not well." Beyond that, the boys could only speculate. But even the wildest flight of their imagination could not approach the gory truth.

Azimullah would have been drummed out of the village long ago for the kind of unsavoury reputation he enjoyed, but he was a navayata! He had his own supporters in the clan, few though they were. Family relationships and endogamous marriages in the navayata clan formed an indissoluble bond. So he was allowed to live in the village on sufferance, instead of being excommunicated. If Masood was not exiled, the clan had less reason to boycott Azimullah.

The navayatas, Nanajan was fond of saying, never agreed on anything except the superiority of their clan and pedigree. And it stood to reason that such superior beings, however evil, could not be treated like ordinary mortals. So Azimullah could even join in the discussions at the tea shop.

The ghost of Karim for once had succeeded in bringing together all the young men of the village at Pyare's tea shop to discuss the apparition and *one measure of rice*. The more the discussion grew heated, the thirstier the participants became. Naturally, if that led to more cups of tea being consumed, Pyare was not averse to it. Azimullah too had found it a good opportunity to creep back into the good graces of the villagers and overcome the informal boycott that the village had imposed on him. He had his own tale to contribute to the growing evidence against Masood.

"I heard from one of Masood's padials that Karim was caught with one measure of rice from the storeroom of Masood's house. He had not been paid his wages for several days," said the Lathpakru.

"So, what happened then?" Pyare took the lead into the enquiry, scratching his stubbly head, a gesture he made whenever his curiosity was aroused. His scalp was always shedding dandruff mixed with grey hair. Since he had opened the tea shop, he was making enough money to free him from the chores of tending to his meagre land holdings. So, he spent most of his time at the tea shop entertaining his guests and impressing them with his knowledge of the world. He was at that stage of his life when youth was fading reluctantly into middle age, unacknowledged and unrepentant, and he craved for some recognition to restore his declining self-confidence. The company of the gossips helped to improve his temper.

"Masood's sons got together and tied Karim to the peepal tree in their courtyard and beat him. They wanted to know how many times he had stolen rice earlier from the store. In spite of several beatings Karim continued to maintain that that was the first and only time he had done so. His mother had gone to bed for two nights running without a meal. He had not even been paid his wages, so he had taken some rice to make gruel for her, he claimed. But Masood and his sons were not satisfied. They believed that if they let him off without exemplary punishment, every padial would become a thief and their silos would be looted. They beat Karim until he was unconscious. They kept the unconscious boy tied to the tree for the whole day in the hot sun. They had given him no food or water. Hour upon hour, one of the sons would go and beat him up a little more. In the evening when they went to continue their torture, they found him dead. So they called the padials and carried the body in the dead of night to Khasab's orchard. Three of the padials and Maqsood, the eldest son of Masood, climbed up the tree and hung Karim's body there, to make it look like a suicide," the Lathpakru reported. Though his story sounded quite plausible, his reputation undermined his credit. The name Lathpakru, given him by the villagers, had something to do with what he did with the boys. Zain knew that much because whenever he was called Lathpakru to his face, and that happened not infrequently when he was in company, Azimullah would fly into a rage and abuse whoever was in sight. Qadeer Ahmad found himself reluctant to believe what Azimullah said about Karim's death, even though he disliked Masood and his ways.

"Who is this padial who has told you all this?" he

asked Azimullah. There was a subtle hint of his suspicious mind in the tone.

"I can't tell you his name. He comes from Kavarai," said the Lakhpakru.

"Why not?" asked Pyare.

"Because he is afraid that if Masood and his sons come to know he has been talking, they will kill him too."

"Does his wife or sister work in Masood's household?" Qadeer Ahmad asked. That was a loaded question.

"Probably," rejoined Azimullah. "You know every one of these padials have their wives or daughters working in the household of their landlords."

"What are you trying to imply?" Pyare asked Qadeer Ahmad, though he understood the implication.

"Well, if the wife of this padial is working in Masood's household, and she is the concubine of Masood or his sons, the padiyal could have a grudge against the family. So I am not sure about Azimullah's story. Moreover, we all know that Masood and his brothers had once thrashed Azimullah."

His story thus challenged, Azimullah hitched up his dhoti and raised his voice, "What nonsense! His thrashing of me has nothing to do with it. I am saying all this for getting common justice for poor Karim. Are we all going to stand here and let that leper get away with murder just because he belongs to our clan? Aren't you too related to him, Qadeerbhai?"

That was a blow below the belt. Qadeer was distantly related to Masood but so was half the village.

"I may be related to him, but so are Pyare and Amirjan, and also Dastagir Sab. That doesn't mean we are trying to shield Masood. Don't you dare impute such motives to me! I don't have to stand here and listen to insinuations, especially from a staff-holder." Even if Qadeer Ahmad had partially believed the padial's story about Karim's death, the aggressive stance of Azimullah was enough to antagonise him. His strong rejoinder, however, put Azimullah's back up and calling him staff-holder was the last straw. Hot exchanges followed. Others joined in. It became a free for all, thereafter. Qadeer had a large number of supporters in the assembly at the tea shop. Had Pyare not intervened to help Azimullah get away, it is quite possible that he would have got another thrashing that day—his fourth or fifth perhaps.

The upshot of all the ghostly sightings, discussions and rumours was that the news finally reached Gingee and the village munsif received orders to send a report to the Tehsildar on Karim's death. For Nanajan this order fell as a thunder clap. Monsoon was round the corner. For the last one week, the skies were covered by dark clouds. Though there was thunder and lightning, there was yet no rain. The monsoon was threatening to break anytime.

Zain was sitting one dark afternoon on the stone-sill of the *osara*, feeding his pet beetle with mulberry leaves. There were a myriad varieties of insect—beetles, caterpillars, butterflies, dragon flies and wasps that inhabited the teeming backyard. And most of these insects came out of their holes on the eve of the rainy season, as though sensing the approach of the monsoon. Zain was not allowed to bring any such insects into the house. He liked to watch the iridescent colours of the seerangi beetle, metallic blue, green and orange, fading into each other. His grandpa had permitted him to keep one seerangi, which is what those multi-coloured beetles were called, as a pet. He did not know that Zain had taken advantage of that concession to secrete a dozen of them in various assorted boxes in the storeroom. He always brought them out, one at a time, to feed them in the light. And since they all looked alike, Nanajan could never know whether Zain had only one, or fifty.

Every time Zain looked at it, the coruscating flashes of colour that the beetle displayed when sunlight struck its shimmering wings fascinated him. Fakhru and Aftab and many of his friends too kept seerangis as pets. Some of the beetles even laid eggs, though none from Zain's stock ever did. So when he saw his grandfather storming in, his pugree askew, his trousers hitched up higher than normal and his face flushed, Zain's first thought was that his secret horde had been discovered, and he would be forced to release all the beetles in the backyard.

Everyone in the house went into suspended animation at the fuming entry of grandpa. Zain recalled his grandmother's tale of the man-eating ogre. Once a poor man had taken refuge in his house. When the ogre returned, he cried "*Fie, Foh, Fum*! *manas gand, manas gand*" (I smell a human, I smell a human). Even the rumbling of the thunder seemed to have ceased at his grandpa's entry. The two maid-servants who were vigorously pounding rice in the far corner of the verandah looked up with the *mussal,* the large wooden pestle, poised in mid-air. The other two servant maids who were grinding rice in the stone-mill stopped their singing. The drone of the granite stone going round and round the base abruptly ceased, leaving Zain with a feeling of alertness in the sudden silence. He took advantage of the paralysing effect Nanajan's stormy entry had on everybody, to slip quietly into the storeroom and hide his beetles in their boxes.

"Now, I will have to go and exhume the dead body of Karim," shouted Nanajan. There were gasps of horror from the family members. The servants did not understand what Nanajan said, for they understood but little of Deccani Urdu, but the plaintive tone of Nanajan's outcry spoke for itself. The stunned Amanna, Bapu and Nanijan realised all at once the implications of Nanajan's announcement. Exhuming the dead had never been heard of in Minambur. Once a man, sinner or saint, was dead and interred, that was the end of it as far as the rest of the villagers were concerned. After every relative had thrown a clod of earth into the grave before it was closed as custom demanded, the assembly of relatives, friends and the congregation of the villagers would withdraw forty feet from the grave and sit on their haunches. The imam sitting on the ground likewise would then intone the *talqin* (a religious lecture) in a loud voice, so that the dead man could hear it clearly, teaching him or her how to answer the two examining angels, Munkar and Nakir, who visit the dead in the grave once he is left alone. The imam would remind the deceased that Allah was his God, Muhammad was his Prophet and Islam was his religion. After a detailed questioning of the faith and practice of the shrouded body in the grave, and depending on the acceptability of his answers, the angels would either leave him alone or administer to him the torture of the grave—*azaab-e qabr*—with a scourge of venomous snakes, scorpions and all kinds of deadly creatures.

No one knew for how long the angels administered this punishment to the sinner in the grave. People swore they had heard mournful cries from the graveyard as they passed by it in the night on some unavoidable errand. Such cries were always heard only at night. Perhaps the angels rested during the heat of the day. Nanajan had warned Zain never to approach the vicinity of the cemetery, especially after sunset. Even the adults avoided the vicinity of the graveyard after sunset, after the body was buried. Nobody in the village had even heard of a grave being opened after a body had been interred.

Zain had heard the imam in the Friday sermons give frightening descriptions of the tortures the dead suffered in the grave. He had woken up on Friday, in the middle of the night, drenched in sweat, with vivid nightmares haunting his sleep. His grandfather, who was a devout Muslim, had read of these tortures in the books of religion which he kept in his dark room.

Opening the grave was a sacrilege. All along, grandpa had dreaded the possibility of an exhumation order. As a devout Muslim, he believed that the dead should be allowed to sleep in peace or in whatever condition Allah wanted them to be. Once the dead are consigned to the earth, every soul has the right to its privacy. Except for special prayers, the graveyard was a place rarely visited; less so after dark and especially after a body had been recently buried. Moreover, he wasn't too sure when Munkar and Nakir would take it into their heads to visit Karim. What if he inadvertently chose to open the grave when they were there? What consequences would accrue to the villagers and to himself personally for the desecration of a grave and interfering with the angels' work? Moreover, the traditions say that a sinner's grave is always full of snakes and scorpions. Everyone believed in God's punishment of sinners in the grave. Karim was not known to be a saint.

He must have sinned so when the grave was opened, would Nanajan be letting loose a tomb-full of poisonous creatures on the innocent villagers, inviting the wrath of the punishing angels. Added to all these forebodings was the impending monsoon, which would make every street of village slippery, and the graveyard one vast field of squelching mud, full of snakes trying to take refuge in dry spots—the mosque, the animal pound, the maqbara and the surrounding houses.

Nanajan gave vent to all these forebodings, forgetting that at this point in time, he had merely been asked to send a report to the Tehsildar. The stage of opening the grave had not come, and if the Tehsildar was satisfied with his report, it may never come. But Nanajan's active imagination refused to remain at peace; he always believed in the worst

"Dadabhoy, why are you getting agitated? You may never be asked to exhume the body." Amanna tried to cool her father's overheated speculation. It was not in her placid nature to remain agitated for too long and she always exerted a calming influence on her parents, especially her father.

"I hope the Tehsildar orders exactly that," the harsh intervention came from the swing. Nanijan could not help voicing her vindictive hopes. She wanted to nail Masood, once for all. Also, she could not miss the godsent opportunity of needling Nanajan. She enjoyed his discomfiture, occasionally. Grandpa had so far been addressing his worries to the walls and the doors but the remark from his wife gave him a focus to vent his pent-up anger.

"Ah, so you are happy! You would like to watch me in trouble, eh? I have never known a woman so eager to ruin her husband. What have I ever done to deserve this from you? I spent a lifetime suffering your tantrums and your gibes; all I got in return is this. I am sure it is your rumour-mongering and gossip that has reached the ears of the Tehsildar." That was, of course, being unfair to Nanijan. Blind and confined to the swing, she could hardly have influenced the course of events on the outside. Nanajan was simply seeking a peg to hang his anger and resentment upon and vent his frustration. So Nanijan's importunate intervention gave him a good opportunity. Having delivered the broadside and before Nanijan could come up with an appropriate rejoinder, he left the verandah in a huff.

He locked himself into his room, racking his brain to draft a reasonably credible report that would satisfy the powers that be avoid the need for any exhumation.

To add to Nanajan's woes, the monsoon rains started the next day and there was a heavy downpour. When it rained in Minambur, it never drizzled. It poured in streams; it rained in sheets as though the clouds were desperate to shed all the tonnes of water they carried and be done with. Sometimes the downpour lasted for days. Few people dared to step out in the open during such days. Neither umbrellas nor mats were of much help. The butchers stopped slaughtering and there was no meat for days together. People fell back on eggs and vegetables and an occasional bedraggled chicken was brought out from the dripping coop.

The household itself would be thrown into turmoil. Half the servants who lived in Kavarai and Shittanpoondi would not turn up for work. Those who missed leaving for home before the onset of rains bore the burden of performing all the chores. The fuel wood lying out in the open would have to be brought in and stacked in the dry shed; the cows and buffalos tethered properly so that they did not break loose and stampede when the peals of thunder and the brilliant flashes of lightning struck their ears and eyes. The heavy curtain that protected the open verandah was lowered and tied down to prevent its flapping in the strong gusts of wind and a myriad other labours had to be performed.

Amid all this hustle and bustle, Nanajan had to go around preparing his dark report on Karim's death. He went about this unpleasant task confined to his room, cursing all and sundry for his discomfiture. First he had to call an uncooperative Masood and take his statement. The village *toti* (assisstant) was sent to fetch him and he came with a *padial* holding an umbrella over him and wearing a look of hurt innocence on his face. The rain of Minambur was no respecter of such flimsy protection as umbrellas. Masood was oozing water from every wrinkle in his face as venom from a cobra's fangs. Though he was restrained in the use of words, the tone of his hoarse replies seethed with suppressed anger. Was this the way for one navayata to treat another, especially one who was related by blood, however thin that blood ran? Of course, Karim was working in his household! Was it a crime to employ *padials*? Of course, he was kind and considerate to Karim, as to all his other servants. He had never even said 'uff' to Karim, even though that ungrateful *kamchor* repaid his kindness by stealing rice, lentils and jaggery from his store. He never did harm the bastard, though he deserved to be thrashed. Neither did his sons or his *padials* touch that *harami*. He had nothing to do with Karim's death.

He believed that Karim had hanged himself out of remorse for all the thefts he had committed. Ask the *padials* and his sons. They would vouch for Karim's thieving ways. And so on and so forth. None of the sons or the *padials* of Masood contradicted his version when summoned. They wouldn't, of course. The story of Karim's being caught with one measure of rice and being tortured to death was a figment of the staff-holder's imagination. Dadabhoy should give no heed to the rumor-mongering of disreputable people with loose character who consorted with boys.

One after the other, the sons and padials of Masood were summoned in the pouring rain and the *talari* (constable) recorded their statements, while Nanajan questioned them. The other independent witnesses who deposed against Masood only cited the haunting cries of the ghost as evidence. Nanajan avoided recording that for fear of being ridiculed by the Tehsildar. By the time Nanajan had come to the last of the witnesses, he found himself in a quandary. Though he had his strong suspicions, there was not an iota of concrete evidence against Masood.

Every time a padial departed Nanajan's *diwankhana*, he left behind a puddle of water. Zain, walking in barefoot with a glass of tea for his grandpa had to be careful maneuvering around the puddles. The street outside was already flowing like the tributary of a river, carrying branches, palm leaves, rotting fruits and other debris to join that vast sheet of water known as the village *talab.*

As Village Munsif, Nanajan had once before experienced floods with the collapse of the talab bund. During the ongoing inquiry itself, Nanajan's mind was on the heavy rains and its impact. He had sent the *toti* (assistant) who did all the official menial work of the village to go and have a look at the talab and assess its rising level. How much water would the talab hold before breaching its bund? Once in the long past, Minambur had witnessed similar rains. The people who had experienced that monsoon still remembered with dismay what had happened then. The bund had broken at several places in the middle of the night leading to disastrous consequences for the village. The mud-walled houses collapsed by the dozen. Some of the old men who could not escape the fury of the flood were killed under the falling roofs. Learning from that experience, a constant vigil was maintained on the bund. The *toti* came back after an hour or so dripping rain water from his meagre covering. He brought along several volunteers with him who wanted to give their own assessments.

The news was not good. The water was rising fast. Once the level reached the top of the bund and the water started overflowing, the earthen embankment could be breached at any number of places. The weakest point was, of course, the one closest to the village. That was the place where bullock carts and cattle frequently crossed the bund on their way to the paddy fields. The bund had a dip there as a result of this traffic. Every time it was repaired, the bullock cart traffic would restore the man-made pass. Once the breach occurred there, the whole village would be flooded. The plinths on which the village houses were raised were not too high so many of the houses were under threat of being inundated. The elders gathered outside in their wet clothes and clamoured for the village munsif to do something about it. Wasn't the Government paying him all of Rs10 every month to look after the well-being of the village their looks implied?

Nanajan immediately organised the barbers' band. Ratnam was the only one who possessed the small drums. The barber was the official announcer for all such events by beat of the drum. In the pouring rain, Ratnam and his gang went around the streets beating their drums. The assistant barbers held umbrellas over the drum beaters. The umbrellas were for the drums, not the beaters, for once the tight skin on the drum got wet, it would refuse to sound. Unlike the drenched village elders clamouring for action, the wetter a drum got the less noise it made. The barbers' band announced to the villagers about the impending crisis and warned them to take all precautionary measures. Of course, the precautionary measures were not spelt out, but the villagers knew that they had to get the most useful household goods to higher ground in the house, or shift to the school or mosque which were built on a high plinth. The old and the infirm had to be shifted from their *kutcha* mud houses to *pukka* brick and cement dwellings. Everone chipped in to help.

In this crisis, the investigation of Karim's death was suspended. Nanajan gathered as many volunteers as he could and rushed to the tank bund to see if it could be strengthened before the water rose to critical levels.

"I will also come with you," Zain volunteered helpfully. He knew that there would be great excitement at the bund. Many of the villagers would have gathered there to see the *tamasha*. Even a few of his friends would have escaped the clutches of their parents and would be there at the bund. Some of the village leaders would be strutting about throwing their weight around and ordering others to do this and that and accomplishing nothing. Quarrels would be erupting now and then, involving even fisticuffs, on the best ways to control the expected floods. The bund was the most happening place to be at this time.

"I don't want you. You stay put here," Nanajan would not expose his grandson to the rain, thunder and possible flood. "Somebody get hold of this brat and tie him down," he ordered. Amanna called to him, "Zain, don't go anywhere. I need you here. If the bund breaches, there will be water entering the *osara* and *dalan* (the lower and higher verandahs). Who will help me carry all the things to safety?" Amanna shrewdly appealed to his sense of chivalry. She knew Zain would not resist the temptation to be helpful, in or out of season, though his help often proved to be more of a hindrance. If he could not go to see the floods, Zain thought, they could come visiting him at home. He was looking forward to seeing the waters enter the house. Oh, what fun that would be! He would be able to float all his paper boats then without going out into the rains.

His grandmother and great-grandmother sat in the dark room off the verandah, praying in loud eerie tones, asking Allah to stop the rains and to have pity on the animals and the birds, if not the sinners. The servant-maids from Kavarai took burning timbers from the hearth, rushed into the knee-deep waters of the courtyard and flourished the flaming torches at the pouring skies. The Fire Dance had been found efficacious in stopping rains in Kavarai—so why not in Minambur? They believed that the rain gods could be frightened into laying off once they saw the flames thrust into their faces.

Nothing seemed to work, however. It was as though the skies had opened up, and refused to close. The roof of the house covered with overlapping country tiles was not made to withstand such torrential fury. It was leaking at several places. The maid-servants went about placing earthen pots below the drips so that the water could be prevented from falling on and eroding the earthen floor and creating runnels to make the floor slushy. From time to time, one pot or the other would start overflowing. Bajijan and Amanna, keeping a watchful eye would shout, "Mampeta, that pot is full." So, Mampeta would scurry around with an empty pot to replace it and then would carry the full one to the *osara* and empty it out in the overflowing courtyard.

"Zain, come here and sit by me," cried Nanijan, in the break from her loud prayers. "Don't go near the *osara*. That is leaking too much." The warning was not so much for preventing Zain from getting wet, as for saving him from getting bitten by the snakes and scorpions which come out from their holes seeking dry refuges. They would slither up the steps of the *osara* and try to crawl under any shelter they could find. In the past, several snakes and scorpions had been found hiding in nooks and corners of the house after the rains. They escaped drowning only to be killed on dry land later. Once, after similar rains, Amanna had placed a hot curry pot on a coiled cobra in the kitchen, mistaking it for a *chummal*, a rope pot holder. The poor cobra had no chance.

Nanijan temporarily forgot the death of Karim in the greater worries caused by the heavy downpour and rising waters.

"*Ya Ghouse al Azam Dastagir*, save us from this great calamity. Pray to Allah to stop this heavy rain. I will perform the next *gyarhveen* with great devotion," she invoked the Patron Saint of all Muslims in India! Hardly anyone in Minambur knew that the great saint Abdul Qadir Gilani was buried in Baghdad. For the Muslims of the subcontinent, he was a living saint and was often invoked in place of God. Zain remembered that the next *gyarvheen* was due in a couple of weeks' time.

On the eleventh of every lunar month the devout Muslims of Minambur, especially the women, took a ritual bath, dried their hair with incense smoke, put on clean clothes and cooked ghee-rice, mutton dishes and other fries. The ladies would sit together on the cotton carpet and sing a few hymns, *qasidas*, in praise of the Prophet and the Saint, recite some of the miracles of the holy man, and then the elder member of the household would recite a short prayer, a *fatiha,* calling the blessings of Allah on the Prophet, the Saint and all those present. Then the special sweets, the *boondi* and *jahangiris*, would be distributed to the participants and sent across to the houses of relatives and friends.

But Nanijan's loud invocation perhaps never rose above the noise of thunder and lightning. The bund broke just after the prayers, before the sun had even set. The water cascaded into the village washing away many of the kutcha earthen houses. The walls of unbaked bricks, already made soft by soaking the rains, could not stand the fury of the rushing waters. Many of them crumbled, bringing down the supported roofs. The streets flowed like brown rivers carrying along the silt of the lake and the mud of the unpaved streets. Bapu who had gone to the bund to join in the fun of strengthening it returned home in haste. He had to wade through waist-deep muddy waters in the street. Even the courtyard had more than two feet of water. The narrow drain between the house and the kitchen found itself unable to cope with the turbulent flow. Luckily the walls of Nanajan's house were made of stronger stuff and withstood the fury of the rains.

"It's God's anger at what the villagers have done to Karim," Nanijan suddenly recalled him. "If the village munsif doesn't do anything about it even after this dire warning, God knows what will happen to all of us." But this prophecy fell on deaf ears. Nanajan didn't hear a word of it. He was busy at the bund.

Zain was dying to see what was happening in the street. It must be in flood, he knew, but the house had no windows to look out of. So he climbed up on the old divan that was kept stored in the space between the *diwankhana* and the kitchen and peered out into the street. He was even willing to risk the threat of the scorpions and snakes lurking in the eaves but he couldn't see much. With some difficulty, he scrambled up to the gap between the tile roof and the wall and hung there, precariously clinging to the beams. He could see the flotsam and jetsam that were being carried away by the fast-flowing stream that was once the Pool Street. There were broken chairs, wooden boxes without lids, manuscript sheets and dead cattle, all floating away on the muddy waters of the flood. Yet, braving all the fury of the elements, he saw people wading waist deep to retrieve the large quantities of fish which the flood waters had brought to the village from the talab. There are no clouds without a silver lining, at least for some. The floods had killed many of the fish; only the murrels and the eels were still alive. Both were succulent fish for the villagers.

Zain was sure that many houses would have a feast that night on the succulent murrels the tank was known to breed. Murrels were not easily available to the villagers. Only those who had private tanks could have a supply at command. They were a highly-prized fresh water fish in the village. Its head resembled that of a snake and it had dark grey spots on the body and grew to a fairly large size, so when it rose to the surface to breathe, people often mistook it for a snake. Those who had muzzle loading guns were lucky for they could shoot it. But first they had to catch a sufficient supply of dragonflies, and then carry them to the talab; throw the half-dead flies on the water, wait for the game fish to rise to the bait, shoot it just when it was snapping at the flies and then dive in to retrieve the dead fish. So the flood waters delivering murrels at their doorstep without all the trouble was a bonanza.

It rained throughout the night. Many of the mud houses standing only on earthen walls collapsed. Many people were rendered houseless and were given shelter by neighbours who had *pukka* houses. Some took refuge in the school building where the village munsif had made arrangements for the welfare of the homeless.

As dawn broke over the clouded horizon, the rains petered off. Perhaps Nanijan's prayers had at last reached the right quarters, though belatedly. As the water receded from the streets, it left behind all the ditches filled with thick slush and puddles wherever the rushing detritus had gouged out the soft earth. It had also left even some pukka houses damaged. Zain was thankful that their house had been spared the fury with comparatively minor damage. The thatched shed that housed the cattle had collapsed, but the cows and bullocks housed there had escaped unhurt. The chicken coop that supplied the household with dozens of eggs daily was totally washed away. All the chickens had drowned, in spite of Amanna's best efforts to save them. She was heartbroken. It had taken years for her to build up the small poultry farm she ran for the benefit of the household and neighbours. She treated the hens as family members and many of them recognised her. She had given them names, and she believed they recognised their names. The Karimans, Rahimans and Muttekaris that came fluttering in response to her call in the evening from wherever they were roosting, had all been carried away by the ruthless waters.

The large earthen hearth in the courtyard on which the paddy was parboiled before being dried in the sun had been washed away. Its iron frame stood naked and forlorn.

The flood had also left many families bereaved. Some of the old and weak who had gone to the fields, unmindful of the rising water and the threatened breach, paid a heavy price. Some old people in the kutcha houses, who could not drag themselves out of harm's way, also lost their lives under the collapsing roofs. Teams of volunteers sent out by the village munsif found dead bodies in the paddies or stuck in the irrigation channels. More than a dozen people lost their lives.

It was not until three days later that Mahmood, the son of Masood came to meet Nanajan without being summoned.

"My father is missing since the flood. We have not been able to find him," he told Nanajan. He did not look unduly perturbed. "He had gone to the embankment to save his strayed cattle; since then we have not seen him."

"Did you check up in Kavarai and Shittanpoondi," Nanajan had asked. "He might have taken refuge there from the waters."

"All our padials have run away. We checked in all the nearby villages; father is not there."

"I will try to find out," Nanajan had assured them. The *toti* was duly sent to Kavarai and he managed to locate Arumugam and Guna, a couple of Masood's *padials*. The *toti* returned with both of them in tow—bedraggled looking specimens, wearing a single string around their waists covering their private parts, dried mud still clinging to their arms and bare bodies.

"Where is Masood?" Nanajan had thundered at them. When dealing with women and *padials*, an intimidatory tone right at the beginning brought quick results. That is what all men in the village believed. *Kill a cat on the nuptial night, and the wife would be obedient for the rest of her life.* At least that is what the proverb promised. Nanajan regretted all his life that he omitted this essential chore on the nuptial night and his wife took the upper hand. He could never control her acerbic tongue even when she could see, much less now that she was blind. He had no intention of omitting the chore with servants wherever his authority was in danger of being flouted. "*Roz-e awwal, gurba kushtan*" (Kill the cat on the first night), he would repeat in Persian before proceeding to the action. The *padials* trembled at his peremptory demand.

"We don't know," they replied. But the tone in which they replied belied their words. Nanajan was quick to notice that they refused to look him in the eye while answering his questions.

"You know what has happened to him," he roared at them. "And I know that you know. You better come clean; otherwise, I will send you to jail." The *padials* cowered under this thunderous threat. Where the peremptory tone had failed, the threat worked.

"Masood is dead," said Guna, the elder of the two. Often, it is the older and more mature man who succumbs to threats, Nanajan would often say. Guna confirmed his suspicion. Nanajan never let on whether he was relieved or sorry to learn this news. Though he never would articulate it, Nanajan believed that some people improved this world by leaving it and Masood was one of them. But as village munsif, he could not let matters rest where a villager, a land-owning villager at that had died, without getting to the bottom of the affair.

"How did he die? And where is the body?" He asked.

Arumugan and Guna both fell silent, as though they were unwilling to reveal anything more. "Unless you tell me the truth, both of you will be arrested for causing his death," Nanajan told them, this time quietly. Both the *padials* recognised the menace in that quiet tone.

"You tell him," Arumugam prompted Guna. "No, no, you tell him," Guna retorted.

Nanajan thought it best to question them separately. "Take Guna out and wait there," he ordered the *toti*. "Now, tell me what you know," he asked Arumugam.

"We were returning from spreading the manure on Masood Saheb's field when the flood caught us," Arumugam stammered, his reluctant tongue breaking up each sentence into several clauses.

"The waters rose high. We saw Bade Saheb's cows being washed away. Ahmad Hussain Sahib's pump house then collapsed while we were standing close to it. There was a great crash. We were really frightened. That is when we saw *ayya* (master) Masood Sahib. He had taken shelter in the pump house. When the roof fell, he was caught in the fallen debris. Half his body was trapped under the heavy diesel pump which had been uprooted. Perhaps his legs had fractured. He saw us and shouted for us to save him. We tried to reach him but the onrushing water kept pushing us back. By that time the water was already upto our chests and the current was pulling us towards the deep tank. We had to save ourselves. We swam with great difficulty towards the bund. We could still hear the faint cries of Masood Saheb for help as we climbed the bund. That is the last we heard of him."

After hearing this story, Nanajan called Guna and questioned him closely. His tale corroborated Arumugam's in all details. It was perhaps understandable that the *padials* had not gone out of their way to help Masood at the risk of their own lives. Masood had done nothing in his lifetime to build their loyalty.

It took another two days to locate Masood's body. Having been in water for five days, it was in much worse shape than that of Karim's. His sons put him in a gunny sack and brought the remains home in a bullock cart. No one was willing to give him the funeral bath, not even his own sons. "He has had a bath for the last five days. He doesn't require one more," said one of them. They wanted to get the funeral rites done and over with as quickly as possible.

Some villagers, out of sheer navayata loyalty joined the funeral procession. Giving the shoulder to the bier and joining the funeral prayers was an ordained duty for all Muslims. It earned them rewards in the hereafter. In spite of copious use of camphor and burning of incense, the odour from the bier was overpowering and the pall-bearers could not carry the bier for even a few steps before surrendering it to Masood's sons.

"Allah has given him his just deserts." Nanijan quoted the oft-repeated proverb—*Allah ke ghar der hai, andher nahi hai* (Allah may delay the retribution, but he always does justice), she said with great satisfaction. "If you take away innocent lives, God will surely punish you in the same way." Had she known the words, she would have called it poetic justice.

Nothing very much came out of Nanajan's report to the Tehsildar. Since the chief suspect himself had died, the Tehsildar allowed Karim to sleep peacefully in his grave.

The Bodymates

When I was in school, I wrote short stories in Urdu and some in English. In those days, I had not heard of short stories in Urdu. Yes, there were Urdu magazines which my mother subscribed to, and they had some stories called '*Afsana*' in Urdu but I rarely took note of them. So, the short stories I wrote, I called them 'novels', an exaggeration, no doubt, but since my schoolmates had rather limited reading experience they were persuaded to believe that what I wrote were in fact novels. The illusion was strengthened by the fact that these handwritten short stories were presented in the form of booklets, with a title page, a frontispiece with the name of the author, the fictitious publisher and all the other fiction which pirated novels contain today on their title pages.

The stories I wrote were also not original. I did not possess a mind inventive enough to weave original plots. At least, I did not in my school days. I developed that creative ability much later after I got married. It has stood me in good stead during my conjugal life! But returning to the theme of my short stories, what I wrote was a rehash of the tales told by my grandmother. After a lapse of more than six decades, looking back at her attitude to how children should be treated, it is remarkable how much in advance of their times the old women of the village were. My grandmother told us stories of adult life—the escapades of husbands and wives, adulteries and sexual peccadilloes, without pulling any punches. It's remarkable to look at all her grandchildren today and note that they grew up none the worse for it. In fact, all of them developed (grandfathers and grandmothers in their own right today) into quite balanced, sensible and tolerant adults.

One of the stories she told us, which I converted into a 'novel' and circulated among my schoolmates, concerned a Prince. I don't know why all stories told by grandmothers concerned only kings, queens and princes, at least in India. Much later, when I read the *Tilism-e-Hoshruba* (The Enchanting Spell), a thirty-volume tale of enchantments, magicians, spells, transformations, etc. I found that even those tales were inhabited only by kings and queens, fairies and ogres and heroes who possessed magical weapons. It appeared to me that the eastern world was inhabited only by royalty and their attendant goblins, ogres and other such creatures. There was no common man in those days; or else, the contemporary media was not alert enough to highlight the concerns of the common man to get reflected in contemporary fiction. What a wonderful and glorious time that was!

The Prince in my grandmother's tale came to believe quite early in life that all women were adulterous and, even though married to kings and princes, were willing to give themselves to the first comer, even if he happened to be a *jinn* or a *rakkas* (the corrupt form of a *rakshas* in the village lingo). So, he decided that he would not marry any of the beautiful daughters of the ministers, the army commanders and other court officials who hung about the court and fattened themselves on the produce of the land. The Prince had learnt magic from a magic teacher in the Court. (It appears that the kings in those days employed astrologers, magicians and shamans in the Court as teachers to the young princes, in addition to experts in martial arts, politics and administration. It is reported that the modern inheritors of the royal mantle, who rule from Delhi, continue this tradition). So, having mastered various occult sciences, the Prince decided that he would create his spouse from his own body. Grandmother called this story *Tan Ka Joda* (Body Spouse).

The Prince sincerely believed that a mate created out of his own body would never betray him, and would remain faithful to him eternally; but he reckoned without human frailty. So, one day, he sent away all his servants from the palace retaining only his closest confidant. Entering the basement, he showed the confidant two large ceramic jars with lids made of the same material. The jars had all kinds of inscriptions in strange scripts in bas relief. Then he opened an ornate wooden chest and took out several swords, daggers, scalpels and other sharp surgical instruments—all made of chased steel and inscribed with hieroglyphics, cuneiform and Arabic calligraphy. He removed a silken carpet, also similarly adorned, sat down cross-legged on it, and for a long time recited many incantations.

The confidant, standing in a corner all the while, was wondering what the outcome of all this charade was to be. When he finished casting the spells, the Prince said to his trembling confidant, "I will now get into one of those jars and stand in it. You will draw a line from the centre of my forehead to my crotch with this magic chalk piece. Then you will take this sharp magic sword and you will cleave my body in half, exactly in half. Let all the blood fall into the jar, but not a drop should fall outside. Then you will take one half of my body and put it into the other jar. You should make sure while doing so that no drop of my blood falls on the ground. Having done that, you will close both the jars with the lids, seal them, then leave the room and lock it up from the outside. You will place reliable guards at the door and make sure that no one enters the room for a full forty days. Then you will open the lock, enter the room alone and remove the lid of the first jar. You will then see what you will see; and bring some robes with you when you come."

The Confidant was horror-struck at these instructions. He was now trembling all over his body.

"But your Highness," he protested, "how can I cut you? If you die, I will be tortured and hanged."

"Just carry out my instructions and nothing will happen to you or to me. This is high magic. You are my most trusted friend, that is why I am asking you to do this service for me, but if you refuse, I will have to hang you. You know too much and as a rebel you cannot be allowed to live. I will then ask someone else to do this for me."

Faced with this ultimatum, the Confidant had no choice. Thereupon, the Prince took off all his clothes and got into the big jar. Taking care to see that the black mole at the left corner of the Prince's mouth was left undisturbed, as also the small red birthmark at the parting of his hair, the Confidant took the wet enchanted chalk and drew the line.

At this point in the story, and recalling my grandmother's pause, there are many questions I should have asked. But then, one doesn't go about asking how, why and wherefore when listening to fairy tales. There has to be a willing suspension of disbelief if one wants to enjoy the story. We do that every other day when we are watching movies, even the best English ones. So, the Confidant too suspended his doubts and proceeded to carry out his master's instructions; but he could not fulfill them to the letter. While he was transferring the other half of the Princes' body, two drops of blood did fall on the ground in spite of all his care and caution, unnoticed by him.

On the forty-first day, he returned to the palace, got the room opened and removed the lid from the first jar. To his amazement and happiness, the Prince emerged as handsome and as radiant as ever, if not more. He thanked the Confidant with a beaming face, took the robes he had brought and asked him to leave. He closed the door, and then removed the lid from the second jar. There emerged from it one of the most beautiful women that the Prince had ever seen. She had a glowing lustrous countenance, a black mole on the left corner of her mouth emphasising the beauty of her face and the red birthmark at the parting of her hair. Her body could have put Canova's *Psyche* and *Venus de Milo* (with both her hands intact) to shame. After covering their nudity with robes, they emerged from the room.

Their nuptials were celebrated with great fanfare and the festivities lasted for months. The courtiers noted their close resemblance to each other and wondered. The Princess and the Prince lived happily ever after—no, not for ever but for some time. Even fairy tales don't always end happily. In this story, it was those two drops of blood that escaped the notice of the Confidant that played the villain.

After a few months, the Prince noticed a change in the Princess' demeanor. Her passionate love for him of the initial days was now tinged with a hue of indifference. Having created his spouse from one half of his body, the Prince loved her as much as he loved himself. He believed that the Princess could not help loving him as much as she loved herself. So, at first, he could not believe that there could be any diminishing of her love for him. But though she was literally his half, for better or worse, she was imbued with a personality of her own, with her own intelligence, emotions and thoughts. So, at first, the Prince gave due allowance to this fact. But day by day, the evidence of her indifference mounted until one night he found her absent from his bed. He got up and searched all the rooms and found her nowhere. She came back to bed in the early hours after keeping him anxiously awake. The next night, he pretended to be asleep. Just after midnight, the Princess quietly slipped off the bed and proceeded noiselessly to the basement. The Prince followed at a discreet distance. She climbed down the few steps and then walking to a jar removed its lid. To the horror of the Prince, there emerged a huge Snake, lustrous and shining like burnished gold with a torso as thick as his own. The Prince found himself strangely attracted to the Serpent. He realised that his affinity to the Snake was because it had been created from a few drops of his own blood and he cursed the Confidant for his carelessness. Meantime, the Princess was engaged in shedding her clothes and embracing the Serpent.

Many questions would occur to the reader at this point. How is it possible for creatures belonging to two utterly different species to meet in conjugal union? But again, such questions do not deserve the dignity of a reply. I can only refer to Leda and the Swan, Peleus and the Merman, Pasiphae and the Bull, Europa and another bull, and the numerous bas reliefs on the walls of the Khajuraho temples. Grandmother didn't tell us the stories from the Greek or Indian mythology, nor of the Khajuraho temples. I learnt all these by myself much later in life!

The Prince was shocked. To say that he was shocked is to put it too mildly. His world collapsed around him. The woman whom he had created out of his own body, endowed her with all the knowledge that he had gained over the years, imparted to her all the values and traditions of his family and upbringing could go and indulge in such an atrocious act was beyond his comprehension. She was not only his bodymate; she was also his soulmate. That is what he had thought. His instinctive reaction at this gross betrayal of his love and faith was to draw his sword and kill both the Princess and the Snake. But then, all the wisdom and patience his teachers had inculcated in him over the years took over, and he paused. He withdrew to a distance and stood for some time thinking. After all, he said to himself, the woman is flesh of my flesh, blood of my blood, literally. If I kill her, I am killing half of myself (a kind of semi-suicide, the Prince could have said if he had summoned his sense of humour). And what is the Snake? He is my own blood! It is also her blood. Let me wait and think some more before I take any action, he rationalised. Thus, the native hue of his resolution was sicklied over with the pale cast of thought, and his precipitate desire lost the name of action. He retired to the bedroom and went back to his pretended sleep.

Much later, the princess returned and silently crept into bed. She tested him with various incantations to see whether he was awake, but he countered her attempts of mental projection by a magic of his own. After some time, the Prince noted from her breathing that she was in a deep satisfied sleep. Then he got up and tiptoed down to the basement with his drawn sword in hand. He had thought over and decided to kill the Snake. After all, he reasoned, as the Snake was created out of a few drops of his own blood, by killing it, he was only losing a very small part of himself. He had lost more blood in the battles and skirmishes than the few drops that made up the Snake. He could afford to lose it. So, the Prince entered the secure basement room and removed the lid of the jar. As soon as the Snake emerged, he killed it and cut it into several pieces. Then he put them all into the jar and recited some incantations so that it could not be restored to life.

The next day, the Prince left on one of the routine raids that princes undertook in days of yore, to enjoy the killing of innocent men, women and children (their successors continue to do so even to this day). The Princess searched and found the pieces of her lifeless lover. She brought them out secretly to her bedroom and mourned over them for three days. Then she used all the force of the magic at her command, but having failed to restore life to the Snake she did certain secret rituals.

After her husband returned, she took up her conjugal duties as though nothing had happened. Having lulled the Prince into complacency, she exerted all her charms one night on the Prince and made him ecstatic. Lovingly, she said, "Let us play a game, Prince," she challenged him. "Why not?" said the Prince in a state of satiated somnolence, accepting the challenge. "Then I will pose you a riddle—a simple riddle. I bet you cannot solve it!" Faced with this challenge, the Prince who prided himself on his intelligence and knowledge, laughed out derisively.

"Tell me the riddle," he said.

"Very well, but if you cannot solve this riddle in forty days, you shall forfeit your life!"

The Prince sobered up on hearing this forfeit. "And what will you bet, if I solve it?" he asked. "My life, of course," said the Princess.

She had put him on the spot, and he could not refuse without appearing a coward. He had to accept the bet.

"The riddle is this" said the Princess
"The beloved lives on the body
The beloved lives on the heart
The beloved lights the lamp
And rests under the bed."

For many days, the Prince racked his brain to solve the riddle. The meaning was simple enough. The beloved, of course, was the Snake. It was as much a part of the Princess's body as his own. Perhaps, she still loved the Snake. So, it lives in her heart. But how does he light the lamp and rest beneath the bed? He wanted to consult his shamans and the sages who infested the Court but that would have amounted to cheating. Also, he would have lost face with them, he who claimed superior wisdom and knowledge. Try as he might, he could not decipher the riddle. One day, he went to his magic carpet and in a state of intense meditation with the best of charms and incantations the magicians had taught him, tried to penetrate the mind of the Princess. To his amazement, he discovered that she had blocked her mind with the self-same magic that he had used. Every day spent in the search for the meaning took him nearer to his doom. He lost interest in the administration of the state and even in the performance of his daily chores. For days, he locked himself in his room and sat brooding for hours on the riddle. As the end of the forty days grace neared, and he had still not found a solution to the riddle, he decided to take leave of his nearest and dearest before his life was forfeited—for as an honorable man he could not go back on his word.

I recall having asked my grandmother at this point in the story, "Why didn't the Prince simply kill his unfaithful wife and save his life? At least he could have told her to go to hell, put her in prison and got on with his life."

"Ah, he couldn't do that. I forgot to tell you something. When the Prince and the Princess made the betting contract, they jointly cast a spell on each other. If the riddle was not solved by the fortieth day, the Prince would never wake up from his sleep on the forty-first morning. He would go into a state of suspended animation. He would live on until someone with greater magic power brought him back to life. Similar would be the fate of the Princess if the Prince solved the riddle before the time was up."

"But he could still have killed her before the end of the forty-day period. He need not have waited till the end to confess failure and go into suspended animation," I had remonstrated.

"You forget," said my grandmother. "She was his bodymate created from half his body. If he killed her, he would also lose half his life and half his strength!"

"Ah, what a cunning woman she was, the Princess!" we all exclaimed. "All women are," my grandmother had said with a smirk. "It's the men who don't realise it."

So, on the thirty-ninth day, after having called on all his ministers, magicians, teachers and sages, he went to have his last supper with his only sister. When he reached her house, he found that it was lit by a thousand lamps. The Prince was taken aback. Was it the festival of Diwali or was his sister celebrating his last day on earth?

"Neither," exclaimed his sister. "Today happens to be the Night of Lamps. As you know, all the lamps from the houses of the courtiers meet once every month in each other's house. Today, it is the turn of my lamps to play host. All lamps from the city have gathered here and will gossip among themselves till dawn."

The Prince laughed. As he sat sipping wine with his sister and nephews he heard a vast murmur. The lamps were all talking to each other and following the age-old traditions were exchanging gossip. With his magic powers, the Prince could understand what they were saying.

"You know," said one lamp gleefully, "my mistress is sleeping with the Prime Minister's son, and my master has no idea."

"He may know it," said another, "but what can he

do about it? After all, the Prime Minister himself is being cuckolded."

"That is nothing," said a third. "My master is cheating the Prince and is siphoning off millions every month. How else do you think he could maintain that army of slaves, the horses, the elephants and the concubines?"

The Prince heard this exchange of gossip with great amusement. He decided he would attend more such soirees if he survived. Then, in the midst of this conversation of the lamps, a rather loud and oily voice intruded.

"I am the Lamp from the Palace of the prince," said the voice dolefully. "My Prince is to die tomorrow for his Princess has trapped him into a bet."

Listening to all the gossip which the lamps were exchanging, and the good wine he had quaffed from his sister's cellar, the Prince had fallen half asleep. He rarely cared to give any heed to gossip, for gossip mostly ended up destroying reputations and breaking up relationships. But since the lamps were purveying first-hand information and had no axe to grind, the Prince had listened to what they were saying with half a mind. So when the lamp took his name, he became alert.

The other lamps all fell silent when they heard the Palace lamp. They wanted to know the details. After all, gossip about the rich and the powerful is always more interesting. Who is bothered if Tom's wife is sleeping with Dick or Dick's daughter has eloped with Harry? The Palace Lamp then proceeded to tell what the Princess had done and how she had concocted the riddle to take revenge on the Prince for having killed her beloved Serpent.

Hearing the details of the riddle and its meaning, the Prince realised the devilish plot his bodymate had concocted to bring about his death.

The Prince was much more cheerful the next day, and went about his chores with great energy and vigour. The Princess was mystified and not a little anxious at this change in the Prince's mood. Had he discovered the meaning of the riddle? she wondered. She attempted to probe his mind but he too had successfully shielded it against outside intrusions. When the evening of the fortieth day shrouded the palace courtyard, the cicadas had started their night-long songs and the chandeliers had been lit, the Prince called for a great feast with many guests. Viands were consumed and wine flowed like water. After all the guests had departed and the servants had been dismissed, only the Prince and the Princess were left. Then he turned to her and said, "You perfidious woman! Here is the meaning of your riddle. You discovered the remains of the Serpent in the cellar. Of his burnished skin, you have stitched a blouse. That is what you are wearing now and that is what is meant by '*the beloved is on the body*'. Then he took out his dagger and cut away the blouse exposing a necklace of polished bones, ground and shaped like pearls.

The bone necklace was adorning her shapely breasts, lodged safely in the cleavage. "Those are the bones of your Serpent which you are wearing next to your heart. That is the meaning of '*the beloved is on the heart*'. You have melted the Snake's fat and are using it in the lamps, especially the lamp that lights your bedroom. That is the meaning of '*the beloved lights the lamp*'. I have dug up the floor under your bed and found the rest of the Serpent's body buried there, '*sleeping under the bed*'."

The Princess went to sleep that night after taking a deep draught of opium and never woke up. The Prince put her in a magic casket and she is still sleeping there in the secret chamber of the palace.

Part II

I sent my grandmother's tale along with other folk tales, of course without my asides, to a publisher in London and it was published under the title *Folk Tales from India.* Many years later, I happened to be in London and as is my wont, went to browse old and second-hand books in my favourite bookshop on Charing Cross Road. There is a narrow lane branching off from Charing Cross Road. It's a cul-de-sac and has many shops containing rare old books and ancient maps of India. My interest in the literature of the occult had been aroused by the tales of my grandmother and my subsequent reading of *One Thousand and One Nights* and other such classics in Arabic and Persian. The bookshop kept its rare books on India, the Orient and the occult in the basement. When I climbed down the narrow wooden stairs into the rather dimly-lit basement, I found the walls lined by many bookshelves. The only other occupant was an English gentleman browsing through the shelves.

He appeared to be in his forties and was dressed in a sports jacket with leather patches on the elbows, and an Oxford tie. With the rather thick woollen trousers which country gentlemen preferred to wear, he looked distinguished but rather eccentric. As he browsed in one corner where books from India were stacked and I focused on the Middle East, we did not approach each other for quite some time. From the corner of my eye, I found that he had chanced upon a book which had caught his attention and was now sitting on a stool in his corner and browsing through it. Suddenly, he closed the book with a snap and stared at the dust cover at the back. Then he stared at me for some moments with a keen gaze. Again, he looked down at the book only to glance back at me keenly.

"Are you the Irfan Mekari who wrote this book?" he asked me abruptly. I was a bit startled at this sudden breaking of the gloomy silence in the basement which had so far only echoed to the rustling of pages. It took me a few moments to recover my poise.

"What book is that?" I asked.

"This one," he said. From a distance I could see neither the colour of the jacket nor read the title of the book.

"It has your photo on the back," he volunteered. Suddenly, it dawned on me that he had chanced upon my book on the folk-tales of India! The book had already acquired the status of a second-hand book in less than twenty years. *Sic transit gloria mundi* (Thus passes worldly glory), I murmured to myself.

"Yes, I wrote that book long ago," I said. He got up and came over to me with right hand extended. "I am John Wickelman, the Duke of Wickelshire. I am pleased to meet you." I shook hands with him. "Where is Wickelshire?" I asked him.

It's a small Duchy in the south of England. You may not even have heard of it," he said while shaking hands with me.

"Pleased to meet you, Your Grace," I said. I had no idea how to address a duke on his home turf. Had I met him in India, I would perhaps have addressed him as Mr Wickelman.

"Oh, cut that out," he said, "just call me John." Having put me at ease, he invited me to have a drink with him at the Bell and Cat, a pub across the road. At the invitation so graciously extended, I had no alternative but to accept.

We sat down in the dark cozy corner of the pub with a pint tankard each. He had bought the book and my old photo was face up on the table, staring at me. The duke proceeded to ask me questions for most of which I had no answers.

"I have read the story of the Bodymates with great interest," he said, "but tell me—where did your grandmother get that story from?"

"Honestly, I have no idea," I said. "Folk-tales as you know have no source and no provenance. They are just there, in the collective memory of the rural folk. She must have heard it from her grandmother, I presume. And she in turn must have heard it from her grandmother."

"Interesting! But there must be some basis, some modicum of truth at the base of such stories, don't you think?"

"Well," I said, "I can't imagine what truth there could be at the base of a story about a Prince who cuts himself in half and with the help of magic spells creates a spouse for himself. Of course, some of our ultra-nationalists will claim that the story is about the discovery of cloning and plastic surgery in ancient India disguised as a myth. They will argue that if we are prepared to believe that a whole cow can be created out of a single cell, why can't we believe that a whole human being can be created out of one half of a human body?"

The Duke laughed. "I have met many people in India who believe in the reality of such myths. I have heard claims of grafting an elephant's head on a human body and people travelling at supersonic speeds fuelled by cow's urine."

"Oh," I said, taking a sip from the tankard, "you have been to India."

"Of course I have been to India," he said. "Paul Brunton was a frequent visitor to Wickelshire. I had read all his books in the sixties and seventies but what inspired me to go to India was his *A Search in Secret India* and the *Message from Arunachala*. However, my interest in India was to learn the Left-Hand tantric path to salvation. Of course, I had read Sir Phillip John Woodroffe who wrote so voluminously on Tantra, but the theory of Tantra was one thing and its practice another. I met many Tantrics in India, mostly in Bengal and Bihar. But most of them turned out to be charlatans, practising their occult rites in cremation grounds, eating half-burnt human bodies and using human skulls for their mumbo-jumbo. Their only achievement is to persuade gullible villagers to sacrifice their sons and daughters for hidden treasurers. Some of them even manage to persuade the urban middle class to perform incest with their daughters to obtain wealth and power. I got disgusted with them soon enough and left for the Himalayas. There, in the mountains, in the hidden caves beyond the source of the Ganga, I found some genuine tantrics—ones with real occult powers. I sat at their feet for many a year and they taught me spells which, I am sure, no Englishman has learnt before."

"And few Indians," I interjected. I felt amused at his claim. I could easily see that he was one of those Englishmen who romanticised India, especially its occult side. He was quite obviously an heir to the traditions of Madame Blavatsky, Annie Besant, Paul Brunton, Sir John Woodroffe and others who came to India and out-Indianned the Indian gurus.

We repaired to the Charing Cross bookshop to finish our unfinished business. I picked up a few books on Rumi, Hallaj and Shabistari. The Duke had left before me. As I came out of the shop after making the necessary payment, I found a Rolls Royce idling at the kerb. The Duke was standing at the door, obviously waiting for someone.

"I would like you to visit Wickelshire House, my ancestral mansion, for dinner tonight. I will get you dropped back to wherever you are staying after the dinner," he invited me with a smile. "By the way, where are you staying?"

"At the Oxford and Cambridge Club, here at the Pall Mall," I said.

"That's a nice place, but I will make an even better offer. Why don't we go to your club? You pick up your nightsuit and toothbrush and whatever and come with me. Tomorrow is the weekend. We could go over my library and browse through the collection of the rarest books of occult science from all over the world."

The temptation was too great to resist and I succumbed to it. So, I collected my nightsuit and shaving kit from the Club. As we drove to Wickelshire Mansion in the English spring, I could feel the nip in the air even without winding down the glass window. Wickelshire was just two hours south of London, one of which we spent getting out of the London traffic; then we turned from the highway onto the village roads and within a short drive were at the mansion gate. It was manned by a security guard who recognised the Duke's car and the electronically-controlled gates rolled aside smoothly. We entered a long drive bordered by well-laid gardens and then Wickelshire house burst on my vision. It looked more like an Indian Palace in the midst of the English countryside. With its exotic turrets and minarets, it had the look of the palaces which abound in Rajasthan and Saurashtra.

"My great-grandfather built it after his return from India. He had joined Gen Harris's campaign against Tipu Sultan where both Arthur Wellesley and my grandfather John Marwell were colonels. Since Wellesley's brother Richard was the Governor-General of India, Wellesley rose rapidly in service. At the battle of Seringapatnam, it was my grandfather who took the Sultanpet Tope and later the Castle of Seringapatnam though Wellesley got the credit. Though Arthur made a great show of imposing discipline on the looters and rapists in the British Army, it was actually his greed which could not stand others taking away any part of the loot."

The grounds of Wickelshire Mansion were a miniature version of Blenheim Castle's extensive grounds, with a man-made lake with god-made geese swimming in it. Inside, the rooms had the usual high ceilings with walls and doors covered with tapestries, and chandeliers with their original candle-holders replaced by bulbs, hanging from the ceilings. I was shown to an imposing room by the butler who informed me that more than half the mansion had been leased to the Stately Homes of England Trust which had opened it to the public. It was the Trust which kept the mansion and the grounds well-maintained and the lease-rent which kept the library of His Grace well stocked with ancient tomes.

When we met for aperitifs and dinner, the Duke resumed his monologue.

"It was during the sack of Seringapatnam that my grandfather chanced upon a strange casket kept in a sealed room of the Palace. It was so ornately decorated with carvings, runic symbols, both Pali and Kufic calligraphy, that my grandfather fell in love with it at first sight. He believed that it contained gold, diamonds, emeralds and other precious stones—the fabled riches of

India. Without the knowledge of Arthur, he secreted the casket to his own tent and later brought it to Madras. It travelled with him wherever he went. It was with him on the Maratha Campaigns, the Pindara Wars and so on. Arthur had become a general before he left India but my grandfather retired as a Colonel. But all those who went to India in those days and joined the East India Company's service were robber barons—Warren Hastings, Robert Clive, Elihu Yale, Duke of Wellington, all of them. Arthur Wellesley is said to have brought back 50,000 pounds. I think that was a fraction of what he really brought back from his loot of Seringapatnam—gold, diamonds, emeralds, swords with jewel-studded hilts and daggers. Some of them you can see in the British Museum, some in the Victoria and Albert."

"Yes, I have seen an ancient Quran looted from Seringapatnam in the Lambeth Palace Library presented to the then Archbishop of Canterbury by Arthur Wellesley himself with his own inscription and signature," I said. "But what did your grandfather bring?"

"Of course, he too was no exception. He built this mansion from the loot, but his most prized possession was the ornate casket, for it was mysterious. He called it the Mystery Casket. He called the best carpenters and locksmiths from England and Europe to get it opened. They just could not discover any joint. It appeared to be carved out of a single log of mahogany. They said there was no way it could be sprung open. They believed that it was no casket but a carved piece of solid log and the only way to prove it was a casket was to break it down. No one recommended that, for it was such a beautifully carved artefact with its runic characters, Kufic calligraphy in gold and Sanskrit letters carved in jade studding its surface, which once broken, could not be repaired. So, it lay there on a trestle table in the basement of the mansion for the next two centuries."

"Is it still there?" I asked, my curiosity aroused to a high pitch.

"Of course, it is still there," said the Duke with a smile.

"And can I see it?" I asked rather hesitantly, not knowing whether the Duke would be willing to show such a prized possession to a stranger.

"Sure," he replied with a quizzical smile, "that is why I brought you here. After all, you are the folklore expert, though you don't believe in grandmothers' tales."

I spent a restless night in a strange bed in the mansion. And my dreams were all about handsome princes, mysterious voluptuous princesses wearing snake skin blouses, ornately-carved caskets containing remains of pythons and anacondas and so on.

I joined the Duke for breakfast—an elaborate English breakfast which you only read about in books, with devilled kidneys and kippers and venison sausages and eggs cooked in various ways weighing down the refectory table and the side-boards. The Duke then took me to the library. What an amazing collection it had! Contrary to what John had said about his grandfather having focused on looting only gold and jewels, I found his ancestors had looted many books which were still in manuscript form, unpublished—books in Persian, Arabic, Brahmi, Sanskrit, Pali, Bengali, ancient Tamil, Kannada, Mandarin and so on. Many of them were on tantra with strange pictures of human bodies with mysterious lines emanating from every organ.

There was a surfeit of linguistic wealth there in that library and I was satiated.

"So, when am I going to see the Mystery Casket?" I asked.

"Now," he said and took me through long corridors and gloomy passages meandering across the palace to a locked part of the mansion. He stopped before a nail-studded wooden door, guarded by two private security guards who came to attention and saluted the Duke. He took out a huge gleaming copper key and opened the door. As he switched on the light, the passage before us was swathed in a dim yellow light. We walked forward for a hundred yards, turned a corner and came to another door.

All the while that we had been walking, the Duke had kept up a monologue.

"You remember I told you about learning ancient

magic spells from tantrics in the Himalayas? They claimed that they had kept themselves alive for hundreds of years. One of them even claimed that he was a soldier in the army of Rana Sanga and had fought against Babar at the Battle of Khanwa. Disgusted at the defeat and loss of life, he had given up the world and retired to the cave. That was five hundred years ago!"

Oh, these gullible English nobility, I thought, they are the stuff of which PG Wodehouse characters are made.

"So, after having learnt all the incantations from the tantrics, I came back to try them on the casket. Many a day and night, I sat before it in lonely vigil with lighted candles, incense and myrrh, reciting the spells," he continued.

"With what result?" I asked sceptically.

By this time we had reached another door and the Duke opened it. There was a staircase leading to a basement. We entered the underground chamber and the Duke switched on the light. I saw the room was littered with half-burnt candles, incense burners with half-burnt coals and ashes, and incense sticks in silver holders with inches of ashes trembling on their tips. There, in the centre of the room, on a low trestle table, I saw the Mystery Casket. It was about eight feet long with a diameter of three feet. It was indeed a marvel of ancient workmanship, such as the ancient artisans of India executed, with elaborate and intricate carvings. The casket had all those various scripts carved into it, and many of the words and letters worked into the mahogany were carved from precious and semi-precious stones. It did appear to be carved from a single log, for the various cursive scripts in gold ran across the surface in a continuous flow. There would have been a break if the casket, if it could be called a casket, had been in two parts. I had seen several wooden sarcophagi both in the British Museum and the Cairo Museum in which the mummies slept. Even though they were made very smooth and very sleek, one could spot the joint where the two halves met, with a little scrutiny.

"So, you could not open it?" I asked.

"I did open it," he said with a smile. "My incantations learnt in the Himalayas were quite effective."

He went close to the casket and with some manipulation found the button hidden in one of the stone dots of the mysterious letters. As he pressed it and stood back, slowly and gently without even a creak the lid opened up revealing the inside.

My heart was thudding with excitement as the lid lifted itself up. I saw that the inside was lined with soft velvet over a thin cushioning all round. There was even a pillow-like bump at one end, and an indentation in the centre. But the casket was empty.

"So much for the speculation of your grandfather about the gold and jewels inside. So, what did you find inside?"

"I will tell you at dinner," he replied. "My wife is joining us then."

I could not contain my excitement and curiosity throughout the afternoon. What casket was that? How old was it? How long had it lain in Tipu's palace? It certainly was not carved during Tipu's regime or even that of his father Hyder Ali. It was far, far older than that, than even the Maharajas who preceded Tipu and Hyder Ali. What had it contained? Did it have any relationship to my grandmother's tale? Why had the Duke asked me about the origin and source of her tale? Do I, a rational man with a scientific mind, believe in all this mumbo-jumbo of tantrism? Like John, all the tantrics I had met in my travels in India happened to be charlatans and street-magicians, entertaining bystanders with sleight-of-hand tricks which they called magic. Many of them had been exposed and arrested both during the British rule and after independence, some of them accused of kidnapping, rape and murder.

But then, the casket was real. It did have all those mysterious Persian and Sanskrit engravings. I was confused, and it was in this state of confusion that I joined John in the smoking room for an aperitif before dinner. We had just finished the glass of sherry when the dinner gong sounded and we rose for the dining room. As we entered from one door, the door on the opposite side opened and there entered one of the most beautiful women I had ever seen in my life. She had no English cast to her countenance. It had certainly an Indian or Persian look—a complexion of burnished gold, long black hair shining like sable, falling on both sides of her body right down her waist, a nose chiselled out of translucent marble, and a figure which would have put Shakuntala, Diana and Psyche to shame. She was dressed in a long resplendent robe which emphasised her height and her figure. Her alabaster arms were encased in a blouse cut in the Indian fashion. I stood rooted to the spot, dazed and witless.

As she advanced towards me, the Duke said, "Meet my wife, the princess of Seringapatnam."

And as she came closer, I saw a small black mole on the left corner of her mouth. When she smiled, the mole distinctly faded in colour. And on her forehead, where the hair parted, there was a red birthmark, small and noticeable only by one who looked for it!

Juniper Cottage

As Vinod parked his Toyota Camry at the foot of the steep flight of steps cut into the side of the rock on which the Juniper Cottage was located, the Himalayan evening was breathing its last lap. In the next half-an-hour, darkness would be overtaking the plateau and the cottage. After the blistering heat and polluted air of Delhi where the mercury hovered in the middle forties, Chail felt almost chilly. June was the cruellest month in India's capital, Vinod thought. For some peculiar reason, the traffic snarls grew worst in that month. Cars massed up at every traffic signal, with drivers honking incessantly on their horns, as though that would cool down the heat. Tempers rose all round and road rage became the order of the day. People snarled at each other at the least provocation. Every morning husbands left home after snapping at their wives and the wife snarled at the housemaid, who was again late for work. Delhi became a city of barbarians every summer. The camouflage of winter made the road users look like human beings, but the heat of June melted away the veneer exposing their real abrasive nature below the skin. Four-letter words became parts of speech and one heard them on the road, in the offices and at parties.

That was one reason Vinod had escaped from the city of the damned. As he stepped out of the car, he took a deep breath of the clean fresh air. It felt like a draught of a cool Kashmir stream. He felt as though he had taken a dip in the Liddar stream in Pahalgam. He took out his suitcase and holdall from the boot and locked the Camry. It was a reflex action. There was no danger of anyone stealing the car from inside the Castle Estate, but after twenty years of driving with caution, it becomes second nature. Cars were regularly stolen in Delhi streets and gangs of thieves enjoyed immunity from local police. They had perfected the art of changing the number plates of the cars, removing the stamped engine numbers and despatching them by trains to far-off destinations where their accomplices took delivery. But these were mostly Marutis, Fords and Hyundais. So far thieves were wary of stealing Camrys and BMWs and Mercedes. There was no ready market for them, and they were too conspicuous.

As he climbed the rough stone steps, Vinod paused midway to look over the top of the darkling pines in the fading sunlight that still lingered on the peaks of the mountain ranges that spread all around. Somewhere at the back of his mind, a vague thought struggled to come to the fore. A depressing thought. Was there some connection between the fading sunlight and his own life? As he had left Delhi that morning, he had known that it would take him a long long time to knit together the unravelled skeins of his life.

The midway pause on the steps gave him time to regain his breath. Though the suitcase and holdall were rather lightly packed, even the short climb had left him a little breathless. Of late, he had given up going to the gym. He was out of condition, he felt. After this lone holiday, he would resume his exercise regimen, he resolved. And he would give up drinking and become a teetotaller. As he bent down to pick up the luggage again and continued the climb, his legs felt rather heavy and he wondered why. He had always prided himself on his stamina and physical fitness, but the daily intake of Chivas Regal, and nights spent with Amita had taken their toll. Amita had an insatiable appetite. He had heard of nymphomaniacs, and Amita sucked out all his energies every night.

He wondered why he felt so weak now that he was out of Delhi. Perhaps the struggle with Priya and the parting had sapped his strength. He knew it was not his fault—the parting with Priya. In the final analysis, Vinod told himself, it was Priya's fault. It was Priya who had refused to give in. He had been willing to go half way. He was prepared to cut down on his drinking, was willing to allow her to entertain her numerous relatives at home (including her obnoxious mother whose sight he could not stand, even when she was at her best), and even permit her to visit her parents in Bombay occasionally. He could not give up Amita, of course. But Priya wanted none of that. She wanted all of him.

As he paused, Vinod recalled his honeymoon with Priya, right here in Chail years ago. They had occupied another cottage then—the Pine Cottage, he recalled. Priya was a beautiful girl and the honeymoon was a dream. He was stunned when he first saw her at the gate of DPS School in Delhi. He had gone to pick up his nephew, Vijay, at the request of his elder sister, Poonam. Priya was standing just outside the gate, perhaps waiting for a bus. She was wearing a pink sari, draped demurely around her comely shoulders and a matching blouse, he recalled. With a complexion that would have put many Bollywood stars to shame, large kohl-lined eyes and a mouth that demanded to be kissed there and then, she made a deep and instant impact on Vinod. He offered to drop her home, at the spur of the moment. Normally, as she later told him, she would have refused the offer. She was not that kind of girl who accepted lifts from strangers. She had read about the fate of some who had taken lifts from predators, and paid for it. But the presence of young Vijay, all of seven years, had reassured her.

They did not share much information during that first ride; Priya remained taciturn. Vinod too kept the conversation banal in the presence of Vijay. But he found himself very attracted to her—her simple looks, demure attitude and sincere commitment towards her wards had made a good impression on him. Even during that first meeting, Vinod had felt that Priya too was attracted towards him. So, his sister was pleasantly surprised when for the next few days, he had offered to pick up Vijay from the school, without being requested. He had rarely done that before.

When his sister first saw Priya, she was even more surprised, for she felt Priya was not the type of girl Vinod was usually attracted to. Though she was quite beautiful, her beauty was of a quiet type, the kind that is formed out of a simple, innocent mind. Vinod was an extrovert. He liked parties, drinks, flirting, dancing in discos and moving around with girls who came to gyms for mala fide exercise. He liked glamour in his girlfriends. He was more attracted to the smart, glib, articulate and party-going girls. As a student he used to bring home many girls, mostly from the Miranda College. With a Harley-Davidson (a gift from his father on his birthday), between his legs—a car was passé—Vinod exuded machismo from every pore. His father was a self-made billionaire who belonged to the old school. He kept Vinod on a tight leash so long as he was alive. After the father died and his only son Vinod inherited his father's business and fortune, he started sowing his wild oats. He had many affairs, mostly temporary and broke many hearts. So, when Vinod brought Priya home his sister remonstrated with him.

"She is a simple innocent girl. And she is a school teacher, for heaven's sake! She is not your type, Vinod. Leave her alone. You have broken too many hearts, but they belonged to girls who could afford to get them repaired. This girl is different. If you break her heart, it will never heal. So, don't do it," she told him.

"But my dear Didi, I am not going to have an affair with her. I am serious. I want to marry her," Vinod had blurted out.

"What!" Poonam had cried out. "You will marry the school teacher; I don't believe it. But why?"

"Because after all those callous butterflies, her innocence appeals to me. She is quite serious about life and she is not impressed with my money or my looks. That is what attracts me to her."

At first, though Priya went on a couple of innocent dates with Vinod, she showed no interest in any kind of flirtation with him, much less in having an affair. A friendly soul, she was certainly attracted to Vinod. As a school teacher, she lived in the company of middle class, conservative gentry. Her male colleagues in the school were rather introverted, staid family men, concerned with the struggle to make the two ends meet on their meagre monthly salaries. Sitting one day over coffee in the India Coffee House in the early days of courtship, Vinod had attempted to hold her hand. Discreetly, she withdrew it and kept it in her lap.

Looking into the dark depths of her eyes, he had asked her, "Do you think you could fall in love with me?"

"Love is a divine gift, Vinod. It is not lightly bestowed; nor can it be casually withdrawn," she had replied seriously.

Vinod had felt a little abashed at her earnestness. On another occasion he had taken her for tea and snacks to the Gymkhana Club, to impress her with his connections with the high and the mighty. As they sat in the oak-panelled lounge, relaxing in old cracked leather sofas, Priya watched the old ladies clad in old-fashioned saris of yesteryear amble in. They were accompanied by their even more ancient looking husbands, in faded suits and limp ties held loosely at their scrawny necks.

"Are these the high and mighty who rule India?" she had asked. "They look decrepit, faded and past their prime."

Vinod felt a bit deflated.

"The man you saw in the wheelchair was once the Cabinet Secretary of India, and the man with the white moustache and walking stick was once the Army Chief," Vinod had mentioned.

"You seem to be enjoying the membership of a Geriatrics Club," Priya had remarked.

Vinod felt all his efforts to impress her were falling flat and it showed on his face. "I don't mean to sound snobbish, Vinod." She had tried to assuage his feelings. "You see Vinod, I come from a middle-class family. My mother, who was a religiously-inclined housewife died when I was still in school. My father married a second time. My stepmother allowed me to complete college, though rather reluctantly. All these high-flown places you are showing me around are alien to me. I have never visited any club. Before you took me out, I had never been to a five-star restaurant. I do not relate to such places; nor to the Cabinet Secretaries or Army Chiefs."

Her lack of interest in his money or his machismo piqued and quickened his desire to overcome her resistance to his blandishments. It was a case of attraction of the opposites. So, he persisted and at last broke through her wall of innocence and indifference. In spite of all her reservations, she fell in love with him and after a year of courtship she consented to marry him. Her love for him was not tinged with an iota of selfishness or greed. She cared nothing for his cars or his money.

Her stepmother was overwhelmed at the prospect of getting such a rich and handsome son-in-law and simultaneously getting rid of Priya. So, the nuptials took place in the Taj Palace Hotel in Delhi. It was a glittering, gala affair but Vinod avoided inviting any of his erstwhile flames.

Vinod took Priya to Chail for their honeymoon. His first choice was Mauritius or Phuket, but Priya was reluctant to go abroad with her newly-married husband, before even having seen India. She was afraid of committing any *faux pax* before foreigners, which may embarrass Vinod.

So, they landed up at Chail in the Pine Cottage which was owned by a business friend of his late father. For two weeks, they hardly left the Cottage except to go over to the nearby Castle Hotel to have their meals. Many times, Priya cooked simple meals for them in the well-equipped kitchen annexed to the Cottage. Priya found that Vinod was a man of high appetites, both at the table and in the bed. Though she tried to satisfy him in every way, there were times when she longed to merely curl up on the sofa and just listen to his voice. But such occasions, rare as they were, soon turned into passionate plays.

Vinod was at first very happy with Priya. After the torrid affairs he had had and the one-night stands, the steady relationship with a devoted sensible girl like Priya made him very happy. Her total commitment to him and her utter devotion to his wishes and his welfare boosted his ego. And he was even happier to note that she was willing to satisfy his wildest demands and most passionate fantasies in bed. He took pleasure in every part of her body. Vinod had a sadistic streak in bed. Sometimes looking at herself in the bathroom mirror Priya saw the red bruises and the bite marks, but she never complained. Vinod never realised the deep reluctance and restraint with which she gave herself to him, merely to make him happy. The passion plays continued for many months after their return to Delhi.

Perhaps the birth of a child would have diverted Vinod from passion to parenthood; but the child never came. Vinod did not feel the failure so much as Priya. She started wondering whether there was something wrong with her.

Within a couple of years of the marriage, Vinod's passion started cooling off. He stayed longer and longer at the office and business demands took him away to New York, London and Paris. Priya never suspected that Vinod was finding different beds in those fleshpots to quench his fire. She accepted that a successful businessman had to travel, and an exhausted traveller required physical rest when he returned. So, at first, she did not remonstrate with him at his lack of interest in her. But she became a bit perturbed when his absences grew longer and longer even when he was in Delhi and he started staying nights in the office. That's when she started getting worried. She suspected things were not what they seemed.

One late night things came to a boil. Vinod had spent the evening with Amita, his college friend, drinking with her and having a good time. He found Priya waiting for him when he returned home in the early hours. "Vinod, how long is this to go on?" she asked. "As long as I think I need it," he said shortly.

"But I have given you everything that you needed. What more do you want? I have even compromised every shred of my self-respect and dignity to please you outside and inside the bed. I take care of you, cook for you, pack your bags for you and wait for you every evening to join you at dinner. Why do you abandon me so? What are you seeking in drink and perhaps in other women?"

"Shut up," he had replied angrily. "Don't you dare to talk to me like that?"

"Why shouldn't I, Vinod? You are losing all your balance, and our marriage is going downhill because of your drinking and your whoring."

That is when Vinod had lost his temper. For the first time in their marriage he had slapped her, but Priya, even then, had not lost her cool. "Vinod, I want you to stop all that you are doing and come back to me," she had pleaded. "Remember all the promises you made to me before marriage. What happened to all those commitments you made to me in Chail?"

"Promises made during courtship and commitments made in bed have no sanctity. They are made to be broken," Vinod had answered heartlessly.

"But I am still your wife, Vinod. We are still married. You don't believe in the sanctity of marriage bonds?"

"No, it is finished," he said. "I cannot live with you anymore. I am divorcing you."

"Vinod, don't say that," Priya had cried. "I love you. You know I cannot live without you. You are everything to me." It was a cry from a broken heart.

"But you are nothing to me," Vinod had said with a note of finality in his voice.

"You are an old woman, in mind and body, and if I live with you, I will myself grow prematurely old. And I never want to grow old," Vinod had exclaimed, with the utter confidence of his youth and vigour.

"But what will I do if you abandon me?" Priya had wailed.

"You are still young. You can marry some old school colleague of yours," Vinod had said callously.

"A woman does not love twice, Vinod," she had cried. It had been as though her soul was being wrenched from her body. There was so much of sorrow in her voice that Vinod was taken aback for a moment, but he hardened his heart, turned and walked out of the house.

Vinod had felt no regrets at parting from Priya. His affair with Amita was progressing well, though Priya did not know anything about it. At least that is what he believed.

And the break happened months ago.

As Vinod's head cleared the lichen covered parapet of undressed stones of the Juniper Cottage, he saw that the word Cottage was a euphemism, for it was a fairly large structure built in the old Anglo-Raj style, so dominantly prevalent in the erstwhile native states in the early part of this century. It had a gabled roof, large windows to catch as much light as possible, slatted window-panes, and green painted wooden walls. It must have been a comely building in its heyday but age had withered its vanity. Many of the wooden tiles were missing from the roof and the paint was peeling off from the outer walls and doors. Many of the wire-mesh mosquito screens that covered the windows hung loose.

Juniper was one of the five cottages located in the vast complex of the Castle Hotel, which had once served as the summer resort of the Maharajah of Bundipore in the glorious days of Pax Britannica. After independence, it was taken over by the state and handed over to the Tourist Department. And like all buildings touched by that department, the once beautiful and well-maintained palace had been transformed into a shabby, rundown, dilapidated collection of rooms, with frayed carpets, broken sofas and non-functional bathrooms. Yet, with all these shortcomings, these cottages had a charm of their own. Those who could afford preferred to rent the cottage rather than a more comfortable suite in the main Castle Hotel. Vinod took in all this at first glance as he stepped in. For a moment, he wondered whether he had done right in renting the cottage, instead of booking a suite in the Castle Hotel, but he had needed the quiet and the privacy of a cottage all to himself. He had had too much of company all of these last few months—the lawyers, the courts, the well-wishers and so on; above all, the reproaches of his sister.

He walked the few steps to the door carrying his heavy suitcase and his bag. His last visit to his cardiologist was not very pleasant. "You have high BP and a weak heart. I notice the first signs of cardio-myopathy. You have to give up your late nights and heavy drinking. Don't lift any weight heavier than five kilos. If you are not careful, your heart may give up suddenly." As he paused, the cottage door was opened by a rather well-dressed lady. She looked at him, noted his exhausted looks and heavy breathing, glanced at the suitcase in his hand and remarked, "You must be Vinod Malhotra."

"Yes, I am," said Vinod.

"You should have told me. I would have sent someone to carry the luggage."

"And who are you?" asked Vinod.

She said her name was Viveka. Putting down the suitcase and holdall that he was carrying on the once

Persian carpet, Vinod asked Viveka to sit down as he himself took a seat.

"Are you the housekeeper?" he asked her.

She looked at him with a smile.

"Housekeeper, conscience keeper, soul keeper..." she said with a laugh.

"And whose conscience and soul do you keep?" Vinod asked flirtatiously, as he recovered his breath and his heartbeat returned to normal.

"Ah," she laughed lightly. "Many people come to Juniper Cottage burdened with cares, both physical and mental. The Cottage gives them back what they bring into it. They say an ancient *rishi* lived here in an *ashram* before the Maharaja built his palace and these cottages for the royal guests. People used to come to him to confess their sins and pray for salvation. It was called the *Punyashram*. You expiated your sins in the solitude of the ashram. Juniper Cottage occupies the same site, they say."

Vinod was amused by the story.

Viveka also revealed the fact that the telephone didn't work and warned him sternly that if he left the windows open, he could expect to be invaded by monkeys. She also told him that the kitchen had the necessary utensils and crockery and the cupboard and the fridge were well-stocked with necessary provisions for a couple of days, if needed. If he needed any more he could always ring up at the Castle Hotel, though she didn't reveal how he was to do this when the phone didn't work. Viveka sat for some time in the sitting room with him and prattled on about the facilities in the hotel, the attractions in Chail, which were not many and, the close-by shopping areas which were non-existent. She tried to comfort him with her presence and her desultory conversation, since the cottage gloom held out no prospect of any entertainment. After she left Vinod felt forlorn.

He switched on the single unshaded bulb of the drawing room and threw himself into a sofa for a smoke. There were several doors opening into the sitting room. He could guess that one of them led through a covered verandah into the kitchen and the rest into bedrooms. He looked out of the window and noticed the juniper bushes crowding the space between the cottage and the parapet. According to the Tourist Office, Juniper Cottage had three bedrooms in addition to the large sitting room and a kitchen annexe. He postponed exploring the rooms until dinner. He did not look forward to the prospect of the walk to the dining room of the main hotel, half a kilometer away, in the dark, particularly in his worn-down state. The sofa, even with its squeaking springs, felt too comfortable to leave.

He relaxed into the sagging upholstery and surveyed the room, which was the main living room. Apart from the sofa in which he sat, there was a long three-seater on his left and an old-fashioned chaise longue on his right.

The upholstery of both had seen better days. There was, of course, the ubiquitous fireplace, with an ancient rusted poker and a pair of broken tongs. Above the mantelpiece, he saw an old painting of a Rajput lady hanging on the wall. The dust and grime had obscured the face and Vinod could not make out whether she was young or old. In the corner, by the door he had entered, was a roll-top desk, the kind that was common in India in the early part of the twentieth century. Vinod knew that such furniture was available now only in antique shops.

With falling darkness, Vinod felt as though the temperature in the room too had gone down by a few degrees. His watch showed it was only seven pm. There was a cold draught coming from one of the bedrooms. He wondered if that bedroom had a door opening on the backyard but he did not have the urge to get up and find out. He found a strange sense of lethargy creeping over all his senses. He had just lighted his third cigarette when suddenly he heard a strange noise coming from one of the closed bedrooms, the same door from under which the cold draught was coming. Normally he would have ignored the noise. One should expect such noises from old wooden buildings, but of late, his nerves were on edge and even small sounds tended to grate on his nerves. At first, he could not recognise what it was, a mix of a screech and a scratch. It sounded like some small animal trying to get out of a wooden trap. He thought that it would be in keeping with the rest of the cottage facilities for the Tourist Department to provide some rats in the bedroom. So, he disregarded the noise and continued to smoke.

His mind meandered back to the messy divorce he had just concluded. He knew that Priya had had an unhappy childhood with an over-dominant and strict step-mother and a recluse father. She had no brothers and sisters, and when he had married her, she had given up her career of teaching to be a proper wife to him. In any case, he himself was a bit old-fashioned in marriage. He would never have stood for a working wife. With his wealth and income, he could afford a wife who stayed home. He believed that a woman could not be a wife and a mother and yet have a career. She had to choose and Priya had chosen. He was still wondering about Priya and her career prospects. She had threatened that if he divorced her, she would kill herself. She could not live without him, she loved him so. She was now divorced, finally. What would she do now? In his heart of hearts, he believed her threat was meant seriously. She was the type of girl who would kill herself if rejected; but he disregarded the threat. Like an ostrich hiding his head in the sand, he stopped reading the newspaper after the divorce. He, therefore, missed the report of Priya's suicide. He convinced himself that she was alive.

Then he heard the noise again. It had grown louder as though some large animal was scratching at the door with its front paws. What animal was it that was trying to get out? he wondered. And how did it get into the room? The scratching sound was now accompanied by a croak.

There must be some animal in the bedroom which must have crept in from the backyard and was trying to get out. The right thing to do was to open the door and let it out. But what animal was it? The forests of Chail had a variety of fauna, including black and brown bears. What might come out if he opened the door—what if it happened to be a bear or a leopard? But the animal seemed to be in pain. Should not one save it from its agony? But he found a strange reluctance in himself to get up from the sofa and go to the door. Or was it the fear of what he might see behind the door once it was opened that was preventing him from getting up?

In the respite from the scratching sound, his mind once again went back to Priya. Now that she was divorced, he wondered what she would do. She did not have even a child to keep her occupied. Would she go back to her parents who had been glad to see her married off? Would she go back to her career? Too old for that. The younger people with their BEds and MEds would give her a tough competition and an inferiority complex. He realised that Priya was facing a *cul-de-sac*.

He heard the noise again. This time he could not disregard it. He wondered whether it could be a large cat, but then a cat did not explain the croaking. Cats never croaked. They mewed and they purred but they never croaked; nor did bears or leopards. The sound reminded him of the large black ravens in the Tower of London and the strange noises they made when hungry. Strange birds, those ravens, their large black bodies made a weird contrast against the pale sickly-coloured walls of the Tower. Their waddling walk on the lawns, their deliberate neck motions, their unearthly croaks all reminded Vinod of a poem he had read in college.

"*Take thy beak from out my heart, and take thy form from off my door!*"

Quoth the raven "Nevermore".

He put out the cigarette in the ashtray on the table, got up reluctantly from the sofa and went forward to open the door. He had hardly taken a couple of steps when some instinct made him pause. What if it was an animal larger than a cat? Were there any wild predators in Chail, and could one have got into the bedroom? Should he open the door without knowing what was behind it? Should he not ring and summon help? But the telephone was dead. As he hesitated, he heard the sound again. This time, it was a loud wail, an unearthly kind of wail wrenched out from the very depths of a tortured soul. It was the sound of someone on whom all the sorrows of the world had descended. His hair stood on end. For a few moments, as he listened to the crescendo of the wail, he felt both fear and a deep welling of sympathy in his heart, for it was no animal that cried in that bedroom. There was a distinct human note in the sound. He had a sinking feeling, as though his heart was falling through unfathomable depths.

He staggered and fell back into the sofa. He needed a drink and a puff badly. He stretched his hand towards the ashtray where he had put his half-smoked cigarette. As he did so, he glanced at his hand. It was trembling. Vinod had always thought of himself as a brave man, a man of steel nerves. How could an unknown animal behind a closed door frighten him so? But what frightened him was not the trembling. What shook him was a feeling that his hand was changing before his very eyes. It was shrivelling and getting smaller even as he watched. As he looked at it, he felt that the skin on the back was becoming loose and wrinkled as that of an old man. Was it really happening or was he hallucinating? The fingers looked as though they were becoming thinner and crooked, the nails bent and serrated, the hair white and lifeless. It was like something out of a film—like a speeded-up film where they show a flower wilting, then shrivelling, drying and crumbling all in a few seconds. He looked at his other hand. He saw to his horror that the same thing was happening to it.

Even as he was attacked by a panic, the wails from the bedroom were growing louder and louder. He turned to look at the door, and as he turned, he felt the belt at his waist loosening. Strange, he thought. He got up to tighten it and took a few steps towards the door again, but his waist too appeared to have shrunk. The trousers were in danger of slipping down. With the first steps he took, he felt his feet move loosely in the shoes, as though the shoes were a couple of sizes too large. It was a strange feeling. His clothes felt loose, his shoes felt loose, his belt felt loose. Was his whole body shrinking in his clothes? As he tried to walk back to the sofa, he felt no strength in his knees. It was as though someone had sucked out all the youth and strength from his body. Meanwhile, the loud keening from the bedroom continued to resonate in the sitting room. The wail would start as a low plaintive moan and then rise slowly in a crescendo to a deep lament, a dirge, a requiem for all the departed joys of the world. And then it would die away and sink into a painful expectant silence. After that pregnant pause, he would hear the pawing at the door. Then the wail would rise once again. As he tottered into the sofa, he knew he had no strength even to call someone. He recalled faintly someone telling him that the telephone didn't work.

As he listened to those deep wails, a feeling of utter sorrow and desolation crept over him. He felt as though the wails were coming not from the bedroom but from deep inside his head. He felt drawn towards the bedroom, towards whoever was crying her heart out there. An invisible force was tugging at his limbs trying to pull him up, to make him walk up to the door. Yet, the weakness in his knees, looseness of his spine, and his nerveless body would not allow him to get up. Who was there inside, imprisoned in that dark bedroom and what animal was it that was scratching at the door? He felt as though he knew her…he had known her sometime far back in the past, aeons ago. Who was it who had wronged that wailing creature? Now, she was calling on him as if those terrible wails were demanding some retribution.

Suddenly, he noticed a change of note in those wails, a tremulous change as though the voice was sinking and unless he went to her quickly, she would die without her wrongs being righted. His youth and strength were already gone. His body had visibly shrivelled. He had nothing left to offer her except his quivering soul, his fading self. He felt he must get up and go to her. He didn't know what he would see once he opened that door. Would he have the strength to switch on the light? What would he encounter in the gloom? Would the bed be empty or would he see some frightening form crouching there? Horrible visions danced before his eyes, frightful forms, nameless horrors. He saw in his mind's eye misshapen figures, twisted limbs, and oh my God, what did await him behind that closed door? He knew deep inside him that once he entered that room, he would never be able to come out. No one would ever know what had happened to him. He would just wither away in the gloom along with that fading wail of that bedroom. The darkness would swallow him.

He spotted a pad of the Castle Hotel stationery on the roll-top desk by the side of which he was sitting. He felt an urge to write something about what was happening to him. The pad beckoned him. With his old, shrivelled fingers, he drew it closer. He took out his pen, which felt heavy in his fingers. He noticed his nails twisted like talons which were coming off the skin. He decided to write down the whole sequence of events before the fatal attraction pulled him into that dreadful maelstrom.

******

Deepak discovered the faded sheets of the Castle Hotel stationery from beneath an old newspaper in the wooden niche of the roll-top desk. That was years later. Juniper Cottage had grown more dilapidated over the years, Deepak found. It had remained untenanted for long intervals. The very first look at the exterior of the building had depressed Deepak. The walls, windows and doors had lost even the vestiges of the old green paint at many places. The rain and snow had whitened the exposed timbers giving it a scabrous look. He had stayed there many years before with his parents and family on a holiday, but he was saddened to see that the leather seats had more cracks than a drought-stricken dry landscape. The paint had peeled off from the wooden walls inside and the carpet was falling apart at the edges. It appeared the Castle Hotel had not bothered to keep it in a semblance of good repair, nor replaced the old frayed carpet or the furniture of old British days. He looked around as he read the ancient manuscript and noticed the bedroom door opposite, which rcmained closed.

Deepak had just arrived from Delhi. Reena was to join him there from Shimla the next day. They were both married, but not to each other. Deepak had decided to celebrate his triumph over his old friend turned business rival Kaushal, whom he had driven into bankruptcy, despair and death. He had been trying to do that for over ten years now. He had adopted every means, fair and foul, and step by step he had forced the man to dispose of all his assets to meet his liabilities. He had ensured that Kaushal's house was seized by the bailiff.

He had seen him beg for mercy from even his smallest creditor. Finally, the man had filed for bankruptcy. The only thing Kaushal believed he had was Reena, his wife. He did not know that Reena too had deserted him and hitched herself to Deepak's shining star. So, a triumphant Deepak felt he needed a holiday to relax and savour his triumph. He had asked Reena to spend a week with him. He had been having an affair with her for the last three years. His own wife believed that he was on a business trip. As he read the old manuscript, he found his glance straying towards the bedroom door from time to time. The manuscript referred to that room. He did not believe a word of what he was reading. The unknown writer, Deepak thought, must have let his imagination run riot. Perhaps he had attempted to write a horror story.

Just as Deepak put down the manuscript wondering who had written that story, he glanced at the old newspaper in which the manuscript was wrapped. There was a small piece of news that had made the front page. The headlines read: "Lonely lady commits suicide". Below, the eight lines written in florid journalese stated that Mrs Priya Malhotra, the recently-divorced wife of the industrialist Vinod Malhotra had been found hanging from the fan in her two-bedroom flat. She left a note behind stating no one should be held responsible for her death. She was taking her life as she had nothing to live for. Her former husband could not be traced, as he was reported to be holidaying in Chail.

As Deepak finished the manuscript, he wondered. Though he did not believe a word of it, he could not help glancing at the bedroom door. He also picked up the telephone receiver to check whether it was working. "Hello," said a female voice at the other end. "What can I do for you?"

"Who is speaking?" Deepak said.

"This is Viveka of the Castle Hotel, Mr Deepak."

"Oh," he said. So there was a Viveka in the Hotel.

Was it the same Viveka mentioned in the manuscript? he wondered.

Just then he heard a noise, a faint noise as though a rat was scratching at the bedroom door. He glanced up, and even as he stared at the bedroom door, he heard a croak, a loud croak as though someone was torturing a raven.

Lisa Ulyanova

I met Lisa Ulyanova on the railway platform of the Moscow terminal in St Petersburg. It was a rather cold morning in September and I had spent an uncomfortable night in the narrow bed of the coach. Lisa stepped forward and introduced herself. "I am Lisa Ulyanova," she said, "and I am to be your guide in St Petersburg, no?" The 'no', I discovered later, was an affirmative challenge whenever Lisa wanted to make an emphatic statement, as though daring the other person to contradict it. In any case, the previous three days of rather tedious negotiations with the Russians had left me in no position to contradict anyone, much less a diminutive but tough looking customer like Lisa. She was dressed in tight jeans, a crumpled cotton shirt and a leather jacket. She was not much taller than five feet with a thin wiry frame. But her stance (she always stood on the balls of her feet), and her bright shining eyes, imparted to her the look of an alert leopard, apprehending unknown dangers from the surrounding scrub but ready to take on any hunter.

"Welcome to St Petersburg," she continued, herding us to the exit and the car park. "We will first go to the hotel where you can have your wash. Then please come down for breakfast. As soon as you eat your breakfast, I will take you on a tour of the city, no?"

"Yes, that is okay," I said meekly in response. So, I and my three companions picked up our suitcases and followed Lisa out of the terminal. There was a huge red bus standing just outside the exit and Lisa led us into it. I thought that a fifty-seater bus was a bit large for the five of us, but Lisa said that anything smaller would not give us the kind of grandstand view of the city's glories. Moreover, the vehicle had the PA system, without which a guide would feel as helpless as Yehudi Menuhin without his violin.

On the way to the hotel, Lisa kept up a continuous patter on the mike.

"St Petersburg was founded by Peter the Great in 1703. Actually, he captured the site from Sweden in a war that year. The first thing he built was the Peter and Paul Fort, no? That was the first real building of the new city. You will see it when we go there. He called it Peter and Paul, perhaps because there was Peter in it. He also called the city Petersburg. Actually, he named it after himself but claimed it was after Saint Peter. All bunkum, as you say, no?" We all nodded our heads, not having had the personal acquaintance of Peter the Great.

As the bus proceeded towards the hotel, Lisa showed us all the important buildings en route and the way she talked about them, Arvind could not help asking her in his gentle voice, "Did you build them, Lisa?"

"You are joking, no? I like jokes. Ognav never liked jokes; he was too serious."

We refrained from asking who Ognav was, for fear that Lisa may go off on a tangent. We were not ready to make the acquaintance of Ognav so early in the day.

"An interesting moment! Petersburg changed names several times. In 1914, the Czar changed the name to Petrograd. You know why?"

"No," we all said in unison. None of us had been born in 1914.

"Because Russia was at war with Germany and the name sounded too German. Grad is Russian, no, and Burg is German. That is why?"

We all appeared suitably impressed. That was a lesson in comparative philology.

"It did not stop there. The name was changed to Leningrad in 1924. That is because Lenin started the

Russian revolution from here."

Ah, said all of us. Now we are getting a lesson in Russian history.

"Then it was changed again?" Bajaj asked. He was curious to know the progressive changes of metropolitan life.

"Yes. In 1991, the people of Leningrad decided to go back to the original name. So, it was changed again to St Petersburg."

"Will you change it again to Petrograd if there is a war with Germany?" Arvind asked mischievously.

"Ah, you are joking, no?" Lisa smiled. She looked quite charming when she smiled.

"St Petersburg has a population of four and a half million today. An interesting moment! Before the Second World War it had a population of three and a half million. After the war the population was six hundred thousand." She was watching us to observe the effect of her shock statement.

"And what happened to the rest?" interrupted Arvind, my colleague.

"Oh, over one million died during the war. The rest went away from St Petersburg—how do you say migrated, no?" Lisa explained.

"The Germans killed one million people?" asked Bajaj, another colleague who was accompanying us. He sounded a bit sceptical.

"Most of them," said Lisa. "Many died because they had nothing to eat. They starved you know. Many children died in the first year of the siege. The Germans surrounded the city and would not let anything in—no food, no medicine, nothing."

"And how long did this siege last?" asked Bajaj.

"Nine hundred days. Actually, eight hundred and ninety-nine days, but it is easy to say nine hundred, no?" Lisa asked quite reasonably.

"The siege of Leningrad was the most terrible siege in all of history you know. People just died out of sheer starvation. Only some little supplies were smuggled in across the Lake Ladoga and these were hijacked by the military."

"How do you know all this? You were not even born then," interjected Arvind with a mischievous smile. Lisa looked to be in her early thirties, but she took Arvind's question seriously. Her face reddened, as though her credibility was being questioned.

"I am not stupid, no?" she said showing her irritation. "I read books. I have read everything about the siege of Leningrad. Also, my mother and father remember everything. My father's two brothers died in the war. My mother's whole family died. I have no brothers, no cousins, no aunts, no uncles, nobody, no? When my parents die, I will be all alone."

Arvind fell back, abashed. There was a sad and

melancholic look on her face when she said this. It was as though she was looking into the bleak future and seeing herself living in a two-bedroom apartment, friendless and alone in that vast bustling metropolis of St Petersburg.

By this time we had reached the hotel. Lisa collected our passports for registration and we went to our rooms to freshen up. As I was standing at the lift, Lisa reminded me, "Please come down at 9.30. We go to the restaurant to eat our breakfast; then we go to the city."

As we sat down for breakfast, I asked Lisa for the day's detailed itinerary. "I take you to the Neva River first. After you see that, I take you to Peter and Paul's fortress. It was built for the war against Sweden. Peter the Great built it, no? An interesting moment—it was never used for the war. Peter used it as a prison." She would have gone on, but I interrupted. "Could we not see the Hermitage first?" Hermitage was one of the four or five best museums of the world.

"Yes, we see it after lunch. First, we see Neva, the summer palace, the field of Mars and other interesting places. Then I take you to the Hermitage," she replied patiently. But I was rather impatient to see the Hermitage, for which specific reason I had come all the way to St Petersburg. I was afraid that by the time we finished with all those places that Lisa wanted to show us and had lunch, we would all be too tired and have very little time left to see the Hermitage.

So we worked out a compromise, rather reluctantly on Lisa's part. We would go to the Neva River first, then see the Hermitage before lunch.

On the banks of Neva, we took the usual photographs and Lisa pointed out the two stubby towers which, at first glance, I took to be some kind of monuments. Lisa said they were old lighthouses which were not in use now. "Across the waters, you see the Peter and Paul Fort. We will be going there later. An interesting moment! The Neva River is only seventy kilometers long but it is very deep. It is navigable for most part of the year but the water is highly polluted. Do you see the film of oil floating on the surface? My boyfriend used to say that in another ten years there will be no fish left in the river."

This was the first mention of a boyfriend by Lisa. So, I took it as a cue and asked her, "Ah, you never mentioned about a boyfriend earlier. Who is he and what does he do?"

Lisa became pensive and remained silent for a while. I thought perhaps I had overstepped the bounds and asked her a personal question which I shouldn't have. Perhaps, Lisa was offended at a stranger asking such questions. It turned out that was not the case.

"He was an engineer. I lived with him for five years. Then he left," she said with a deep sigh. That simple statement in three short sentences seemed to cover a deep tragedy. Lisa appeared to be close to tears when she said them. Abruptly, she turned away from me towards the parapet and peered down into the waters. I could sense that some suppressed pain was widening the cracks in her memory and she wanted to hide its obvious effects from me. I diverted the subject back to the Neva River and its shipping.

On the way to the Hermitage, we passed through the other sites.

"That is the house of the Yusupov family. It is called Moika Palace. They were one of the richest in the times of Czar Alexander. An interesting moment! It was the Yusupov family which hatched the conspiracy to kill Rasputin. Rasputin used his hypnotic powers to persuade the Czar to actually go to the front to lead the army against the Germans. That was in 1916, just a year before the Revolution. It was to remove him from the scene. He used the absence of the Czar to influence the Czarina to remove all those Ministers whom he did not like. He replaced them with those he liked. Some of the Ministers he removed were pro-British. The British government was unhappy. It is rumoured that they ordered their Secret Service to kill Rasputin. He had already become very unpopular with all the influential families of St Petersburg, especially Prince Felix Yusupov.

So, Felix took the help of Raynor, a British Secret Service officer, and along with other friends they lured Rasputin to their palace and took him to the basement. First, they gave him enough cyanide to kill five men.

When he did not die, they beat him with clubs. He survived that, so they shot him. Yusupov shot him three times in the back. That also did not kill him, so Raynor shot him in the forehead. They then wrapped his body in a carpet and threw it in the river Neva. But he still lived. They say he had supernatural powers, no? You have such people in India also, I have heard. Godmen, no? Rasputin tried to claw his way up from the frozen river. His body was found the next morning; he had died of drowning. All those weapons had not killed him. He was a real magician, no?" concluded Lisa. "After his murder, the Czarina took revenge and ruined the whole Yusupov family."

Whenever Lisa wanted to draw our attention to any particular fact of her narration, she would preface it with the phrase 'an interesting moment'. Since I had noticed so many interesting moments occurring in her patter, I asked her, "And what is the interesting moment in your life?"

I seemed to have touched a raw nerve. But this time, the words came out in a gush. "My five years with my boyfriend were the most satisfying. He was a very powerful man, very high in the Communist Party in Yugoslavia. He had come here to be trained. He was very ambitious. He wanted to go back to his country and rise very high in his career, so he left."

"And why didn't you go with him?" Arvind interjected.

That was a zero point. She took some time to reply. "I was so happy with him. We suited each other well, no?

His name was Ognav which in his own language meant 'fire'," she said.

"What language was that?" asked Bajaj.

"He was a Macedonian," Lisa replied. Ognav, I thought, must be the Greek cognate of our Sanskrit 'Agni'.

"The name suited him well for he was all fire. He wanted to do many things. I was willing to do whatever he wanted to help him. I knew he was much higher than me." Here, Lisa pointed to her head. "But he left me and went away. I was even ready to give up my own career."

"What career was that?" Arvind asked.

"I am a mining engineer. I qualified from the Institute in St Petersburg; I stood first in my class. Then I worked for a Design Organization," she replied.

"Was Ognav married?" I asked.

"No," said Lisa. "He was not married. He had many things to do in his own country, he said. He had no desire to marry and get tied down."

"And now that Yugoslavia has broken up into so many parts, which side is he on? You said he was a Macedonian who went away to Belgrade. Is he with the Serbs or the Croats who are fighting with each other and with the Bosnians?"

"I don't know," said Lisa with a helpless shrug. "It was seven years ago he left me. I have had no words from him—no letter, no phone call, nothing."

"Didn't you write to him?" Arvind asked. Those were the days before the all-pervasive internet and email killed the letter writing.

"I did. I wrote several times in the beginning but there was no reply." Lisa's face became more and more pinched as she said that.

"But you must have had his telephone number. Why didn't you ring him up?" I asked.

"When I rang, his father picked up the phone. He did not speak well with me. I cannot tell what he spoke. I was not happy, no? So I never phoned again." There was a tragic note in her voice, as though she was speaking through choked tears. Obviously, the memory of Ognav's father and his harsh response still hurt.

By this time, we had reached the Hermitage—the green and gold winter palace of the Czars of Russia, where Peter the Great ordered the execution of his own son and Rasputin held sway over the Czarina and her handmaids. Lisa became a guide again with her 'no's' and 'interesting moments'.

The Hermitage Museum was established by Catherine the Great in 1764. Lisa showed us the grand architecture of the palatial building. "It has three million items, no?" she said waving her hands. "But only a few of them are put on display. There is not enough place to show them."

"And where do they keep the rest?" Arvind asked.

"All of them are kept safe in underground vaults,

but no one is allowed to see them. I suppose only the Director and the high level officials can go down there."

We entered the vast complex of the museum which consisted of the Winter Palace, the small Hermitage, the old Hermitage and new Hermitage. The collection was so vast that we could merely breeze through most of the rooms and the loggias.

"This is the room of the Great Vase. You see that huge vase?" Lisa asked us in one of the exhibit rooms. "It is called the Kolyvan vase. It weighs nineteen tonnes and it is made of jasper. It was made in 1843." The huge vase which was well over eight and a half feet tall towered over all of us.

"So, how was it brought into this place?" I asked.

"It was installed here first before the walls were built," Lisa explained.

"Has anyone attempted to steal it?" Arvind, with his quiet sardonic humour asked.

Lisa had by now understood Arvind. She laughed with all of us.

We breezed through the paintings of Classical and Renaissance masters. We saw Titian, Veronese, Leonardo, Raphael and Murillo.

I halted at Canova's *Three Graces*. Canova is one of my favourite sculptors. Every time I have visited Paris, I have never failed to visit the Louvre just to stand and gaze at his *Cupid and Psyche*. And the *Three Graces* almost equalled that magnificent sculpture.

The Hermitage has one of the largest collections of Impressionist and post-Impressionist paintings. We saw hundreds of Picassos, Matisses, Renoirs, Manets, Van Goghs, Gaguins and what have you. When you see too many paintings of great masters at one go, in a museum or gallery, your sight gets jaded. One painting merges into the other and they all look similar.

As we halted before Rembrandt's *Danae,* Lisa got into her stride again.

"That is *Danae*. We used to come here often, Ognav and I. He liked to gaze at the nude, with his arm around my waist." Lisa was lost in reverie for a few moments, recalling faded memories of lost intimacies.

"Actually, Rembrandt used his wife Saskia as the model, but only her body. He put the face of his mistress on it. Double benefit, no?" Lisa explained. "The painting you see on the wall is a restored Rembrandt. Just a few years ago, a madman threw sulfuric acid at the painting. Perhaps he was a lunatic; perhaps he didn't like the nude figure. Not content with throwing acid on her, he slashed the painting twice or thrice with a knife. It took almost two years for the experts to restore it, no? Now you are seeing *Danae* behind reinforced glass. That is not how a painting should be seen."

I recalled that due to the threat posed by vandals, many works of art have gone behind armoured protection.

Mona Lisa in Louvre can be seen only behind armoured glass. Someone broke the arm of the statue of David in Florence which used to stand in the open plaza. I saw it in the open when I first saw it. Now, it has been removed, along with all other statues that used to adorn the plaza, and put in protective custody.

As we were coming to the end of our visit of the Hermitage, I was curious to see the copy of the oldest extant Quran in the world. The Third Caliph of Islam, Usman, is reputed to have appointed a commission of the closest companions of the Prophet to collect and prepare written copies of the Quran. Four copies were prepared and sent to the Governors of the various provinces. One copy was retained by the Caliph. He was reciting from this copy when he was assassinated. It is said that some pages still bear the marks of his blood. It had been taken by Tamerlane from Damascus to Samarkand. And when the Russians conquered Samarkand, the Russian general brought it to St Petersburg. It was reported to be housed in the Hermitage Museum.

"Where is the oldest copy of the Quran housed? Can we go and see it?" I asked Lisa.

"Ah, you are somewhat late for that. At the request of the Government of Uzbekistan, our Government has restored that Quran and today it is housed in Tashkent," Lisa explained.

I had to wait for three more years to see it in Tashkent

where I went later.

As we came out after seeing the Museum, I noticed that Lisa was still preoccupied with the memories which we had provoked by our questions. It was as though she wanted to unburden herself of them.

"What will happen to me after my parents are gone, I wonder?" she said pensively.

"You don't have any boyfriend now?" I asked. "Ognav left you seven years ago."

"Yes, I met one or two people but there was no fire in them," she said.

"The best thing for you Lisa is to forget Ognav," I said. "He has been gone for seven years. He has not written to you or spoken on the phone. His family obviously doesn't want him to marry you; that's perhaps why his father was short with you on the phone. They have disowned you. Forget about him and look for someone else. Marry him and settle down."

As I gave this advice, I realised how hollow it sounded. Here was a lovely girl whose family had been wiped out in the siege of Leningrad, living with her old parents about whose death she was obviously worried. She had given the five best years of her young life to an over-ambitious Commissar who was more interested in his political career than in marrying a Russian girl who would perhaps be a drag on his upward climb. Here was a girl who had been willing to sacrifice her career to help her man and who was still in love with him, even though he had left her seven years ago. How could she forget him so easily? I wondered.

"I cannot forget him," she said as though echoing my thoughts. "He should have told me why he left me. I don't know anything. Is he still alive? He may still be loving me; he may be under compulsion. Who knows?"

I could see that she was still hoping that one day Ognav would come back and take her with him. It was cruel of that rascal, I thought, to have kept the poor girl in suspense. If he wanted to abandon her, he should at least have had the kindness to have told her so, but just disappearing like that smacked of a ruthless cold bloodedness.

As we drove along the downtown area, I saw a huge azure dome and two minarets rising above the other surrounding buildings. From a distance the building appeared suspiciously like a mosque. So I asked Lisa, "What is that beautiful dome?"

Lisa was always happy to be asked questions about her native city. So, on my query, she became expansive. "It is the Saint Petersburg Mosque, no?" she said. "It was opened in 1913. When it was built, it was the largest mosque in Europe; that was before the First World War. Though only eight thousand Muslims lived in St Petersburg at that time, the mosque was built to accommodate five thousand worshippers. A very optimistic project. An interesting moment! The mosque was designed by a Russian architect, Nikolay Vasilev."

"Was he a Muslim?" asked Arvind.

"No, he was a Christian. And it was the Czar Nicholas who gave permission to the Muslims, actually the Mufti of Orenburg, to raise funds and buy land. They raised more than seven hundred and fifty thousand roubles and bought land in the downtown area. Vasilev patterned the dome on the tomb of Tamerlane, the Gur-e-Amir in Samarkand. In 1940, the mosque was taken over by the Government and was used as a warehouse during the war."

"Is it still used like that?" I asked. "No, no," said Lisa defensively, as though she was being personally accused of being sacrilegious. "When President Sukarno of Indonesia came to visit us in 1956, he also went to see the mosque and offer prayers. At his request, the Government restored it to the Muslims. So for last more than three decades, it is with the Muslims."

"Can we all go and see it?" asked Bajaj.

When we got down at the gate of the mosque, we wanted to go into the compound and have a look at the interior, but Lisa was a bit apprehensive. "No, no, we can't go in. They don't like strangers to come in, especially women are not permitted."

"Even as a licensed guide?" I asked.

"Yes, I have never been inside," she said.

As we proceeded on the driveway, a tall man in a jacket and heavy trousers with an Uzbek cap on his head came out of the side entrance and waved his hands at us, signalling us to go back. But I advanced and called out loudly "Assalam-O-Alaikum." The moment he realised I was a Muslim, he assumed that we were all Muslims. He welcomed us with a broad smile and took us into the mosque through the side entrance. It turned out that he was the Akhun, that is, the Chief Priest. There were very few people in the mosque. Through Lisa's interpretation, we learned that the building of the mosque was mainly funded by Abdul Ahad Khan, the then ruler of Bukhara, to commemorate the 25th anniversary of his reign. I asked him how many worshippers came to the mosque for prayers. He laughed bitterly and said only the old men came to the mosque and they were very few in number. The younger generation had lost faith in religion and most of them had joined the Communist Party; and the Party frowned upon its members going to the mosque.

When we came out of the mosque, Lisa thanked me for helping her see the interior of the mosque for the first time.

Lisa showed us the Nevsky Prospekt, the main thoroughfare of St Petersburg, after lunch. We had to leave the same evening for Cherepovets by train. As we were driving to the station, I asked her, "Tell me why did you leave your career of a mining engineer and become a guide? You must have been getting a much better salary there."

"After Ognav left, I found I could not sit before the computer and press keys anymore. I had learnt English; I wanted to be out. I find that taking tourists out and telling them about St Petersburg is more interesting than sitting in an office at the drawing board. It is boring," Lisa explained.

But that was not the real reason, I could guess. After Ognav abandoned her, it was Lisa's loneliness that drove her to find refuge in crowds of strangers. Taking out tourist parties, talking to them about the history of Czars and Czarinas kept her away from the thoughts of her tormentor. She wanted to be in neutral territory where she could lose herself and her identity in a sort of no man's land, populated by the living strangers and dead heroes of history.

As we got into the train compartment, I waved to the forlorn diminutive figure of Lisa Ulyanova, standing on the huge platform drawing the lapels of her leather jacket closer against the cold. Once again, the tourists were departing leaving her alone with her memories. She was back into the war zone until next morning when the new tourist party would arrive. But I knew that whatever happened, she would continue to keep the lamp burning in the niche of her heart for the return of her fiery warrior, who had perhaps long forgotten her existence.

Munshiram of Ayodhya

As Munshiram watched the last dome of the Babri Masjid come down, he found he had no emotions at all. No happiness, no elation. The fall of the dome did not affect him in any way. Of course, his mind was occupied by a more serious concern. The pressure on his bladder had reached an unbearable level. All day long, hemmed in by the crowd of chanting kar sevaks, he had suppressed his urge with great self-control. Moreover, even though he was within walking distance of the compound wall of the mosque, which he could have used to relieve himself, he had been told the whole area was sacred precincts. No corner of it could be desecrated. Who knew where the young feet of the child Ram, Ram Lalla, had left their footprints? To urinate anywhere in that vicinity was sacrilege, Munshiram knew. He had withheld his urge for hours until the old building had fallen.

For years Munshiram had thought that he would feel a sense of elation, of triumph when the structure fell, as all the leaders had been proclaiming that it was a symbol of the foreign invaders of India. It was a symbol of India's shame. Some foreigner from Afghanistan had come all the way to Ayodhya, the birthplace of the most sacred Hindu God, Lord Ram, demolished an old temple that stood at the site of Lord Ram's birth and built a mosque with three domes there. Munshiram who had been listening to the fiery speeches fulminating on Babar had been half-convinced that he should support the move to right the ancient wrong—it was utterly wrong for the conquerors to have built a mosque to worship Allah where Ram Lalla was once worshipped. Those invaders had demolished a sacred place of worship dedicated to Ram Lalla to build a hated symbol of the conquerors, a mosque. That was what his leaders had told him and his fellow citizens of Ayodhya, not once but ad infinitum.

Sometimes in the past one year, he had felt a mild sense of guilt that he was not doing anything to help the movement to restore the temple. All around him, as he stood there in the gathering dusk, he heard the large crowd of kar sevaks, the saffron-robed volunteers with headbands of the same colour with Ram's name inscribed on them, who had come from all parts of India, raising cheers of "Jai Siyaram". But Munshiram felt nothing, and he wondered why? The tempo had been building up for the last seven years.

The Babri Masjid, the ancient brick and mortar edifice had stood there with its three moss-covered domes for over four centuries. It was reputed to have been built by Mir Baqi, the commander of Babar, the first Mughal conqueror of India, who had come from Kabul. Munshiram had been told that Mir Baqi had raised the mosque after heartlessly demolishing a temple to Ram that had stood there for centuries. Ram was the most sacred Hindu God, who all Hindus believed had been born there two million years ago. Hence, the destruction of the mosque was the only way to restore India's pride in itself, Munshiram had heard. But only yesterday, he had been assured by the leaders of the movement that once the mosque was demolished the temple would be rebuilt. A magnificent Ram temple would be raised on the ruins of the mosque. The new Ram temple would be the pride of India, may be the pride of all the Hindus of the world. Consecrated bricks had been collected from every village of India. Sculptors had been engaged for years to carve the idols and the doors and lintels of the planned temple. But Munshiram felt no surge of pride, no elation and no sense of triumph as he saw the brick-and-mortar walls of the mosque crumbling under the hammer blows of the kar sevaks perched precariously on the slippery domes. He heard the jubilant roar rising from a hundred thousand throats, as the domes fell.

As he stood watching the destruction, he asked one of his neighbours, "What will happen to the idols of Ram Lalla and others inside the building?" Some decades ago, a miracle had occurred. Three idols of Lord Ram and his companions had suddenly appeared at exactly the spot claimed to be the place where Ram Lalla was born. Except for a few sceptics, all Hindus were convinced that it was a miracle. The government had closed down the mosque, but permitted priests to go in and perform the morning and evening puja to put the deities to sleep. No Muslims were permitted to go in. Their very presence near the gods would defile the divinities. So, Munshiram was rightly perturbed about the safety of the deities if the debris of the crumbling domes fell on them.

"Don't you worry," his unknown neighbour had reassured him. "Ten of our devoted kar sevaks, Ram Bhaktas every one of them, sneaked into the mosque and quietly transported all the deities, with due devotion and respect to a safe place. They will be restored when the new temple comes up."

In fact, the only thing Munshiram felt at that moment was a strong urge to relieve the pressure on his bladder. He looked this way and that to find a way out of the crowd and a secluded spot well beyond the sacred precincts to relieve himself. The pressure had been building up for quite some time, but all his attention had been focused on the sight of the flying debris and falling bricks. But now that the job was done, Munshiram suddenly found himself in desperate need of physical relief. For the moment, it appeared a forlorn hope. He could spot no secluded corner away from the sacred precincts, for the crowd was everywhere as far as he could see. His desperate glances did locate a spot where he could have stood with his back to the cheering crowds and 'do the needful'. He could have forced his way there through the milling crowd, but Munshiram had a psychological block. He could never urinate if there was anyone close by who could observe him in the act, and seeing the press of people all around, he knew there was every chance of his being observed. And he was more than certain that not a drop would come out.

His mental block came about this way. When Munshiram was four years old, he had developed some chronic urinary infection. He and his family had been living in Ayodhya from time immemorial. His father came from a farming community, but his landholding of two bighas was not enough to sustain the extended family of Ghasiram. So, when the village moneylender decided to become an entrepreneur and set up a handloom manufacturing factory, Ghasiram joined there as a weaver. Ghasiram, a traditional orthodox Brahmin like the rest of the villagers, had believed in the expertise of the local Ayurvedic medicine man. Every village in India had a medicine man, the vaid, who took care of the minor ailments of the villagers. So Munshiram had been taken to the vaid by his father. Herbal medicines would give symptomatic relief for some time but the problem would recur again and again. Antibiotics had not reached Ayodhya then and the village barber, who also doubled as the local vaid, thought that the only permanent cure for Munshiram's chronic problem was circumcision (surgical removal of the foreskin of the penis). Once the offending foreskin was removed, the barber assured Ghasiram, the infection would find no place to lodge and flourish again.

In the beginning Ghasiram demurred at this drastic remedy. Circumcision was a practice which distinguished the Musalmans from the rest of Ayodhya's Hindu population. It was certainly anathema to the Hindus and more so to an orthodox Brahmin. But then the infection persisted and when the barber repeated his advice, Ghasiram reluctantly agreed. The Hindu barber did not have the skill to pull out the foreskin and with a single stroke of his sharp blade cut out the small bit, pour hot clarified butter on the bleeding penis to cauterise the wound and prevent any infection. So, the Muslim barber had come quietly to Ghasiram's house one early morning before the village had fully awakened, with his primitive kit for the operation.

The surgery had to be done before the village woke up and learnt about the sacrilege that was being perpetrated in Ghasiram's house. Ghasiram and his brother Radhey Shyam had held the frightened young Munshiram on a large inverted earthen pot with his thighs held apart. A red cloth covered the pot. The barber had pulled out the foreskin and had put a wooden clip on the upper end. Then he had taken out an old-fashioned cut-throat razor and sharpened it on a wetted leather strap. Munshiram's cringing eyes had followed the movement of the barber's hand dreading the moment when it would descend. With a dramatic flourish, the barber had pulled the prepuce taut and cut it off with one stroke. As Munshiram went into a deep faint he dimly saw the copious flow of blood from his penis. The memory of those moments haunted Munshiram for the rest of his life. For a full one month, Munshiram was not allowed to leave the house until the wound healed completely.

While the infection never recurred, Munshiram had to pay a heavy price for the cure. The boys of his school who enjoyed communal morning chores on the banks of Sarayu River, found out that Munshiram's penis looked different. They knew at once that Munshiram had undergone a Muslim operation. He had lost his caste. He had become half a Muslim.

Whenever he went along with his friends to the river bank to relieve himself, they would shout at him

"*Musalman, Musalman, teri kati gand,*" referring to his circumcised organ. At first, he had tried to ignore the taunts with a show of indifference. Then he fought with some and came home with black eyes but when the needling had not ceased, the eight-year-old Munshiram had become almost convinced that by the act of circumcision he had perhaps become a Muslim. And that was a terrible thought, for the Musalmans, he had been told, were a terrible, cruel and evil people, who didn't even have the second chance of a rebirth to atone for their sins, but went straight to hell the moment they died. They never found *moksha*.

Ayodhya was a small town where Munshiram went to school. It had a population of less than forty thousand. Though Faizabad, the district headquarters nearby had a larger population of Muslims, Ayodhya itself had less than four hundred Muslim families. Mythology claimed that Ayodhya had seen glorious days when Lord Ram ruled it, but history had not been kind to the city. Though Ayodhya claimed that Buddha himself visited it, and the very first Jain Tirthankar, Rishab Dev, was born there, all vestiges of Buddhist and Jain glory had been obliterated. The local Hindus never acknowledged that Buddhist and Jains ever lived and thrived in Ayodhya. There were hundreds of Hindu temples in the town, many of them claiming to be the real birthplace of Ram Lalla. Faith bolstered by politics and money had focused on the Babri

Masjid as the only birthplace or Janmabhoomi.

There were similarly over a hundred mosques scattered in and around Ayodhya, most of them in ruins; but a majority of those not in ruins waited for devotees in vain. Even the call to prayers was not heard in most of them. As a child, Munshiram hardly came into contact with the Muslims of Ayodhya, but he knew they were there, hovering in the background as an evil presence. The very fact that they circumcised their children, ate meat and slaughtered goats was anathema to the Hindus. It was even rumoured, horror of horrors, that they sacrificed the sacred gau-mata, the holy mother cow, on their festival and ate its meat.

Munshiram felt horribly tainted every time he looked at his penis. As time passed, he had stopped going to the river bank with his school-mates. Not only that, Munshiram found that he could not relieve himself in any sort of company or even in a public toilet. He could do it either in his own house, or someplace where there was total privacy and where no one could see him. Even a human voice heard from a distance would inhibit his urinary urge. Over the years, this became an obsession with him. He just could not find relief, however much the pressure, unless complete seclusion was assured.

As he stood away from the debris of the mosque watching the rejoicing kar sevaks dancing on the rubble mound, the pressure on Munshiram kept mounting—

the pressure of his need and the pressure of the crowds. The Babri Masjid had come down and the people had stopped cheering. The raucous shouts had been replaced by a continuous roar; but there was a different note to this roar that now rose from thousands of throats. It was not a roar of triumph but a groan of frustration of an unsatiated predatory hunger. The hated structure, the symbol of Muslim rule had come down in a cloud of dust, but the hated Muslims who had raised that mosque—if not they, their progeny—were still there. They lived on the very sacred soil of Ayodhya. They lived in every village and city of India. What about them?

This was the most dangerous moment. The kar sevaks had come from all parts of India. In fact, Munshiram had been intrigued at first by hearing the strange accents in which Hindi had been spoken in the concourse. Some other languages too had been heard by him. Later, he had learnt that the kar sevaks with saffron headbands had come from Gujarat, Rajasthan, Maharashtra and even from far-off Karnataka and Tamil Nadu. Many of the kar sevaks who had climbed on to the domes of the mosque, he had been told, had come from Maharashtra with clear orders from their leaders not to return home without demolishing the mosque. Only a few of them had been fortunate enough to be allowed in the sacred task of demolishing the hated structure; but the thousands of kar sevaks who had trekked from far-off places braving the cold December weather had played the role of mere spectators. How much merit had they earned for their next birth by merely observing the fall of bricks and mortar? Was that enough to earn them *moksha*? They had to do something more. The rising crescendo of triumphal expectations the crowd had felt collectively since morning required an outlet to be relieved.

While the demolition was going on the crowd of spectators had vicariously participated in the destructive process, but once the edifice had come down, they felt cheated of their prey. They felt deflated. There was a strong but unspoken feeling that not enough had been done. Just the fall of the three domes was an unsatisfactory denouement for the thousands who had trekked to Ayodhya from distant lands. The Ram Bhaktas who had climbed up the mosque at the risk of their lives and limbs, had achieved their triumph over the hated symbol of the Muslim invaders. They would go down in history. They would achieve *moksha*. But what of the rest? Unless the crowd that had just stood and watched also achieved a matching triumph, how would they justify to themselves the years of slogan shouting, churning emotions, marches on the dusty simmering roads and gatherings in the burning sun they had gone through?

Munshiram felt none of these things, neither the triumph nor the frustration, but he felt the menace in the continuous growl that was reverberating all around him.

He was a part of the crowd, yet not a participant. For him, Babar the Mughal Emperor, the hated figure who was accused of having destroyed the old Ram mandir, was a vague and fuzzy figure—someone who was said to have invaded India long ago from Kabul, one of those who lived in the stories recounted by grandmothers at bedtime. He could not visualise the figure of the destroyer who had lived four centuries ago nor could he bring himself to hate a Musalman enemy, somebody whose very existence was mere hearsay. For him, the Musalman was his neighbour, Shabbir Hussain the weaver.

For Shabbir Hussain was a man of flesh and blood whom Munshiram met every day at the factory and in the market place until the kar seva against the mosque was announced, and most of the Muslims shifted out of his neighbourhood and went to live with their co-religionists in a different part of the city.

Munshiram had met Shabbir Hussain in school. Later, to earn a livelihood, they both worked in the same cotton handloom factory. At first, Munshiram met Shabbir with many reservations hovering at the back of his mind. But soon he discovered that in their dress, food habits and way of thinking, there were no differences. Familiarity bred understanding. Shabbir Hussain was a Musalman but he certainly did not look like an invader to Munshiram. For Munshiram, an invader was somebody like what you saw in the films—a warrior wearing a helmet and chainmail, riding a fierce brown stallion and charging the fleeing enemy with his blood-dripping sword waving in the air. Munshiram could not relate Shabbir Hussain to the portrait of Babar and his armies that his leaders painted in their fiery orations.

Shabbir Hussain wore the same dhoti and kurta that he wore, spoke the same language and ate the same food. Many a time, Munshiram had dropped in on Shabbir Hussain of an evening and had been invited to join in their spare repast. He always found Shabbir dining on a few chapattis and lentils, supplemented with raw onions and pickles. There was nothing else. There was no meat, no kebab, no korma, only the same drab chapattis and lentils. Though he could not break the taboo against eating food cooked by a Muslim, Munshiram could relate to Shabbir, for he too dined on similar fare, day in and day out. Both Shabbir and Munshiram had not known any world beyond Ayodhya and neighbouring Faizabad. They both worked in the same handloom factory and sometimes ate their lunch together which they carried from their homes. Munshiram never saw any meat in the aluminium box that Shabbir's wife packed for his lunch. Shabbir went to a small mosque in the vicinity of his house for his Friday prayers and Munshiram prayed at one of the hundred temples near his house. The temple priest had assured him long ago that that was the real janmabhoomi (birthplace) of Lord Ram.

As the pressure mounted on his bladder, Munshiram remembered Shabbir Hussain and wondered what he was doing at that moment. He could not think of any reason why he remembered Shabbir Hussain just then. His mind was entirely preoccupied with his bladder, but he must have, without conscious effort, heard shouts around him from the crowd and the word 'Musalman' was repeatedly mentioned. He subconsciously noted the word and that brought Shabbir to his mind. Shabbir and he had grown up together. As young boys, they had played marbles together on the streets of Ayodhya and had gone swimming in the Sarayu River as young men. Once Munshiram had saved Shabbir from drowning when the river was in spate. Shabbir had gone for a dip with him. Munshiram believed that a dip in the holy river washed away all sins; Shabbir believed a sip of Zamzam water from the holy well in Mecca cured all illnesses. Shabbir respected his friend's faith. He had no idea that there was a strong underwater current near the bank of the Sarayu. He realised it the moment he had stepped into the waist-deep water. He found the sand slipping beneath his feet and the current pulling him into mid-stream. Munshiram was getting ready to enter the water, but seeing Shabbir in trouble and crying for help, he had bent down and pulled him back by sheer brute strength.

It was, however, Shabbir who had come to Munshiram's rescue and had carried his son all the way to Faizabad on his back when the boy had come down with an acute attack of appendicitis. Munshiram recalled the long exhausting walk, their bodies dripping with sweat and their breath coming short, and their stopping every few hundred yards to exchange the burden of the groaning boy. Once they reached the hospital, Shabbir had stayed with him for the operation. Even though Munshiram knew that Shabbir would lose wages for his absence, he could not persuade him to leave.

Munshiram's mind was suddenly pulled back from these reminiscences by the sound of fresh shouts. The large crowd was now breaking up into smaller mobs. "*Chalo, Chalo, maro, maro*" ("move on, move on, kill, kill"), Munshiram heard voices shouting amongst the mob. Though Munshiram's subconscious knew who were the objects of "maro, maro", his conscious mind rejected it.

He recalled that Shabbir Hussain lived close by and it came to him that that was the place where he could go and relieve himself in seclusion. He was rather frightened of the shouts raised by the mobs, and the menace of their tone; but he also knew that the menace was not directed against him. Also, he did not believe there would be actual killing. Nobody had ever killed anybody in Ayodhya that Munshiram remembered. The individual mobs consisting of the kar sevaks from Delhi were now moving out of the Masjid complex. The breaking-up of the crowd into mobs and their movement opened up avenues for Munshiram to slip out. Holding his dhoti up, he hurried on. As he turned toward the exit, the pressure of the milling crowd pushed him out. He saw that the streets of Ayodhya were practically deserted. Most of the Hindu population was still in the Babri Masjid grounds, and the few Muslims who lived in Ayodhya had locked themselves up in their own houses apprehending serious trouble.

Munshiram hurried through the narrow unpaved bylanes, his destination being Shabbir's house. Shabbir lived in a quarter of the city which was close to a small mosque. Muslims tended to build their houses close to mosques, so their colonies clustered there. Part of the reason was devotional, and part, a feeling of security in numbers. Muslim colonies in cities and towns generally tended to decline into slums. Neither the government nor the municipal administration bothered to allocate enough funds for cleaning the drains, the streets, lights and garbage removal. It was a rather dingy area with single-storey houses huddled close together. Since there was no drainage, all the waste water from the houses flowed out into the lane and kept it always smelly, wet and slushy. The dirty water mingled with the soil and stagnated in muddy pools here and there. Munshiram had visited Shabbir in his house many times and recalled the dusty street. Not that the street where he lived was any better. But his house had a septic tank so the street was generally dry. The Muslim area was always dirtier than the rest of the town.

The mayor and the other officials of the Municipality refused to soil their sandals by visiting the Muslim slums. Munshiram had been told time and again that Muslims were a dirty people. Looking at the mohalla where they lived, that seemed to be true. He had observed Shabbir washing himself five times a day before prayers, but that was only ritual ablutions, not really hygienic. As he walked on, Munshiram wondered again as to what Shabbir was doing at that moment. For one thing, he hoped that Shabbir, his wife Sabira and their three children were at home. They could not be anywhere else, for since the kar sevaks started arriving from all over India, business in the town had come to a standstill. The handloom factory where they worked had been closed this last week and all the workers had gone to join the crowds; some had returned to their hometowns.

Most of the workers lived a hand-to-mouth existence on their meagre wages. They survived on the daily wages they earned from the factory. If the factory remained closed for more than a couple of days, workers starved. Remembering this, Munshiram felt a sense of vague guilt. He had not visited Shabbir these many days. Munshiram and his father Ghasiram came from a background which followed a regimen of frugality in daily living and saving for a rainy day. Shabbir, being a Muslim, did not believe in savings; in any case there was no surplus to be saved.

Not that Munshiram could have done much to alleviate the sufferings of Shabbir. He himself was without wages for the last one week since the kar sevaks had come, but he had been drafted by the organisers of the kar seva to cook for the multitudes who were camping in the various open spaces of the town. He could at least share that food with them, and provide his family. Shabbir being a Muslim could not be allowed to perform the holy task of cooking for kar sevaks or partake of the prasad cooked for the bhaktas.

Walking along, Munshiram reached Shabbir's house. Shabbir lived in a two-bedroom single-storey house, with a tiled roof. Munshiram knew that Shabbir had inherited it from his father. Shabbir's family had lived in Ayodhya for twenty generations or more; so had Munshiram's. Gingerly stepping across one puddle after another so as not to soil his sandals, Munshiram climbed the two short steps that led to the narrow low door and knocked. There was no response. He waited for a few moments but still there was no response from within. He paused and knocked again, this time a little more loudly. Still there was no answer. He wondered whether there was anyone at home. Perhaps Shabbir had fled with his family to another part of the town, or he might have gone away to Faizabad. He cursed himself for having come this far only to knock on the door of an empty house. If the house was empty, Munshiram knew that there was no relief for him. Was he condemned to carry his burden until he reached his own house on the other side of the town? he wondered. But then, where could Shabbir go? As far as Munshiram knew, Shabbir had no friends or relations even in Faizabad.

The pressure was still mounting. If anything, it had gotten worse since he had thought that relief was at hand. As he was convinced that there was no one at home, Munshiram turned to descend the two steps that had carried him up. His foot was on the first when he heard the sound of some movement inside the house. He paused, turned back and knocked again and called out, "Shabbir, Shabbir, please open the door. It's me, Munshiram." Abruptly, the door creaked open. Through the small crack he glimpsed the outline of a face in the gloom. It was Shabbir. His famished face looked terror-stricken, and his eyes in that gaunt face looked haunted. He looked at Munshiram as one looks at a stranger and asked, "Yes, yes, don't shout. We don't want anyone to know that we are here. What do you want?" There was no friendliness in Shabbir's abrupt tone. Munshiram was taken aback. He had expected a better welcome or at least a more polite response.

Directly challenged to state the purpose of his visit, Munshiram was at a loss for words. He had expected Shabbir Hussain, his old friend of many years, to greet him first and then invite him in. He had not been expecting to be challenged so peremptorily. He would have welcomed a friendly exchange of words first and then he had planned casually to ask Shabbir for the use of his bathroom. Now, Munshiram felt that while the pressure was still there, he would be unable to state his purpose and still perform the chore.

"Why don't you let me in, Shabbir? How are you? I have come to enquire after you," pleaded Munshiram.

"You chose this time to come to my house? Your people must have destroyed the mosque by now. It will be our turn next. They will come to kill us now," said Shabbir, his hands trembling and his haunted eyes darting hither and thither as though expecting to find a mob following Munshiram.

Munshiram was bewildered. The idea had never occurred to him that anyone would want to kill his friend Shabbir. All along, he had believed that the kar sevaks were gathering in large numbers driven by their devotion to Lord Ram. He had also believed that after all the fiery speeches, *yatras* and *sammelans*, some amicable solution would be found for the mandir-masjid dispute. Maybe the mosque and the temple would be constructed side by side and he and Shabbir would then go together to pray there. He had not even believed that the mosque would be pulled down till the reality struck him. He recalled that the mosque had been demolished right before his eyes and the realisation came to him that something which he had not imagined had come to pass. He had heard the mobs chanting "Musalman, Musalman", and recalled the shouts of "*Chalo, Chalo, maro, maro*". Once his mind was off his bladder and he thought of all that had happened in the enclosure since the fall of the mosque, everything fell into place. He knew that the mobs would now be searching for the Muslim houses to kill.

Looking at Shabbir's haunted face, Munshiram recalled all the stories he had heard of the pogroms in far-off cities of Uttar Pradesh, Bihar and Gujarat where Muslims had been killed, homes looted and burnt and women raped. But Ayodhya had never undergone such a pogrom. Was it going to happen here now? He did not think so. In school, Munshiram had learnt that Ram, the great Ram was a *maryada purshottam* who upheld the rights of people and justice, who never killed innocents but helped the oppressed and downtrodden. How could anyone kill innocents in his name? Munshiram asked himself. That too in his own birthplace!

Just as this realisation struck, he heard shouts behind him, the same shouts that he had heard from the crowd earlier. He turned around to see a mob of hundreds making for the house of Shabbir Hussain and other Muslims in the vicinity. "Quick, quick," he said, "let me in." Reflexively, Shabbir opened the door and Munshiram stepped in. He saw Sabira cowering behind Shabbir. Irfan and Iqbal, the twin teenagers were standing behind her, and the youngest, baby Salima was staring with round, frightened eyes, too young to understand what was going on. The tableau of the five huddled figures with the look of stark terror on their faces communicated its collective fear to Munshiram. While his mind told him that he had nothing to fear as a Hindu, his heart trembled, more for the Muslim family than for himself. He tried to put on a brave front and reassure his friend.

"Don't worry," said Munshiram. "I will tell them that I live here, if they come." He tried to give some assurance to Shabbir and his family which he himself did not feel.

"They won't believe you," said Shabbir. "They have been collecting names and addresses for the last one week. They have the electoral rolls with them. They even came and marked my house with chalk, though I have tried to wash it off," he said hopelessly.

Suddenly, he looked up at his old friend and asked with a bewildered note in his voice, "Munshiram, why are they doing this to us? What have we done to them? What have Salima and Sabira ever done to them? If they wanted to pull down the mosque, they have already done it. Did we come in their way? Are they not satisfied with that?"

Munshiram himself was confused. He did not know how to answer Shabbir. He knew that the Muslims of Ayodhya had done no harm to anyone. They too had lived for centuries in the small town just as the rest of the Hindus. Both had suffered the pangs of hunger whenever the rains had failed and both had been equally exploited by the zamindars and factory owners. Both had been equally taken in by the false promises of the politicians and both had blindly supported the leaders who had held out any faint hope of relieving their misery—so why this blood lust? asked Munshiram of himself. Why does the crowd want to kill all the Muslims who had not even visited the Babri Masjid in decades? That derelict monument had ceased to be a Muslim place of worship since idols were installed in the main niche of the building. Now, everything had been demolished. So why kill the Muslims? He found no answer.

In the meantime, the mob had reached the door and there was a roar of "kill, kill" coming from hundreds of throats. They were beating down the flimsy door with staves and iron rods. "Come out, come out *haramis*," some of them were shouting. Shabbir and his family were looking this way and that for an escape route. Sabira drew her dupatta close around her as though the flimsy scarf would protect her like a coat of armour. Irfan, the elder son, put a protective hand around his cowering mother. Iqbal his younger brother drew Salima closer. She was crying quietly. They were all glancing around the room anxiously seeking an escape route, as though a mysterious door would open in the wall and they would escape through it. The small house was hemmed in by buildings on all three sides. There was no way of exit from that trap. The six of them stood there, looking at each other and wondering what to do, which way to go, where to hide from the storm that was crashing against the door. The door was not very strong and it could not withstand the repeated blows for too long. There was no hope of any help from outside. Shabbir knew that the local police supported the kar sevaks. He had all too frequently heard the mob shouting in processions *"Yeh andar ki baat hai, Police hamare saath hai"*. So, the mob knew from inside information that the police was with them. No help could be expected from that quarter.

"Don't worry," said Munshiram, "the police will be on the way. They will come to our help any time." Munshiram was a simple soul. He still had faith in the administration and the machinery of law and order.

"Ha," said Shabbir, "the police are not going to come. You know it and I know it. They are all with the kar sevaks." Munshiram knew it all too well in his heart of hearts. He had seen the large contingent of police in the precinct of the mosque. They had stood there idly as the kar sevaks had brought down the domes. Perhaps in their heart of hearts, they too rejoiced at the fall of the mosque. After all, they came from the same society that had demanded the destruction of the mosque.

As the door gave way suddenly under the heavy blows, dozens of wild-looking men with saffron headbands, their eyes bloodshot, rushed in. More than a score of them had crowded into that small room and more were pressing to come in. Most of them carried thick bamboo sticks and some of them even had swords and long knives. The shouts of "*maro, maro*" were rising from all throats, both inside and outside the house. And then a fierce looking tall man with a thick handlebar moustache, in a saffron vest and headband, with his bulging biceps lifted his lathi high in the air. It fell on the head of Shabbir with a solid thump and he went down. Sabira received the next few blows and she too fell down. Baby Salima shrieked and suddenly wet herself. Her urine formed a pathetic puddle at her feet on the ground. Even at that moment, Munshiram looked at her and felt a pang of envy. How he wished he could relieve himself like Salima!

Within moments, the mob had surrounded the fallen group and was raining blows on them with bamboo staves and iron rods. Munshiram shouted, "Stop, stop, I am Munshiram, I am a Hindu. These are all Hindus. Don't kill them. Don't kill them." But the mob had gone berserk. They were in the grip of a fierce blood lust. Within moments, Salima, Irfan and Iqbal too were lying bleeding on the ground, but the rain of blows did not cease. The pitiful cries of Salima were lost in the shouts of "*maro, maro*" raised from a score of throats. She was lying on the floor, writhing in her own blood and urine, bleeding from half a dozen deep cuts on her head, face and arms. Someone from the crowd caught hold of Salima by the legs and lifted her. As she hung upside down, he swung her limp body once or twice and then dashed her head against the wall. There was a crack and her brains splashed on the wall. This time there was no cry from Salima. Her lifeless body was flung into a corner.

The horror-stricken Munshiram cowered against a wall asserting feebly that he was a Hindu. He had received a dozen blows. Covering his head with his arms, he continued to shout feebly, "Stop, stop, I am a Hindu, I am a Brahmin." Shabbir was kneeling trying to hide his bleeding head between his wobbling knees. Sabira had already died but the mob was pummelling her lifeless body into a pulp.

By this time, Shabbir and Munshiram were the only ones left alive. Both were lying on the floor bleeding from their heads, their broken hands and legs twisted in all directions. Someone from the mob had heard Munshiram's cries and was asking the others to stop. A few of the mobsters were holding back the blows. In desperation, Munshiram decided to recite the Gayatri Mantra, the most sacred mantra of the Hindus, the mother of Vedas, in as loud a voice as he could with his bleeding lips.

"*Om bhur bhuvah swaha.*"

As the sound of the mantra, the great utterance from his quivering throat, one or two kar sevaks reined in their blows.

"*Tat savitur varenyam, bhargo devasya dhimahi.*" (We meditate the effulgent glory of the divine light. May he inspire our understanding).

"Hey, stop hitting him. He is reciting the Gayatri mantra," someone from the crowd had at last recognised the words which were coming out of Munshiram's bleeding lips.

"*Dhiyo yo nah prachodayateh.*" (Direct our understanding to the right path).

"He is a Hindu," cried someone else from the crowd. Suddenly the blows stopped. They all stood around the two limp figures staring with wild puzzlement. Another voice cut in—it was the hefty man with the handlebar moustache who had landed the first blow.

"These bastards would do anything to cheat us. He may have learnt the Gayatri Mantra from someone."

For a moment, the mob had felt a pang of guilt at the possibility that they had been raining lethal blows on Hindus. The suggestion that it might after all be a Musalman who had learnt the Gayatri Mantra relieved them somewhat. Then a third voice suggested, "Let us take them out and find out." This replanted the doubt.

"Yes, before killing these bastards, it's better to ascertain who they are." The mob welcomed this suggestion enthusiastically.

So Shabbir and Munshiram were dragged out of the house by their feet. Two or three of the killers dragged them down, the bodies bumping over the steps. "Okay," said the handlebar moustache, who appeared to be in some kind of control, "Strip them."

In no time, a couple of rough hands pulled down Shabbir's trousers and Munshiram's dhoti. "Ah, Ah," shouted a dozen throats.

"Look at the bastard's penis. He is a Musalman, and this rascal even had the gumption to recite the Gayatri Mantra to cheat us. Let's kill him first."

There was an enthusiastic response from the crowd. After all, these two had turned out to be Musalmans, both of them. So, two hefty young men held down the enfeebled Munshiram, sitting on his chest with redoubled vigour for his temerity and the third took out a large butcher's knife. And as a butcher slaughters a goat, he held up Munshiram's head and with calm deliberation, slit his throat from ear to ear. As the dark red blood spurted out of Munshiram's neck, his bladder voided and with a sigh, which sounded like "Hey, Ram", he relieved himself. At last, Munshiram had found his relief.

Later in the night, a group of Muslim voluntary workers found the naked bodies of Shabbir and Munshiram lying in the middle of the street, amidst a puddle of blood, urine and slush. Their heads had been bashed in. The only way to recognise them was by their circumcised organs. "Must be brothers," one of them surmised. In the dead of night, quietly, all of them were buried in the same grave in the Muslim graveyard. There was no time to dig separate pits. They also found the four bodies of Sabira and her children inside the house. Mobs were still prowling around and it was better to perform the burial as quickly as possible without any ceremony. There was no priest around. So, one of the volunteers recited the only prayer from the Quran he remembered, the *ayat-al-kursi*—the heart of the Quran—"*Allahu, la ilaha illa huwal haiyyul qayyum.*" The volunteer read the prayer in a subdued voice not to attract any attention. The rest of them bowed their heads in reverence for the dead, not understanding a word of what was being recited. All of them recited a few *surahs* of the Quran in their prayers.

Ghalib had written a century earlier:

"Loyalty, when it is steadfast, is the essence of Faith;

If the Brahmin dies in the temple, bury him in the kaaba".

Shireen of Samarkand

For a long time, Aslam had believed that Samarkand was a mythical locale like More's Utopia or Hilton's Shangri-La, and only existed in the fertile imagination of romance writers and poets. He had mixed it up with Kubla Khan's *Xanadu* which in any case was only a hazy vision in the opiated daydreams of Coleridge. Aslam was an avid reader of historic fiction and English poetry.

As the journey took him over the lush Ferghana Valley, he recalled bits and pieces of Indian history. The first Mughal invader of India had come from this very valley. Babar always felt a deep love and nostalgia for this valley of mountains, rivers, fruits and flowers. He always felt he was an exile in India. Samarkand was his birthplace, his hometown, and he hankered to return to that city and be buried there when he died. His desire never got fulfilled. He is now lying buried in Kabul, a place as alien to him as Agra or Delhi.

As the Aeroflot plane took a turn over the city of Samarkand before landing, Aslam, looking down at the city spread below, was hit by the reality of the once-famous capital of Central Asia. Even from the height of four thousand feet, the stately domes of Samarkand, decreed by Tamerlane and his successors, asserted their proud existence by rearing their spires high in the clean, unpolluted air of the Ferghana Valley. The sight of these magnificent medieval monuments, even from a distant height, went a long way in compensating Aslam for the uncomfortable and cramped flight in the obsolete Russian aircraft.

There had been an interminable wait at the VIP lounge of the Tashkent airport while his escort, a deputy minister in the newly-independent Uzbek state, had gone to complete the bureaucratic formalities. When Sokrat, for that was the name of the worthy deputy minister, did not return for a long while, Aslam had started wondering whether the Aeroflot staff, recently liberated from KGB control, had gone on a lightning strike. Back home in India, he had experienced the constant inconvenience of airline staff going on strike at the drop of a hat. Perhaps, the disease was catching on in Uzbekistan too,

Aslam thought. So when a beaming Sokrat came back, flourishing two pieces of paper as though they were passports to heaven, Aslam knew that everything was all right, and they would leave on the flight for Samarkand.

Sokrat had been his escort for the past one week in Tashkent while Aslam made the rounds of the various ministries on his official mission schedule. Aslam suspected that Sokrat was less of an escort and more of a government chaperone to keep an eye on the Indian visitor. Aslam's grandfather, an Arabic and Persian scholar, a retired professor of those languages from the Delhi University, had filled Aslam's brain with romantic visions of the ancient Persia. He found Sokrat singularly lacking in any knowledge of the history and religion of his native land.

Sokrat was a highly-refined product of the long communist regime that had ruled Uzbekistan for close to a century. And that regime had practically erased the influence of the old Persian culture in all walks of Uzbek life. There was hardly anyone in the bureaucracy who could even read the Persian script. In any case, Aslam had come on a purely business mission. The language and religion of Uzbekistan was no concern of his.

So when the flight landed at the airport, Aslam had the feeling of a mission half-achieved. He was at last going to see the city which Tamerlane had believed to be the capital of the world, and so named its rural suburbs after Baghdad, Cairo, Delhi, Damascus, Isfahan and Shiraz—the city which Hafez, the greatest of the Persian poets, offered to squander along with Bukhara if only the Turkish beauty from Shiraz were to take in hand his devoted heart. The story goes that when Tamerlane conquered Shiraz, the first thing he did was to summon the poet in chains and demand from him, "You profligate, I spent a lifetime to build Samarkand and Bukhara into the greatest cities of the world, and you dared to sacrifice them for a single mole of your beloved's face?"

"Had I not been that extravagant, your Majesty, do you think I would have been reduced to such a poor state?" replied Hafez.

Sokrat, of course, had no idea of Hafez or Turkish beauties.

Aslam had not come to Samarkand as a tourist. His real mission was to meet the Secretary of the Communist Party of Ferghana. Sokrat had promised to arrange the meeting sometime during the course of the day. She was away on tour in the valley and was to come to Samarkand later for the meeting. In the meantime, Aslam was to enjoy himself going around the beautiful city. Sokrat had kindly engaged a guide for him who would take him to see the old monuments.

When Aslam was driven to the guest house where he was to stay for the next two nights, he met the guide, a Turkish beauty from Shiraz whose paeans had been sung by Hafez a thousand years before. She reminded him of the figures he had seen in the Persian miniatures and in a modified form in the Mughal paintings. Slim and tall, with the original oriental features softened by a liberal intermingling of Persian and Uzbek lines, and large eyes underlined by kohl, Shireen Shirazova was the most beautiful woman that Aslam had met in his life.

Sokrat did not allow him to linger long at the portico. After the brief handshake with Shireen, Sokrat had whisked him away to the spacious but sparsely-furnished bedroom. Sokrat had left him there asking him to freshen himself up and join him in the sitting room. So, after a quick wash, when Aslam came to the sitting room, he found Shireen waiting for him. He was glad that he was going to have such a beautiful guide to take him around Samarkand and his opinion of Sokrat's taste improved considerably.

Having spent a full day with Sokrat, Aslam had concluded that his escort shared at least one trait with his ancient namesake—a poor judgment of women. But the choice of this beautiful guide now persuaded Aslam to revise his opinion. Sokrat, after all, did have some wisdom, and he did not need the Delphic oracle to confirm that view.

Aslam had eyes only for the guide. The sitting room and its ambience had no attraction for him even though its décor was a striking example of Central Asian art, in its baroque and highly ornate form. The walls with carved panels, the intricate arabesque patterns of the walnut screens, the plush low-flung sofas and divans, the colourful tapestries, all held his glance but briefly. However, there was nothing baroque or ornate about the lady who now came forward to meet him. "Good morning, Mr Aslam. Welcome to Samarkand. I hope you had a comfortable flight," she said in a lilting voice, a voice that held the hidden tinkle of a mountain stream gently flowing down on rounded pebbles to meet the Syr Darya.

"Well, whatever discomfort I might have had on the flight is now dispelled by your warm greetings," Aslam responded gallantly, walking around the table in the centre to take his seat on the sofa closer to Shireen. "I am really glad that Sokrat has chosen you to guide me around Samarkand. I am sure your company would enhance the beauty of the city."

"Ah, ahem," said the lady looking a little embarrassed at the unabashed effusiveness of Aslam's compliments. "Well, I don't know about that," she said with becoming modesty. "We will have to see where Mr Sokrat is? I hope you will excuse me for a few moments; I will just go and find where he is."

Before Aslam could say anything, Shireen had exited from the room. He had now time to look at the wood carving, and the ceiling in particular which was done up in the Kashmiri *Khatamband* style. Perhaps that art had been brought to Kashmir by the artisans in the entourage of the greatest ruler of Kashmir—Budshah, or Zain-ul-Abideen, to give him his real name. But thoughts of Shireen kept intruding in his observation. She appeared to be in her early thirties and spoke English rather well for an Uzbek. But then, a guide had to know more than two languages. He recalled that the Intourist department of the erstwhile USSR trained its guides rather well not only in history and archaeology, but other more useful arts—useful to the regime.

"Well, it seems your friend Mr Sokrat is indisposed. He will not be accompanying us on our tour of the city," said Shireen, returning from her search. "But I rather think that is only an excuse. He has been escorting so many VIPs around Samarkand that he has come to hate the sight of every monument here."

In a way, Aslam felt relieved that Sokrat would not be joining them and he would have the exclusive company of Shireen. With her around, Sokrat would have been an unwanted intrusion. Aslam was reminded of a saying in his mother tongue—a bone in the kebab.

"But what about my appointment with the Secretary of the Communist Party of Ferghana? That was for this morning and Sokrat was to arrange that," Aslam asked, with mixed feelings of pleasure and guilt. In fact, his visit to Samarkand was primarily to meet that important and powerful official of the regime. Even though the USSR had withdrawn from the Central Asian states, seventy years of their communist reign had left behind a powerful machine. So Aslam did not want to go around sightseeing without having attended to business first

"Oh, you had an appointment with the Secretary? I have no idea about that. You will please have to check with Mr Sokrat," said Shireen, without showing any concern for Aslam's anxiety.

This time it was Aslam's turn to go in search of Sokrat. The corridors of the large guest house baffled him. He lost his way several times in the labyrinth. He located his room with some difficulty in that huge complex. The communists of Russia always built large edifices, whether it was an apartment complex, a hotel, or a department store! Aslam found Sokrat lying in bed when he entered the large room after knocking. "What has happened to you?" he asked with some concern. "You appeared perfectly all right in the morning when we landed." Sokrat did not look.tired or ill.

"Yes, but when I went in for a wash, I felt suddenly faint. I have talked to the doctor; he has advised me complete bed rest today. Perhaps, I will be able to join you in the evening. Please do forgive me. The guide will take care of you until we meet," Sokrat looked rather helpless and quite embarrassed as he made his excuses.

"But what about my appointment with the Secretary of the Communist Party?" Aslam asked.

"Oh, I forgot to tell you, the appointment has been

postponed. There will be no meeting this morning. The Secretary is away on an official tour of the valley and is expected to return shortly. I am sorry; I regret the inconvenience."

Aslam was disappointed. The whole purpose of his visit to Samarkand was in jeopardy and he felt let down. His feeling of guilt was getting reinforced. "Have you been given any other time?" he asked Sokrat anxiously.

"No, but I expect to get that information sometime today. But don't worry, Mr Aslam, I will see to it that you meet the Secretary, if not today, then tomorrow."

That was somewhat reassuring, but it did not fully reassure Aslam.

It all went back to three months earlier when the Government of Uzbekistan had decided to throw open a mining concession for gold in the Ferghana Valley. After the fall of the USSR, Uzbekistan had gained its independence but the President of Uzbekistan, Islam Karimov, ruled the country with an iron hand. Islam Karimov wanted to shift the economy of Uzbekistan from a supplier of 'white gold' to the textile mills of Russia, to the vast resources such as red gold, oil, steel etc. of which Uzbekistan had a good potential. Hence, he had invited international investors. Along with the Australians and the South Africans, the BMZ Conglomerate of United Kingdom, Aslam's employers, had also made a bid for the goldmine. The conglomerate was shortlisted along with the Australians who had made an aggressive bid. The competition had become tough. There had been several rounds of negotiations with the officials at Tashkent but nothing much had come out of them. They were all perhaps waiting for a signal from the Secretary of the Communist Party of Ferghana who was the real decision-maker. The gold mines were located in the valley.

Unlike other Muslim countries, Uzbekistan had educated its women and some of them were occupying high positions. They moved around freely and were not veiled or in 'hijab'.

As a senior executive of BMZ and as a lover of Persian poetry and literature, Aslam was called in by the President of the Company in London for consultation. He had protested that the people of Uzbekistan no longer spoke Persian; they spoke Russian and Uzbek, both languages not known to him.

"The Secretary of the Communist Party of Ferghana speaks Persian we have learnt, and our feedback is that the final say as to who gets the exploration and mining rights will be with the Secretary. Also we have no one else in London who is better qualified than you to establish contact with that bureaucracy."

So Aslam had packed his bags and left for Tashkent.

"Why do you look so crestfallen, Mr Aslam? Something wrong?" Shireen was solicitous on his return to the sitting room. Her look of concern tempted Aslam to confide in her. "You see, Shireen, I had hoped to meet the Secretary with a rather important proposal. It would have been to our mutual benefit, to your country and my company. But it is most unfortunate that the appointment has been cancelled."

"Oh, I am sorry to hear that. Don't be disappointed. If the Secretary has promised to meet you, I am sure that the appointment will be kept. However, since the Secretary is not in town, let me at least take you around the city. There should be some compensation for your disappointment." So saying Shireen took Aslam's arm and they moved to the large Zil limousine that had been placed at Aslam's disposal. Even though the Communist State was crumbling, the infrastructure it had created would serve the successor for some time to come, Aslam mused.

Their first stop was the Gur-e-Amir, the Mausoleum of Tamerlane. It was built in the Turkish architectural style with an elongated dome. As they alighted at the gateway, Aslam saw a number of Uzbek men and women getting in. There were no tourists. Aslam observed that most of the women, though Muslims, were dressed in frocks or skirts of bright multi-coloured fabrics. Aslam realised that seven decades of communist rule had changed the culture and appearance of the Uzbek population. The men wore trousers and jackets and all of them wore the typical black square Uzbek cap embroidered with white thread. That was a concession they made to their heritage.

"The women here appear to be far freer than in most Muslim countries," remarked Aslam who had just come from London. "Yes," responded Shireen, "that is about the only benefit we got out of the Soviet rule." Her voice held a note of bitterness. Aslam was rather surprised at the remark. During his interaction with the officialdom of Uzbekistan, he had noticed that the senior officials still nominally adhering to the Communist ideology were all rather restrained in their comments on politics and government. Sokrat never spoke freely. He had not expected a guide to be freer. It was a measure of the hostility to Soviet rule and the partially opened liberal rule, he thought, that even a guide was so open in her comments.

Tamerlane's mausoleum was a massive complex of buildings surmounted by a rather high and elongated double dome sheathed in turquoise-coloured glazed tiles. Shireen showed Aslam the large stone bowl in the spacious courtyard. There were many legends associated with the larger than like figure of Tamerlane, many of them related to the gigantic stone bowl, carved from a single piece of rock. Tamerlane, Shireen explained, would get the bowl filled with wine, sit in front and take the oath of fealty (allegiance) from his cohorts on a smaller bowl of wine. The interior of the mausoleum was equally striking. Blue, red and gold were the dominant colours of the tile work and the dazzling patterns shimmered even in the dim light of sparse bulbs hanging from the roof. Richly decorated with onyx tiles with gold painted inscriptions, the ceiling had numerous decorations with jaspar carvings. Among the several graves in the mausoleum complex, Tamerlane's grave was covered by the largest block of black jade in the world, fully eight feet long and three feet thick.

"Do you see the crack in that block?" Shireen pointed to a dark wavy line, a centimeter wide, zigzagging right across the massive block of jade. The stone had cracked. "It is said that whenever Samarkand faces a crisis, Tamerlane strains to come out of his grave. Even in death he is said to be so strong that the heavy block of jade has cracked due to his straining from inside. However, he has so far not succeeded in coming out."

"Do you believe that story?" Aslam asked smiling. "No, I don't," said Shireen. "But Uzbekistan too is straining to come out of its Communist past. Tamerlane only cracked the block that covered his grave, but we will have to break every block that is pressing us down, and every shackle imposed on us by our colonial rulers that has blocked our progress." Shireen had become vehement and her voice had risen.

"And I hope to be a partner in that attempt," said Aslam getting a word in.

"Tell me more about it," said Shireen. "Maybe I can give some advice."

As they proceeded from the mausoleum to the Registan, the place of sands, a large ornamental square, Aslam found himself telling Shireen of his mission to Tashkent and Samarkand and why it was important for him to have met the Secretary.

"But what would you have achieved with the Secretary that you could not with the officials at Samarkand?" Shireen asked, perhaps not comprehending the nuances involved in the negotiations.

"You see, my Conglomerate has offered a lumpsum payment of fifty million pounds for the mining concession plus a royalty per kilogram of gold extracted. Your government has demanded a hundred and fifty upfront. That is too much, particularly as we don't still know how much of gold we can take out annually. My company cannot afford such upfront cost. In any case, the concession is not worth that much," clarified Aslam.

Aslam was aware that all newly-emerging economies had an exaggerated notion of the value of their assets.

"So what does your company consider to be the true value of the concession?" asked Shireen.

"Ah, wouldn't the Minister in Tashkent like to know that?" exclaimed an amused Aslam.

As the car stopped at the kerb near the Registan, a large ornamental central square said to be the first of its kind in Islamic urban planning, Aslam got down first and held the door open for Shireen to get out. They were surrounded by a number of local tourists who had come to see what their ancestors had built. They surrounded the couple, as though they had seen an Indian for the first time. There were smiles of welcome on all faces. Aslam noticed that some of the men and most of the women had gold-capped teeth.

"Is that an indication of a fluoride deficiency, or is it a fashion here to have your teeth capped with gold?" remarked Aslam to Shireen. "Neither," said Shireen, taking Aslam's arm and leading him towards the central courtyard of Registan. "During the early Soviet regime people felt so insecure that they started hoarding wealth for security, particularly gold in the form of jewellery...."

"We have been doing that for centuries in India; we still do so," interrupted Aslam.

"Yes, but here the Soviets prohibited hoarding of gold. One had to obtain permission from the authorities even to buy a gold wedding ring. So the only way people could have gold was to go to the dentist and get gold capping for their teeth," Shireen's explanation amused Aslam. Even the most zealous Russian officials could not devise ways and means of getting at the gold hidden in an Uzbek woman's mouth. Aslam recalled the elite of Delhi attending wedding receptions, weighed down by tons of gold jewellery, but the Income Tax authorities could get at that openly displayed treasure.

By this time, they had reached the centre of the

courtyard. It was originally surrounded by three madrasas, a mosque, a *khanqah* and a caravanserai. It was built by Tamerlane's grandson and successor, Ulugh Beg. Ulugh Beg's successor added to the complex. Only the madrasa had survived the ravages of time but the massive pillars and arched portals bore witness to the grandiose imperial conception of those times.

The square surrounded by those massive structures was used as a public meeting place where people gathered to hear the royal proclamations and enjoy the executions of the condemned.

"That family didn't believe in anything small did they?" asked Aslam.

"Oh, no, Tamerlane hated all things small. When he was generous, he was profligate. When he killed, he massacred in thousands. The story goes that a calligrapher spent years to write a miniature Quran which could be fitted under the bezel (groove) of a signet ring. When he presented it to Timur, the king instead of rewarding the calligrapher did not even deign to acknowledge it. Of what use is a Quran that would require a magnifying glass even to look at it? he must have asked. It was too small for the conqueror to take notice. So the artist went back and spent a few years more to script another manuscript of the Holy Book with each page of ten feet and lines six feet long and brought it loaded on a wheelbarrow. Tamerlane went out to meet him in full panoply with all his courtiers, amirs and clergy, and rewarded the calligrapher with great favours."

"And do you also go for big things?" asked Aslam.

"And why not, if that is possible?" Shireen asked archly.

From the Registan they went to an Uzbek restaurant. It was furnished in the traditional style, with raised square-shaped benches covered with carpets. While Shireen nimbly climbed up on the bench and reclined languidly on the covered bolster, Aslam unaccustomed to such style of dining room furniture found it difficult to sit tailor-style. They managed to get a couple of meat pastries and the typical Turkish Kahwa, infused with cardamom and mint.

By the time they returned to the guest house, Aslam had walked more than a score kms through mausoleums, necropolises, bazaars, *chai khanas* and sundry ancient ruins. Shireen left him at his room and said that she would meet him after he had refreshed himself, and take him to dinner at her house. When he returned to the sitting room after having refreshed himself with a change of clothes, he found Shireen already waiting for him. She was dressed in a multi-coloured silk dress, which emphasised the contours of her figure to great advantage. Aslam could not take his eyes off her as she took him to a small car parked at the portico.

"But before we go for dinner, I want you to see one of

our great assets—the tomb of the Living King," she said. That intrigued Aslam—tomb of the Living King?

The Shah-e-Zinda complex built in the fifteenth century by Tamerlane, surrounding the tomb of a seventh-century saint was discovered on a mound in the city.

"His name is Qutham. He was the son of Abbas, the uncle of Prophet Muhammad; so he is a first cousin of the Prophet. In his heyday, he had functioned as the governor of the sacred city of Medina and he came to Samarkand in the seventh century in the Muslim army. He is reported to have been killed leading a sortie against the massive gateway of the city. As a martyr, he has become immortal."

The legend goes that his head was cut off from his body during the fight. His death then would have demoralised his troops and thwarted the sortie. It was believed that Qutham picked up his severed head and carried it in his left palm and continued fighting. The sight of a headless body fully-clothed in armour must have unnerved the defenders. Once the gateway was breached, Qutham walked up to a mound, dropped his head and fell down dead. That is why he is called Shah-e-Zinda, the Living Saint," Shireen explained to Aslam.

As they climbed the narrow steep lane flanked by ornate buildings, Aslam saw the ornate cenotaph containing the graves of the members of the royal family, who all wanted to be buried close to the Living Saint. He could see that the famous blue tiles that had formed the intricate patterns of most monuments had vanished from the facades at the lower levels of these buildings, exposing the bare plaster underneath. Was it natural decay? Many a tourist in the past centuries must have prized out those irreplaceable tiles as souvenirs and carried them off, but the upper parts of the arches where the vandals could not reach and the domes were in a comparatively better shape. Suddenly, Shireen spotted a Russian tourist who was standing at a turning and trying to prize out one of the remaining tiles from the wall. She flew into a towering rage at this crass vandalism and spoke to the man in excited Russian. The embarrassed vandal quietly slunk away with a guilty look on his face.

"What did you tell him?" Aslam asked.

"Oh, I told him to get off. Look at the temerity of that rogue. He thinks the Russians are still ruling Samarkand so he can still destroy our heritage with impunity. These Russians have exploited us for a hundred years. They took away everything of value from our land—our golden vessels, our calligraphed manuscripts, our engraved swords and daggers and the clothes of our rulers with diamonds, turquoises etc. They are all in Petersburg! They made us into mere suppliers of cotton and other raw materials for their mills and factories in Ukraine and Russia proper. While Russia was moving towards a space-age technology, they kept us in a backward agrarian economy, working our cotton fields for a few kopeks a kilogram. Even the cotton was taken away to feed the textile mills in Ukraine and Georgia. They killed our scholars and burnt our priceless manuscripts in public squares. They even changed the names of our cities calling them after Russian generals who had conquered them. They allowed our monuments to go to ruin and their tourists stole whatever of value they could lay hands on, including the blue tiles."

The vehemence of Shireen's reaction and her intensity of feelings left Aslam somewhat surprised but not too much. He felt the same when he thought of the British.

By this time, they had reached the apex of the large mound that had formed the complex and entered the central tomb of the Living Saint. While from outside it looked like a medieval Central Asian monument, the inside was gloomy, barely illuminated by low wattage bulbs here and there hanging from the high ceiling. Uzbekistan as yet had no surplus to allocate funds for its mausoleums and for preserving its heritage. As the afternoon had far advanced, the keepers of the tomb were herding out the few tourists who still remained inside the tomb.

"We will have to hurry up," said Shireen. "The lights in the whole necropolis are put off at 6 pm. If we are not out of the place by then, we will have to grope our way out of this darkened town of the dead. I, for one, don't like the prospect of spending the evening with the ghosts of these ancient dead," Shireen laughed nervously.

So Aslam and Shireen walked up to the main mausoleum where the Shah-e-Zinda's cenotaph was perched. After paying his hurried respects to the Saint, Aslam turned towards the exit. There was a crowd of the local and Russian tourists all exiting out of the main hall and Aslam found himself pushed this way and that in the crowd. In the melee, he was separated from Shireen. Before he could locate her, the hall had emptied of the visitors and he found himself standing alone by the grave of the Living Saint. The lights had gone out. He called out Shireen's name loudly, only to hear his voice echoing eerily in that vast edifice, reflected back from dome to dome. But there was no answering call from Shireen.

He came out of the door of the central chamber into the wide surrounding corridor which branched off into several narrower corridors. He saw no one there. All the tourists had left the complex by then. Even the keepers of the tomb seemed to have left with them. As he wondered which way to go to get out of the labyrinth, he heard a scream from beyond one of the corridors. It sounded like the voice of Shireen and she seemed to be in deep trouble, as though someone was trying to kidnap her. Aslam rushed towards that corridor from where he thought he had heard the scream. Just as he reached the turning, the remaining lights went out. He vaguely recalled Shireen having told him that the keepers put out the lights at 6 pm, and locked up the complex. Aslam knew that now he himself was in trouble. If Shireen had been forcibly carried off and he had been left locked in the Tomb complex, it would be hours before they both were missed. Sokrat knew that they were to return after dinner; so he would not be unduly perturbed. And if he had gone to bed before that, they would not be missed before morning.

Aslam was not given to nerves normally, but to be lost at night in a vast acropolis in a strange city was not a comforting prospect. He tried to explore every corridor from which he saw a glimmer of light, but the darkness was becoming darker every minute and each glimmer of light turned out to be mere illusion. Wandering about on uneven and broken paving stones in total darkness was not the kind of adventure Aslam fancied. Several times he stumbled on low steps leading from one corridor to another. There were many missing paving stones and he could not help stepping into cavities in the gloom. Instead of spending the night stumbling around, he thought it wise to select a corner and squat down there, waiting for help or the morning. By this time, his eyes had become a little accustomed to the darkness and he could see the open door of the central room which contained the tomb of the Living Saint. Since that was where he had been parted from Shireen, he selected one of the massive pillars nearby and sat down with his back to it. The exercise had left him somewhat hungry and thirsty.

The ground was hard and the semi-dressed granite of the pillar was rough and cold. Aslam felt most uncomfortable sitting there with his back to it. He felt that time had stood still in the tomb. He looked at his watch frequently. That itself took an effort, since he had to cup it with the palm of his right hand to read the faintly glowing tips of the hour and minute hands. The day's long walk of a score of kms in the Gur-e-Amir, Registan and Shah-e-Zinda had tired him out. Time passed very slowly. His frequent look at the watch did not speed up the time. He must have dozed off. Just before midnight something woke him up. It was the clang of iron striking iron, the kind of noise which an ironsmith makes while hammering sheet metal. He woke up with a start and the first thing he did was to peer at his watch. It was exactly midnight.

He glanced up to locate the source of the ominous sound. To his horror, he saw a score of men emerging from the door of the central tomb in twos and threes. They were dressed in medieval era chainmail and had solid steel helmets on their heads with visors down, their hands encased in gauntlets. Each one was carrying a tall lance in the right hand with a long sword tied around the waist. They made an impressive show, had Aslam been in a mood to admire the fine armour-clad warriors and their finer workmanship.

He was in the grip of terror, not comprehending the sight of this strange group of anachronistic men, in medieval armour, marching to the sound of clashing iron. He had eyes only for the central figure whose body seemed to be glowing with an aura even in that faint light. He walked along sedately, his armour clanging, his lance held upright. But Aslam's terror was compounded when he noted that the warrior was carrying his own head in the palm of his left hand. He still held the lance in his right hand; that was what had riveted Aslam's eyes. He found his heart beating so violently that he thought it would burst. The company of lancers led by the headless warrior came out from the tomb's door, climbed down the few steps to the corridor, and marched with slow steps in deep silence but for the clanging of the armour towards a dark corner which must have been not more than fifty feet from the door.

Even though Aslam was sitting hunched up with his back to the pillar, his knees felt as though they had turned to jelly. He could not control their knocking against each other. Even if he had wanted, he could not move for fear of attracting the attention of the warriors. As the company of lancers reached the dark corner, Aslam could perceive that the headless leader descended into a pit which Aslam had not noticed before. Within seconds, he had vanished. One after another, every lancer stepped into the pit and disappeared, until the vast corridor was once again empty. An eerie silence reigned after their clangorous exit. Aslam stared for some time at the vacant spot where the company had vanished, but could not muster enough courage to walk up to the pit and investigate the strange apparitions he had seen. He sat there by the pillar, stunned and silent.

Dawn found him still dozing by the pillar, shivering in the cold air of the tomb and from the events he had witnessed during the night. As the filtered light of the morning sun crept into the room, he heard his name being called. "Aslam, Aslam, where are you? Please answer." Someone was calling him. He came out of his somnambulistic state with great difficulty and managed to answer, "I am here." The beam of a moving flashlight found the pillar below which he was sitting. It was Sokrat with half a dozen Uzbek security officers who had come to find him.

One of the tomb keepers had found Shireen lying unconscious on the steps leading down to the main exit around 4 am. He had called for an ambulance and sent her to the hospital.

"She regained consciousness about an hour ago and contacted me. It took me another hour to reach you. I am really glad to see that you have come to no harm. Shireen was frantic with anxiety when she rang me up," said Sokrat.

Aslam was relieved that he had been found. His

experience with the warriors had unnerved him, but he did not want to share it with Sokrat or anyone else, for he knew that no one would believe him. Now that he was safe amongst his hosts, he wondered whether what he had seen was not a dream, after all. Earlier during his tired walk, he had heard the story of the headless warrior, Shah-e-Zinda. Perhaps the tomb, its semi-mysterious ambience and the power of suggestion evoked by Shireen's telling of the tale had all combined to evoke that vision. In his comatose state, it appeared real to him.

"How is Shireen? Where is she?" he asked Sokrat. "Oh, she is quite okay. She had fainted out of fright. Her abductors apparently could not carry her off so they left her on the steps. She has recovered and gone home to rest. I think you should also rest after spending the whole night in such inhospitable surroundings. Shireen said she would see you in the evening today for dinner."

It was more than half-an-hour before Aslam could reach back to the guest house. He spent the whole day in bed, dozing off and on, and reliving the terror of the previous night in his mind.

It was evening when he dragged himself out of bed and showered and changed for the upcoming dinner. As he entered the sitting room, Shireen sprang up from the sofa and grasped his hands.

"I hope you have gotten over the terrible experience of last night. Let us go now for the dinner that was so unexpectedly sabotaged last night. I have dispensed with your Zil car. My parents are poor people. My father was a worker in the cotton ginning factory and my mother worked in the Arts & Crafts emporium; both are now retired. They would be embarrassed no end if a Zil limousine was found parked at their house."

As Shireen drove Aslam to her house in her small car, he found himself relating what he had seen the previous night in the Shah-e-Zinda tomb.

Shireen looked at him with a strange look in her eyes, "I am sure you know that the graves of the martyrs on the frequented level are empty cenotaphs. The real graves are in the basement below. In the olden times, they used to build an ornate, much-decorated grave, right above the earthen grave down below. This was to circumvent the Prophet's ordinance not to have a permanent, cement and concrete structure. So they left the body buried in an earthen grave and built a structure above. The spot where you saw the warriors disappearing is where the staircase to the basement is located. Aslam, not many people have seen what you saw last night. It is said that this vision is granted to only a select few. And those who are fortunate enough to see it go on to achieve great success in life," she continued.

Shireen's house turned out to be not so modest. There was a central courtyard with a raised verandah on three sides. There were large rooms at each end of the verandah.

The open space between the two rooms was used as the living area. There were the typical raised benches covered with carpets and furnished with soft bolsters. Shireen's father Ikramov and her mother Zeinova turned out to be a very pleasant couple. They knew no English. They could speak only Uzbek. Shireen acted as the interpreter. Sitting cross-legged on the bench that night, Aslam dined on cold cuts of lamb and horse tongue, samosas, kebab and pilaf, all deliciously cooked. There were innumerable toasts quaffed on the Russian national drink and he found that Shireen matched him drink for drink. Aslam returned to the guest house in a euphoric haze, induced by the excellent food, the drinks and the company.

The night was still young when he put on his pajamas and got into bed. Aslam did not at all feel sleepy. The intoxicating fragrance of jasmine was being wafted into the bedroom through the open windows. Jasmine, Aslam recalled, always had an erotic effect on him and he found himself yearning for Shireen. Just as he thought of her, the door creaked open and he saw Shireen walking in, in a diaphanous night dress.

"I thought you must be feeling lonely," she said. "I have brought a bottle to share." Aslam sat up in bed and asked her to sit by his side. She complied gracefully and he put his arms around her.

"You are leaving tomorrow morning, and I would perhaps never see you again," she said. "I came to tell you how much I enjoyed your company today. I know you have not been able to meet the Secretary, but you should not be too disappointed. Why don't you offer the Minister what is the right price given by your assessor for the mining concession? Perhaps you may be able to strike a deal, even without the intervention of the Secretary."

As Aslam sipped from his glass and drew Shireen closer, he thought over her suggestion.

"You see, Shireen," he found himself confiding in her, "our consultants have assessed the right value at ninety million pounds, but if I were to offer that, my company would make no profit."

"They would make a profit at what price then?" Shireen asked, her hands playing with the hair on his chest.

"They would make a great profit at fifty, but as the price increased, their profits would go down. I am afraid they will break off at eighty, but I don't want to go up to that limit. And I don't ever even want them to guess that figure."

"Obviously, they would make a profit even at eighty if they are willing to go up to that figure. Moreover, Aslam, we are a poor country exploited for a century and just emerging into the light. I think you should help our country with every pound your company can spare."

Aslam spent the whole night in a haze. He was to catch the Aeroflot flight at 8 am but that never bothered him or Shireen. Aslam found himself in full sympathy with Hafez, the dead poet. If his Turkish beauty was anything like Shireen, Hafez would have been justified in sacrificing not one but ten Samarkands and a dozen Bukharas.

The return to Tashkent was a damp squib. Sokrat remained silent and subdued all the way. Aslam thought that perhaps the poor fellow had not yet recovered from his indisposition.

That afternoon, Aslam went back to the negotiating table. Azimov led in his team and Aslam found that the official attitude had hardened over the weekend. He tried to put forward his best arguments to keep the price between fifty and sixty million, but his heart was not in it. He kept thinking of the wondrous night that he had spent in the guest house. By the time the negotiations ended, he found he had conceded upto seventy-nine million. He knew that a million more and the negotiations would have to be broken off. Mercifully, just as Aslam was about to throw in the towel and call off the deal, Azimov gave in and they struck at seventy-nine million. Aslam knew that he had conceded far more than his company would be happy with. They had set the limit at eighty and he was just a million short of that.

Having lost the game, as he thought it, Aslam wanted to enjoy the formal dinner that followed. He barely had a few minutes to go to his room and get spruced up before he was picked up by no less a person that Azimov himself. "You know the dinner is being given by the Secretary of the Communist Party of Ferghana. She came back this morning from her tour. The Secretary is very happy with the deal we have struck."

When Aslam entered the dining hall, he was pleasantly surprised to find Shireen there. "Mr Aslam, meet the Secretary of the Party, Shireen Shirazova of Ferghana." Shireen laughed at the look of consternation on the face of Aslam. "I am glad to learn, Mr Aslam, that you gave the most reasonable price for the mining concession. After all, eighty would have been too much."

The God of Crippled Shapes

At first glance, Sharmila was repelled, utterly repelled, by the strange idol of Rakshadev. On a close look, she found it was not any man-made idol at all. It was a protruding part of the mahua tree, an ancient mahua tree which had thrown out its branches over many years in a haphazard manner. As they withered and died during the decades that the tree grew into a magnificent canopied giant, they left behind odd misshapen stumps, each with a distinct shape and characteristics. Some tribal Michelangelo saw the trunk and noticed the odd shapes all those stumps made collectively, and by removing an unnecessary outgrowth here and an unwanted protrusion there, he fashioned an idol out of the wood in a kind of bas relief like a statue chiselled out of a large granite slab. Sharmila stood rooted there, gazing at the strange indescribable structure which at once repelled and fascinated her.

Once she had seen a king cobra in the grounds of Balaram Palace, coiling upon itself and rearing its hood and staring at her with its black, depthless beady eyes. Half its body was off the ground and the rest coiling and uncoiling in a shapeless lump. She was much younger then but instinctively knew that it was a most dangerous reptile to encounter in the wild. One part of her mind told her to run away but her feet remained rooted and would not step back. Strangely, she found herself attracted to the serpent, the attraction of Eve in Paradise before the fall. It was her father who had pulled her back.

"Don't you know that the king cobra is an aggressive snake? It's not afraid of humans and will advance and strike if it feels threatened," he had admonished her.

"But I was not threatening it," she had protested. "Yes, but you stood close and stared at it. It does not know what your intentions are. Also, you must remember that even if it does not advance and strike, it can throw its poison for ten to fifteen feet. If the venom falls in your eyes, you could be blinded. If it falls on any part of your body which has even a small scratch, you could be poisoned!"

Sharmila, now grown up into a beautiful young woman with a doctorate in anthropology in her curriculum vitae, was still fascinated by the Rakshadev. As idols go, it wasn't a masterpiece of art. Many large semi-detached lumps of the tree's trunk formed the body of the feature. Another lump, broad at the base and narrowing at the top, where it merged back into the parent tree formed its main torso. But the tribal artist, who had shaped it perhaps a century ago, had taken full advantage of every protrusion, every convolution, every knot and natural feature of the trunk to fashion something extraordinary. He had used every curve and indentation and every hole to create an awesome symbol of the forces of nature at their terrible best. The head of the idol was just a roundish projection, with only mere suggestions of deep-set eyes, misshapen nose with flaring nostrils, teeth set awry and wide ear flaps. Old withered and dried lianas had left behind wispy strings of hair, if one could call them hair. At the same time, the dried vines appeared to be live and wriggling as in the head of medusa. Below the suggestion of flared nostrils, one could see the upward curving tusks of the wild boar dripping with oozing blood. Sharmila knew that it was only the vermilion applied by the tribal devotees. Yet, she could not rid herself of the feeling that it was blood.

On both sides of the trunk, there was a suggestion of curved horns. It was the minor branches of the trunk which imparted a shape of the large horns of the wild buffalo. She could not see but felt the hint of the opal eyes of the man-eating tiger, the open jaws of the river alligator full of cruel teeth, and the awesome claws of the black bear. Obviously, the Rakshadev was an object of great veneration and regular worship for the tribals. The tribal devotees had made libations of milk, oil and ghee to the idol. The torso glistened in the morning light of the sun, which had penetrated the leaves of the mahua tree and was creating a light and shade effect on the idol, changing its expression from moment to moment with the stirring of the leaves. Sharmila could see the art of the tribal artist who had carved myriads of wriggling slimy creatures into the body, which at one moment looked like the intertwined forest vines and at another took on a pulsating life of their own as the light shifted. All in all, the artist had given that lump of tree trunk an artistic unity, for all the creatures that lurked in the holes and stumps and which struggled in the trunk looked like parts of a living whole.

"What do you think of the idol?" Dr Raman, who was accompanying Sharmila asked. She turned warily to look at him—warily, because Sharmila liked neither his company nor his appearance.

Though Dr Raman held several academic degrees from various foreign universities and was held in high regard for his technical experience, his colleagues in NEERI, especially those of the opposite sex, avoided him.

Sharmila had met him just a week ago and she recalled her first impression of the scholar. It was a case of dislike at first sight. With his old-fashioned, round-rimmed thick glasses, a rather sharp beaked nose and puffed up cheeks, he reminded her of an owl. He had extended a rather limp hand with lean fingers which curled around her palm like a claw. That strengthened her impression of him—an owl of a man. His screeching voice too resembled that of the nocturnal bird and Sharmila decided that she did not like his proximity, decidedly not!

"I wouldn't call it an idol," Sharmila had replied. "I think the artist was trying to create a representative of the forces of nature."

Dr Raman smiled. "You are still riding your hobby horse, Sharmila," he remarked, "idealising the tribal culture and art."

Dr Raman was in his early forties, but dressed as though he was still in his twenties. His frayed and faded jeans, his tight half-sleeved T-shirts, his Nike shoes and his mop of thick hair falling all around his face showed his self-image. And he was, of course, trying since their arrival at the Guest House to impress Sharmila with his youthful vigour and his man of the world manners. Sharmila thought of him more as a predator than a lady's man.

"I am not riding any hobby horse. I am merely giving my impressions of the artistic figure we see before us," Sharmila remarked, rather tartly.

"I know, I know," said Dr Raman, placatingly. "You see, Sharmila, these tribals have no artistic sense. Of course, we know all about the cave paintings of the ancient man but our forests have not produced any such artists. What has happened here is that over a period of years, every Bhil or Gond who visited the tree added a touch here and a touch there. And at some point of time, the local shaman decided that this looks enough like an idol and gave it a name. And you know these shamans—they would go to any length to hype their objects of worship. Actually, it is they who create the local gods and the poor tribals are bilked into believing whatever mumbo-jumbo they invent."

Sharmila did not want to argue with him on the subject of myth-making in the middle of the forest. They had had long arguments since the Environment Assessment Committee had arrived at the Guest House in Dantewada. They were to produce an 'agreed upon report' without any dissenting voices. Any bitter arguments between her and Dr Raman would result in a disputed report and that was not in the interest of the poor adivasis.

The Guest House in which they were put up contributed to the contrary moods of the guests.

Actually, the Guest House was once the hunting lodge of the Maharaja of Bastar, and was located away from the town of Dantewada itself in the midst of a forest. Dantewada was a part of the Bastar district of Madhya Pradesh before the state was bifurcated and a new state of Chhattisgarh was created. Dantewada was to become the southernmost district of the new state. With a high concentration of mineral wealth, especially iron-ore, in the hills of the district, every major steel-maker of India and abroad was making a beeline to that place. One of these influential contenders had obtained a mining lease and had applied to the government for permission to open up the mine after cutting down tens of thousands of forest trees, laying roads and perhaps a railway line later. Eventually, he proposed to set up a ten million tonne steel plant, but in the meantime he would extract and export the ore to Japan and China. It was to assess the environmental impact of all these invasive activities that a team of experts had been formed by the Ministry of Environment and Forests. The expert team had decided to make a first-hand study of the situation before making their recommendations.

Dr Shrivastava from Dehradun headed the team. He had earlier served the Madhya Pradesh government as the Chairman of the State Pollution Control Board. Sharmila was his eldest daughter. As an anthropologist, Sharmila had always been interested in the tribals of Bastar, so when the team decided to visit Dantewada, she cajoled her father to allow her to accompany him.

The hunting lodge of the Maharaja of Bastar had

seen better days in the heyday of the Raj. Years of neglect helped by the ravages of time and the humidity had robbed it of its royal sheen. The large buffalo horns, the tiger skins with their massive glaring heads mounted by the expert taxidermists of Mysore, still stared down with their bright yellow glass eyes, and the sloth bear still stood on its two hind legs in the corner of the sitting room, its forearms extended as though to engulf anyone who drew near in its deadly embrace. Even the bedrooms had panther skins on the walls and displayed deer horns.

This display of the legacy of the predatory royalty and their colonial masters left Sharmila rather cold. As a lover of the wildlife she believed that a tiger prowling in the thick forests of Dantewada, a wild-buffalo with its magnificent horns charging at a hunter and the sloth bear protecting its cubs were far more beautiful in their natural habitat than adorning the walls of any royal hunting lodge.

The evening before, the team members had all gathered in the sitting room under the baleful stares of the stuffed tigers and the wild buffaloes before going in to dine. Though the dim bulbs hanging down from the high roof struggled to brighten the gloom, the large room still remained in semi-darkness creating an eerie ambience. However, the gloomy atmosphere was made quite lively by the spirited discussions that took place when the diversity of opinions clashed.

Dr Raman's was the first salvo. "I think we have seen enough of Dantewada. We have seen the poverty of the tribal villages. Their development and prosperity depend on the infusion of capital into this region. The government obviously does not have the wherewithal to invest the much-needed large sums. Only a private investor would be able to invest the money necessary. The country's interest demands that we should clear the mining project. Let us agree on that." Dr Raman had been hustling the Committee since arrival to come to a quick decision.

Mr Batra, the retired Chief Conservator of Forests, was not to be silenced into acquiescence by this forceful advocacy of Dr Raman.

"Do you realise Dr Raman how many sal trees, how many saj and teak trees, and how many mahua trees will have to be destroyed to open up this area to mining?" asked Dr Batra

"Bah!" said Dr Raman. "All these can be replanted. In any case, we do stipulate in the recommendations that for every tree cut, the company will have to replant four trees in twice the area lost."

"And where is that area to come from? Do you think the company, all powerful that it is, will create additional land to fulfill your stipulations?" asked Dr Johnson, the Ex-Chief Engineer. "We all know what happens once the permission is given and the mines are opened up.

Look at what happened in Goa, in Bellary and in Andhra Pradesh. None of the conditions were ever fulfilled. The gaping wounds in the land remain mute witnesses to the rape of mother earth—the quarries have only stagnant water, breeding fungi and…"

"Now you are growing poetic, Johnson," said Dr Raman. "Just because some fly-by-night company in Bellary or Andhra Pradesh did not observe the stipulations, are we going to deny all well-reputed companies which have been mining large areas in the State for a hundred years the opportunity to create wealth for the nation?" He contrived to inject a note of righteous indignation.

"What about the flora and fauna, especially the various wild animals? Dantewada is home to the last surviving wild buffaloes in the country. It also gives sanctuary to the spotted deer, the sambhar, the wild boar and perhaps the last surviving tigers. Are we going to destroy the habitat of these creatures and in the process make them extinct?" Batra remonstrated.

"And let us also not forget that Dantewada has some unique species of grasses and medicinal plants. I don't want to name them, but they or their extracts are used extensively as tonics for the body and brain; their oil for perfume, hair vitalisers, longevity drugs, piles, rheumatism, kidney stone, jaundice, blood pressure, many kinds of skin diseases, asthma, birth control, leprosy and so on. Most of you have already read that some of these plants are claimed to be useful even in the treatment of cancer. Are we going to destroy all these, just for a few more million tonnes of steel?"

Dr Raman, however, was not to be put down. "Yes, I know most of what you have said is true, but those are cures only for the tribals. I know that our social workers have kept the adivasis from using modern medicines and they still believe in these wild grasses and plants as the universal panacea for every disease in the world. And their shamans and witch doctors perpetuate these illusory beliefs. The sooner they are brought into the mainstream and forget their witch doctors, the better for them."

Dr Srinivasan, the former Vice-Chancellor of Jabalpur University, who had remained silent all this while, now joined the debate.

"We have been discussing all this while about the flora and fauna of Dantewada. Are these the only ones going to be affected by the mining company's activities?" he asked mildly. "Are we not forgetting the tribals in the process?"

"Yes, we must talk about them," intervened Dr Ravi Das, the economist from the National Council of Economic Research. "We have done a study on the economic impact of the mining and steel mill in Dantewada and our study shows that within ten years of the start of the operations, the per capita income of the tribals would increase three times and the GDP of the district would go up in the same ratio."

"Provided the tribals survive the onslaught of our civilization for the next decade," said Dr Khan. "We have seen what our civilization has done to the Jarawas of Andaman and Nicobar, the Bhils of Dangs, the Irulas of Nilgiris and so on, even without any large-scale industry going into those areas."

"Yes," piped in Sharmila, who was sitting in a corner listening quietly to the discussion among her elders. The cicadas outside had been making a terrific racket since twilight and they had now been joined by the frogs in their cacophony. "All that our civilization did to them was to take away their land and push them into the hills and forests. And then we built roads, railways and dams there and sent in moneylenders to exploit them. Then we pushed them out of the hills and forests because we discovered valuable minerals there too. We take away and destroy their way of life, introduce new kinds of diseases like AIDS, swine-flu, chickungunya, diabetes etc. into their system—all this in the name of progress, development and national interest. And to add insult to injury, our leaders go in and hold *shivirs* (camps) and *sammelans* (conferences) and lecture to them about the benefits of progress and civilization!" Sharmila's outburst even silenced the cicadas for a while.

"My dear," intervened Dr Raman in an irritating and patronising tone, "We don't have to be emotional about it. Some damage will occur when the world has to progress. I agree that some trees will be cut, some animals will die, some vegetation will be destroyed and some tribals will suffer; but for the larger good of the nation, these sacrifices have to be made."

"Collateral damage," said Sharmila in an acerbic tone. "That is what you are saying. 'Stuff happens', Cheney had said after destroying the ancient civilization of Baghdad. To civilize Iraq and Afghanistan, we have to rape and kill a few thousand women and children. That is your justification for the destruction of the last habitat of the adivasis of Dantewada!"

"Now, now," remonstrated Dr Raman. "I never said that. Don't you go around putting words in my mouth. All I am arguing is that to save a few sal trees and some species of squirrels let us not halt the wheels of progress."

And so, the arguments had gone on until the *khansaman* (cook) came in to announce dinner.

Sharmila's fascination with the Rakshadev did not abate with one visit. She had to see it a second time. The next morning found her standing before the ancient mahua tree, staring at the misshapen idol built out of the trunk.

To her surprise, she found Dr Raman Singh also at the Rakshadev. She recalled the unpleasant arguments of the night before. As they stood watching the idol, some tribals in their traditional attires wandered in. They carried some wooden objects in their hands. They were wooden figurines of buffalo heads, some artistically and some crudely carved. They stood before the Rakshadev in deep reverence for a few minutes, bowed down and placed the figurines at what could be thought of as the feet of the idol. Then, without a single glance at Sharmila and Dr Raman Singh, they glided away in utter silence.

Dr Raman stepped up closer to have a look at the figurines that the tribals had offered to their deity. He extended his hand to pick up one.

"No, no, don't do that, those are offerings," Sharmila protested. Dr Raman drew back with a jerk.

"I just wanted to see the crude figures they have crafted. You seem to believe that these tribals have nurtured Michelangelos and Da Vincis," he said in a sarcastic tone.

"The tribals of Dantewada are excellent artists. For centuries these experts have been crafting artistic items with clay, stone, bamboo, wood and metal. They can make really beautiful figures by adorning them with shells and peacock feathers."

"You seem to know quite a lot about the tribal art," remarked Dr Raman Singh.

"Oh, I have made many friends among them. Two of them, Sudran and Hirma, had come to visit me in the guest house last evening. They brought me some dolls which their wives had made. We are visiting their village this afternoon, I believe," she said.

That afternoon the members of the Committee were scheduled to visit Chilada village, which was not too far from the Rakshadev.

The previous day, just as the team was sitting down to lunch, Mr Batra, who had gone to Chilada, came back in great excitement. "We have an excellent opportunity of observing the collective worship of the Baurakis tonight if we hurry up!" he had said. The committee was happy and there were murmurs of excitement.

Prof Raman, the sceptic of the team who usually played the devil's advocate whenever the team was on the point of formulating a thesis, asked, "So what is so special about this collective worship, Mr Batra? Haven't we seen thousands of them before? Why all this excitement?"

Mr Batra, who had shown some unscientific enthusiasm took control of himself and said, "Well, from what I have learnt after questioning the tribals—mind you they talk very little and are extremely reluctant to reveal any of their rites—this worship is a survival in symbolic form of the ancient rite of human sacrifice."

This was a bombshell, for the team had no previous inkling that the Baurakis had ever indulged in human sacrifice in their history; but if Mr Batra was right, the opportunity was not to be missed. So, it was decided to leave for Chilada the next day after lunch. Dr Raman Singh tried to persuade Sharmila to stay back, but she was keen to observe the rites. Moreover, she did not fancy staying back alone in the Guest House with him hovering around and with his eyes boring into her. The Guest House itself frightened her, with its four large suites, each as large as a Bombay flat. Sharmila did not find the creaking staircases, the high wooden ceilings, the cracked mirrors and the leaking bathroom faucets prepossessing. She preferred to be with the team out in the open rather than spend an evening alone in that vast crumbling edifice.

When they reached Chilada that afternoon, dusk was falling and the sound of the tribal drums was reverberating from the surrounding hills. The drums had been going on the whole day. Sharmila had heard them while standing before the Rakshadev. The tribals used the drums to communicate with the neighbouring villages, in a form of Morse code. They also had developed over centuries a system of using symbols to communicate important messages; for instance, a Jamun branch and a piece of meat left on a doorstep at night meant "your man was killed in hunt", a bunch of chillies meant "please assemble at such and such village", depending on the number of chillies.

When the team arrived at the village, they were received by the headman with a gift of a large yam and then were taken to the large hut, the *ghotul*. The *ghotul* was the spacious hut where the boys slept and held a dance once a week. The eligible girls of the village went there on that day. A boy who chose a girl and wanted to propose to her offered the girl a drink. If she consented to the proposal, she accepted the drink and returned home the next morning at dawn.

"A sort of debutante ball," remarked Dr Ravi Das, "with minor differences."

"Each culture has its own mores and traditions," remarked Dr Srinivasan.

As soon as the members had been seated, they were served with sulphi. "What is this?" asked Dr Raman, making a wry face. "It tastes like dilute sulphuric acid."

"They get it from the sago palm," explained Mr Batra who had worked long years in tribal areas as a junior forest officer. "They tap the sago palm which yields a colourless fluid, much like the neera you get from the palmyra tree, but less sweet. Then they allow it to ferment in the sun for some hours and it becomes a potent liquor. It also develops into an aerated sparkling drink–our native champagne only ten times stronger."

As they all sat sipping the sulphi, the tall pine trees were crowding in and the large gathering of the Baurakis in the clearing before the *ghotul* was swaying to the beat of the drums. There was no moon and the only light came from half a dozen torches placed around on tree stumps. The swaying at first was relatively gentle and sedate. As Sharmila standing in the midst of her friends watched, the swaying of the dancers became more frenzied and suddenly a tribal leaped out of the crowd. He was dressed in a skirt of reeds, his bare body painted in stripes of red, as though he was bleeding from a thousand wounds. He was wearing a black hideous mask with white spots. There was a sword in his hand.

He started a weird dance, leaping from side to side, weaving his sword and making menacing gestures towards the crowd of tribals surrounding the clearing. From time to time, he halted abruptly and bowed before an imaginary deity. With his weapon he made ritual symbolic movements as though he was dismembering something lying in front of the imagined idol. Perhaps this was the symbolic altar on which in days of yore, a human victim lay half-drugged but semi-conscious. But now, there was a bulging gunny sack over which the Gaita, the witch doctor, was making all those ritual gestures with his sword. He was leaping back and forth and with every slash, he shrieked out some strange words. The crowd joined him in this and every shriek raised Sharmila's hackles. She shivered involuntarily.

The ritual lasted for half an hour and after the witch doctor had slashed and cut the imaginary victim to his heart's content, he slowly wound down and the crowd started chanting. That too went on for some time and then slowly the chanting faded away. Then, one after another, the gathering dispersed, and the clearing was empty.

"Shall we go and take a look at what is in that gunny sack?" suggested Dr Raman adjusting his spectacles on his hooked nose.

"I don't think that is advisable," said Dr Shrivastava. "The Baurakis may not like it."

"But then what sort of research are we doing if we don't even know what that priest was sacrificing?" said Raman, the devil's advocate. However, better counsels prevailed and the sack was left alone.

Sharmila decided to walk across to the Rakshadev which was close by before returning to the Guest House. Other members too decided to give her company.

"There it is," said Dr Raman. "The bag has been brought by someone and placed at the feet of the idol. That stone represents the altar where votive offerings are made." But no one dared to open the sack. They stood there like little children, eager to eat the mangoes but afraid to throw the stones, until Dr Raman hesitantly broke the spell and gave the sack a tug. The sack which had been loosely tied opened and out spilled hundreds of small statuettes, carved from wood. They were all crude human figures, some of them merely half-formed.

"These are the symbolic human sacrificial victims," said Dr Raman. "Perhaps each devotee carries a figure and makes a votive offering to the god."

"Yes, I think that is right," said Johnson.

Sharmila picked up one of the figures and examined

it closely. This specimen was better formed and it resembled the Rakshadev itself. It was carved out of some black wood, resembling ebony, and it too had some of those wriggling convoluted reptilian forms that formed the body of the Tree God. She felt frightened handling it. Quietly she put it down. The she saw Dr Raman stoop and furtively pick up the statue and surreptitiously slip it into his pocket.

Suddenly, they found that a hush had fallen on the forest clearing where they stood. The moon had come out from behind the clouds where it was hiding and cast a soft glow on the Tree God. But the moonlight, instead of softening the figure, made it look even more menacing. They huddled together, as children often do while watching a horror movie on TV, and stood staring for quite a while at the Rakshadev. Then with an unspoken accord, the group of environmentalists trooped back to the jeep which was parked a little distance away. Dr Raman took the driver's seat, inserted the key and turned it. The engine gave a splutter and fell silent. "Strange," he murmured. "I had got it checked thoroughly before leaving the Guest House."

He tried several times, but the jeep would not start. After a few attempts even the splutter died out, replaced by a low whine every time the key was turned. Batra too tried his hand but without any success. He got down and opened the hood. He had a rather good opinion of himself as a motor mechanic since he maintained a jeep of his own. But he could find nothing wrong with the engine. All the parts were intact and the starter too had nothing wrong with it, yet the engine just wouldn't start. "We cannot spend the whole night here trying to start the damned jeep. Let us walk," said Johnson. They decided to abandon the jeep and walk back to the Guest House which was only a few kilometers away by the winding hilly track. If they could cut across through the forest, they could even shorten the distance.

As they trudged along the forest path, they could all feel a vague menace in the air. Except for Sharmila, they all had had long experience of field trips, with months spent among tribal territory, forests and mountains. They had all lived in forest huts and wandered around alone in the jungles, but some of them had never felt the kind of unreasonable dread and fear that they were experiencing now on this walk through the forest of Chilada.

Suddenly, Dr Raman halted and said, "I feel as though someone is following us. I saw someone moving in that clump of trees."

Mr Batra looked at the clump of trees to which Dr Raman was pointing but he could see nothing, yet the sound of twigs breaking and dry leaves crackling underfoot could be distinctly heard.

As they proceeded, the feeling grew that someone or something was either following them or keeping pace with them amongst the dark trees that lined the path. They heard vague sounds behind them, sometimes like the beat of footsteps with a distinct non-human quality to the sound, and sometimes the breaking of dry branches and the rustling of the bushes as though some heavy body was stumbling across through and over the undergrowth. One or two of the group looked behind apprehensively but they found the path clear as far as the eye could see.

"Do you think it could be a tiger that is the stalking us?" Raman Singh asked apprehensively.

"No," said Batra, the forest man familiar with the wildlife of forests. "There is no report of a man-eating tiger in Dantewada. Only a man-eater stalks humans, that too single ones. It would never stalk a group of adults. No ordinary wild tiger comes near humans. It avoids them."

Suddenly Dr Khan caught a glimpse, a vague glimpse of some unrecognisable but menacing form which kept coming closer and closer as they continued. It could be his imagination playing tricks, or the remark of Raman Singh triggering his sighting. He refrained from saying anything for fear of being thought a superstitious scientist. Everyone felt the presence but no one could say with certainty that he or she had seen something tangible.

"There is something there," said Sharmila at one point. "I think it is a large tiger. I'm sure I saw its bright yellow eyes for a moment, and a large body slunk across those trees."

"But my dear," said Mr Batra, "as I said just now, there are no tigers in the forest of Chilada."

A few minutes later it was the turn of Dr Raman. "I'm sure I must be wrong, but I think there is a crocodile in those bushes. I think I saw its long squat body moving across the clearing hugging the ground."

Dr Shrivastava laughed. Where would a crocodile come from they all wondered? "It's our nerves. That macabre dance of the shaman has affected all of us."

But a few moments later, it was the turn of Dr Shrivastava himself. As he jumped across a small depression in the ground, he was suddenly face to face with an apparition ambling along in the dark shadow of the trees. He thought he saw a figure, a tall figure like a broken tree stump, almost black in colour. His first impression was that it was a bear, but before he could recall whether there were any bears in Chilada, at least in that area, the apparition had vanished. Apparently, nobody else had seen it, and like Mr Khan, Dr Shrivastava had no desire to mention his impression and frighten an already demoralised group. He himself was quite shaken.

They were now quite close to the Guest House, for they could see its dim lights. That was when Dr Raman decided to cut across the remaining part of forest, leaving the beaten path. He took the steep hills to climb through the clump of trees and the others followed. The path took a winding turn and by the time Dr Shrivastava and Sharmila who were following Dr Raman reached the turning to rejoin the path they were panting. Dr Shrivastava could now see the Guest House quite clearly in the moonlight.

"Ah, Raman, we are there at last," he said.

But there was no answer from Dr Raman. The path was clear all the way to the cottage, and there was no sign of the scientist. He had vanished into the air.

"Dr Raman, Raman!" Sharmila shouted, but there was no response. By this time, Johnson, Khan and the others too had caught up with them. "Dr Raman just vanished, within a few steps of the Guest House. One moment we saw him and the next, he was gone," said Dr Shrivastava. They stared at each other with dismayed eyes and mystified looks. There was a lurking hope that he might have gone into the Guest House without their noticing it. Their combined shouts brought out the half a dozen servants from the Guest House.

"Where is Dr Raman?" asked Dr Shrivastava of no one in particular. "He was just ahead of me. It took us less than a minute to reach the point where the path took a turning. Where in hell could he have gone in that one minute?"

They all spread out and searched long and far but of Dr Raman they found no trace. They made enquiries of the servants, only to learn that there were no wild animals in the forests of Chilada. They had all been hunted down to extinction by the Maharajah and his English guests long before independence.

It was an utterly demoralised group that met in the drawing room of the hunting lodge. They could only speculate as to what could have happened to Raman Singh. Had the earth swallowed him or the sky lifted him up? One moment he was there and the next he had vanished. He could not have left of his own volition. There was some outside agency that was responsible. What was the figure that had followed them–was it the apparition of a tiger? But it was too large for a tiger! Was it a sloth bear? Was it a crocodile?

Sharmila was the one who gave words to what they all vaguely felt but no one was willing to articulate.

"It felt like the Rakshadev to me," she said. No one said anything, but they all felt she was the child who had spotted the emperor's new clothes.

There followed the inevitable police enquiries. Senior police officials came down from Raipur. They interrogated all the members of the team asking interminable questions, cross-examined the servants, probed into any possible animosities between the various scientists and generally made a nuisance of themselves. But at the end, they could not come to any conclusion. They sent search parties in all the surrounding areas. They made enquiries in each of the nearby villages. Every nullah and ravine in the forest was probed in the belief that Dr Raman might have fallen into one of them, or some unreported tiger had taken him away. But neither their searches nor their probes and questionings produced any clue to the whereabouts of Dr Raman.

The team was disheartened after the disappearance of their team-mate. They had no spirit left in them to pursue their study any further. Sharmila felt a little guilty. She had disliked Dr Raman but she had no ill-will towards him; and his mysterious disappearance had affected her the most. She wondered whether his pocketing of the votive offering to the Tree God had anything to do with his disappearance. Had he committed a sacrilege by purloining the offering made to the Rakshadev?

Once the police enquiries were completed, the team decided to return to Delhi; but one last chore had to be performed. They had to take leave of the Baurakis. The Baurakis had been very friendly and hospitable. By this time their jeep had been recovered by the police from Chilada, so they were able to drive down to the village. After taking leave of the headman and promising to come again, they decided to take a last look at the Rakshadev.

The menacing ungainly wooden idol stood under the tree. It looked as fierce and menacing as ever. If anything, Sharmila found it more fascinating and more repellant than before. She found herself wanting to go closer, yet was reluctant to do so. Then she glanced down at the altar stone at its feet. The bulging sack of offerings was gone, but on the altar stone she saw a single statuette, a statuette carved in black wood of the same shape as the Tree God. It looked very similar to the one which she had handled and which she had seen being pocketed by Dr Raman. How had it got back to the altar stone? Sharmila wondered.

Then she glanced up and got another shock. In the body of the Rakshadev, where all those serpentine forms wriggled amongst claws and talons, she saw a vague form of a thin hooked nose, and just above that a hint of a pair of spectacles with round lenses. They had not been there when Sharmila had first seen the Rakshadev.

Weekend in Athens

Sameer Kapadia came out of the Ellinikon Airport, pushing his hand-trolley loaded with his single suitcase. It was a battered old piece of Samsonite, bearing labels from many airports and many airlines. During its travels around the many airports it had lost one of its wheels, but Sameer knew that if he got it replaced, the ground handlers would break the other wheels. He had flown straight from Madrid and the long overnight flight, with a changeover at Frankfurt, had left him bleary-eyed and groggy. His company had not permitted him travel in business class. In the early nineties, when economy was the mantra, even ministers were ordered to travel only by 'Cattle Class', as a wag later named the economy class. His company did not believe in being generous to its employees, unless such generosity was convertible into profits.

The first sight of Athens was not very prepossessing, in spite of all the favourable literature on Greece, from Homer to Byron, that Sameer had read before undertaking this visit. He had hoped to be met by someone from the shipping company at the airport, but apparently their hospitality did not extend beyond a routine welcome fax message he later found in his hotel bedroom. Those were the days before smart phones, emails and internet had invaded the airways.

The drive to Illyria Hotel, which was the only one willing to accommodate him at short notice (all others being full), too, did not predispose Sameer favourably to this capital city of Greece, once claimed as the cradle of all that was civilized in the western world. As he sped in the taxi towards his hotel he found no Socrates holding forth to a band of budding Platos at the street corner. None of the girls he saw on the roads had a face that could launch a thousand ships. Even the hotel lobby was devoid of any Aphrodite, Ariadne or Medea. All in all, Sameer felt rather disappointed with Athens, though strictly speaking he had no cause to be, for he had not come to Athens on a pleasure trip or as a tourist. He had to come because his company had sent him to settle a year-old insurance claim against the local shipping company, which had blocked a few million dollars of Sameer's employers.

It had all started when the Nagpur Textiles Ltd, Sameer's employers, had decided to import twenty thousand tonnes of viscose fibre from Spain. Viscose was in great demand in India as a cheaper alternative to fine cotton. Its silken feel, shiny appearance and ability to take on fast colours had given it the name of 'art silk', short for artificial silk. Spain was one of major producers of this art silk. It had contracted to engage the transport and bear the freight. The Spanish company, in their wisdom and to save on freight, engaged a tramp Greek steamer, SS KNOSSOS, registered in Panama, from a chartering firm in Athens to transport the viscose to Bombay. As the ship was carrying the fibre bales through the Mediterranean, the captain reported some engine trouble and took it to Piraeus, the harbour that serves Athens and the headquarters in Athens of the original owners of the ship, some Greek shipping tycoons. They had some legal disputes with the Spanish company, so they impounded the ship with the goods. Greek tramps flying Panama flags and captained by a Levantine, enjoyed the kind of reputation which even the pirates of the Caribbean would have envied. It was suspected that they were all in cahoots. He and his crew abandoned the tramp and left for happier climes.

Before the tangle could be sorted out, the inflammable viscose fibre caught fire or perhaps was made to catch fire and the SS Knossos was gutted. The issue became more complicated, what with the Spanish Insurance Company refusing to settle the claim until it was satisfied that the ship with the goods had actually got burnt, and the Greek charterers pleading inability to do anything as the ship had already been impounded by the owners and they could not even go near it. The owners of the ship refused to cooperate until the charterers paid them their outstanding dues, and the Piraeus port authorities refused to allow anyone to approach the ship until their enquiry into the causes of the fire was completed and they had recovered their port dues from the owners. After all, a fire in a ship could be contrived arson to swindle the owners, the insurers or the charterers. In the process, the main sufferers were the Nagpur Textile Company who had already paid twenty million dollars to the Spanish company, with not a fibre of the viscose in hand.

Sameer was first sent to Madrid and then to Athens to meet the various actors in the play, bring about a satisfactory denouement and recover the insurance money from the Spaniards. His job was first to visit the 'scene of the crime', so to say, and start afresh from there. As to what he hoped to achieve by visiting Piraeus and having a distant look at the derelict ship, he had no idea. But as Sameer said to himself, one has to start somewhere. However, he learnt that that was easier said than done. He had his visit to Spain, and extensive discussion with the Managing Director had given him some idea. He had seen a bull-fight, visited Escorial, seen Cordova, visited Granada, the Alhambra and spent an evening watching the flamenco performed by the beautiful gypsies of Albaicin!

Illyria of Athens turned out to be a small hotel with tiny cubical-sized rooms. His room could accommodate him and his suitcase with some difficulty. Its saving grace was a small en suite bathroom. The hotel had a single restaurant or rather dining room which served only Greek food. It was managed by a brawny, stocky Greek, Yannis Viziraki, the owner himself, who registered each guest personally and believed in getting on first name basis from that moment onwards. Yannis was a very jovial character who greeted every guest as a long-lost friend. Sameer found Yannis had a moustache obsession; he was always twirling and stroking the large prominent protuberance on his face lovingly. After checking in he took a warm shower to wash off the aircraft odour from his body, and went down to the restaurant for breakfast. The spread was rather limited—just bread rolls, cheese, olives and olive oil, sour cream and yogurt, and boiled eggs. After breakfast Sameer got some directions from Yannis for his destination and left the hotel. Yannis was good enough to call a taxi for him. His first port of call was the lawyer's office. He represented many of the actors involved in the fracas.

Spyro Kazantzakis turned out to be a rather pleasant old man who spoke English rather well, but with a slight Greek accent and knew his law backwards and forwards,

Greek law that is. "I am doing the best I can, Mr Kapadia, but you know the bureaucracy," he said with a shrug. "They always make you run around in circles before coming to the point if they ever do. Often they don't come to the point at all! I have met every one of consequence in the Maritime Office here. I have been shunted from one pen-pusher to another, but none of them is willing to put himself out, for love or money, to solve the complicated issue. There are so many parties involved in this affair. All of them have claims—some of them against others. The main hurdle seems to be the suspicion of each party as to whether Knossos really got burnt and the viscose bales gutted. No one is willing to concede that unless authenticated photographs are produced; but since no one is permitted to approach the ship, how is one to get the photographs? All we require are those photographs. That will satisfy the Spanish Insurance. Eventually, I am sure we will get permission to get the gutted hold of the ship photographed along with the burnt-out bales of viscose, or what is left of them, but it will all take time."

"But that is a commodity in short supply, Mr Kazantzakis," said Sameer, his annoyance reflected in his choice of words. "You see, my company has been trying to get this issue resolved for almost one year. Twenty million dollars of our money is locked up. We have already lost four million in interest. Every day of delay is costing us thousands."

Sameer came from Gujarat and like many of his compatriots believed every dollar lost was crucial. The lawyer shrugged again. "Call me Spyro," he said affably, "you see Mr Kapadia…."

"My friends call me Sameer," interrupted Sameer, not to be outdone in civility.

"Thank you, Sameer. I met the Port Officer yesterday afternoon in anticipation of your visit. He happens to be a distant cousin of my wife. You know relationships matter a lot in our society. I requested him to allow me, as a personal favour, to board the SS Knossos and take a few photographs. I told him I would guarantee not to disturb anything on the ship. In any case, there is nothing left to disturb as everything inside is reported to have been gutted. All we wanted to do was take a few photographs, I told him. But the Port Officer was adamant. Relationship in this case did not count for much; I believe in India it does. He says there is a Commission of enquiry investigating the fire. Until they complete their enquiry and submit their report, no one is permitted to board the ship. They have even posted a guard on the deck. I asked him how it would affect the enquiry now if we go there, since the ship was burnt more than six months ago. All possible evidence must have been gathered by the Commission long ago, but the Port Officer is not willing to listen."

The lawyer spoke with a note of despondency in his voice.

"So, when do you think the enquiry will be finalised?" asked Sameer.

Spyro laughed. "Anytime, says the Port Officer. I checked with the Chairman of the Commission through my own sources. He is good man, a former judge here in Athens. I appeared before him a few times many years ago. He confirms that estimate—anytime. But you see, Sameer, anytime in Greece means from a day to a year," concluded Spyro, with a Grecian shrug.

Sameer felt rather let down. He had come with warm hopes of a quick settlement and he had expected the lawyer to come up with some helpful suggestions. But Spyro's remarks came like a splash of cold water. "Did you attempt to go on your own to the ship ever?" asked Sameer.

"Yes of course; that is the first thing I did as soon as the Spanish Company engaged me. I took a boat at Piraeus and went up to the ship. I even took some photographs of the hull from the boat, but the security guard on the bridge or what is left of the bridge, refused to allow me up the ladder. He shooed me off. So, I had to come back empty-handed. You can take these photographs for whatever they are worth," said Spyro, proffering an envelope to Sameer. "They are of no use now. I was able to photograph only the hull from a distance. The insurance company wants photographs of the hold showing the gutted bales of viscose, certified by my firm. Unless I go up there, I can't take those photos."

"Where do we go from here then?" Sameer's voice still held the residual fatigue of his travels, overlaid with some faint hope. "We wait," said Spyro with the typical Mediterranean shrug.

"So, when do I meet you next, Spyro?" asked Sameer.

"Tomorrow is the weekend; nothing will happen. Go around and see the sights of Athens for the next two days. Let us meet on Monday and see what we can do," Spyro suggested. "I will try to think of something during the weekend."

It was lunch time when Sameer left Spyro's office. Spyro had advised him to go to Sintagma which had many restaurants. Sameer noted there was a bus stop opposite Spyro's office. He found a long queue and joined it. There were a couple of Greek Orthodox priests standing in the queue. When the bus arrived, they all got in. Before the bus could move, Sameer was overpowered by a strong smell of unwashed bodies and clothes which had absorbed years of rancid perspiration. He got off the bus in a hurry and took a taxi. Sintagma Square had a number of cafes and restaurants. He chose a medium-sized restaurant. When the waiter brought the menu card, Sameer studied it very carefully. He had read somewhere that the word Pilaf stood as a cognate for the Indian 'Pulao', a dish of rice and meat cooked in a spicy sauce. That, Sameer thought, should suffice for a light lunch. When he ordered 'Pilaf' the waiter looked askance at him.

"Anything else to go with it?" he asked.

"No, that is enough," said Sameer. What more does one require when you have rice, meat and spices?

The waiter went away with a piqued look on his face.

When the dish came, Sameer found it was nothing like the Indian pulao. It was a plate of plain white rice topped with a blanched tomato. That was all. Sameer was nonplussed. He understood the pique of the waiter. Meanings of words are not the same in every country.

He ordered a half-bottle of ouzo, more to satisfy the waiter's resentment than with any desire for alcohol at lunch time. He ended up lunching rather frugally on a dish of Greek pilaf, and half a bottle of ouzo. Though the Nagpur Textile Company had given him ten thousand dollars for business expenses, Sameer's innate sense of frugality would not allow him to spend two cents where one would do. Moreover, if he could settle the insurance case without having to spend anything out of that fund, he could take it all back to swell his own bank balance. He decided to postpone his sightseeing tour to the weekend and returned directly to Illyria after lunch.

He had been warned that Athens was not kind to tourists, particularly those who went in search of pleasures other than the study of Hellenic architecture and sites of classical heritage. Before he left Bombay, he had been told a harrowing tale by a colleague of how he had been waylaid by a young couple at midnight in Monastiraki Square and robbed of all his money and papers, including his passport. Sameer's timid soul blanched at the thought of the Greek sharks who lie in wait around street corners to waylay unwary Indian visitors. So, he decided to spend the evening with the TV in his room.

When he switched it on, he found to his dismay that all the channels (there were three) ran only Greek programmes. Greek and Latin, for Sameer, were Greek and Latin and he soon started getting bored. He went down early to have his dinner in the only restaurant that Illyria boasted but one could relish only so much of sautéed capsicum and stuffed eggplants in spite of their exotic Greek names. As he came out of the dining room, he saw Yannis about to close the reception counter for the night. Yannis Viziraki was typically Greek looking, with a broad face, leathery complexion and rather fierce moustaches surmounted by a sharp aquiline nose. Yet, he had a pleasant booming voice with which he greeted Sameer as he came out of the dining room.

"So how are you this evening, Kapadia Sir?" he roared. "Not dining out? Any plans for the evening?"

"I am not going out anywhere," said Sameer, rather despondently. "I have yet to come out of my jet lag. I just finished dinner."

"What? A young man like you, Sir, spending Friday

evening in the hotel room? Shame on you, Sir. There are many places of interest to see. You should be able to walk into any of the night clubs within walking distance. You should go out and enjoy the night life of Athens, Kapadia Sir. If you want I can recommend two or three night clubs. Would you like me to call you a taxi?"

In one breath the proprietor came out with several suggestions. "No thank you," said Sameer recalling the harrowing experience of his colleague. "I will just go back to the room and watch TV, but I don't know Greek and all your channels are only Greek. Why don't you run some English programmes on the TV?" Sameer, typical of his frugal background was not attracted by Yanni's suggestion to visit night clubs. They all cost money.

"This is not a five-star hotel Sir. We don't have many English knowing foreigners staying here. We get only the Greek middle-class tourists here. The Americans and the English go to the five-star and four-star hotels. Besides, cable connections don't come cheap, particularly when there aren't many takers for them," said the proprietor.

"I am feeling so out of touch with what is happening in the world, what with all your Greek programmes and no English papers. Can I have an English newspaper at least?" Sameer enquired.

"We don't keep any English newspapers either, I am sorry. I will tell you what you can do. Take a walk. Just go out of Illyria and turn to your right; walk a couple of furlongs and turn left. Ten minutes will bring you to the Hilton. You will see it as soon as you take the turn. It's the tallest and best building on that road; they keep English newspapers. You can buy one," suggested the proprietor helpfully.

Sameer faced the alternatives—a lonely bored evening staring at the Greek programmes on TV, or a long walk to the Hilton Hotel. The second alternative at least promised some post-dinner exercise and reading material. He decided to walk to the Hilton. As he came out, he felt the cool autumn breeze of Athens caress his skin soothingly, which he welcomed after the stuffy atmosphere of the Illyria Hotel. There was a gentle nip in the air. Illyria was located on the outskirts of Athens. The rural area started just beyond the hotel. He ambled along following the directions given by Yannis. He was also thinking simultaneously of how to resolve the impasse that faced him—how to obtain the all-important photographs of the ship and the gutted viscose bales. Where Spyro the experienced lawyer with his professional and family connections had failed, what chance did he, a Gujarati from India who did not even know the local language have? he asked himself.

He did not have much hope of Spyro finding a way by Monday. What he could not do in so many past months, how would he do it in two days of the weekend? Was he condemned to remain a prisoner of Athens, confined within the cubicle of Illyria and compelled to subsist on the Grecian fare, day in and day out? Accustomed as he was to home food—his farsaan, fafda, Kadi and Kichidi, he was unable to relish goat cheese, dolmades, moussaka and such other unpronounceable viands. Gujaratis going abroad for days and weeks always carried with them enough stock of Khakras and the imperishable farsaan. Sameer's stock had got exhausted in Spain itself; now he had to live on Greek food alone. As he walked along deep in thought, he found that he had forgotten which turning to take to go to the Hilton. He looked around for some passerby to ask for directions. There was none!

Illyria being on the outskirts of Athens and away from the downtown areas, Sameer found himself on a rather lonely stretch of the road. As far as he could see, there was no soul astir on that road at that time of the night. There were tall trees and shrubs in the open spaces between shops. Neon lights glittered on the shop fronts all around and, as he passed along, he could hear loud music from a couple of disco joints. But he saw no one going in or coming out. Sameer realised that he was lost and wondered what to do. He did not like the prospect of taking another wrong turning and ending up in the middle of nowhere. Even retracing his steps might lead him further astray. He had already covered more than a couple of furlongs and there was no sign of the Hilton anywhere on the horizon.

He was getting really worried and recalling all the horror stories he had heard on the eve of his departure. If he was waylaid on this stretch, he was sure to lose his wallet and his watch. He tried to recall what his wallet contained and the thought came as a consolation to him that it held less than fifty dollars worth of drachmas. His passport and cash were safely locked up in the suitcase in his hotel room. There was no safe in the hotel room. As he was trying to calculate the written down value of his watch, he spotted two extremely beautiful girls coming out of a disco. Sameer sighed with relief as one meeting a long-lost relative in the middle of the Sahara. Here was someone who could direct him to the Hilton. As they stepped on to the pavement and came towards him, he stopped them with an, "Excuse me." The taller of the two girls looked up and said in very good English, "Yes, what can we do for you?" Sameer was thrilled to come across an English-speaking girl.

"I seem to have lost my way. Can you direct me to the Hilton Hotel, please?" he asked her hesitatingly.

"Are you staying there?" asked the girl. Sameer was still staring at her intently. Having been starved of a beautiful face for many days, he found both the girls very attractive.

The question and the tone in which it was asked made Sameer look at her rather closely. He had expected the girls to give him the directions and walk on. He certainly had not hoped to be engaged by them in light conversation. There was a quizzical smile playing on the girl's lips. Sameer acknowledged to himself that she was extremely beautiful. She had a fair complexion with an eastern fairness rather than the freckled skin (which most European girl's sported), dark hair falling to bare rounded shoulders and a shapely nose and full lips. She was wearing an off-the-shoulder evening gown of some dark material. Sameer's eyes continuously slid down from her eyes and lips to her bosom. Instead of being offended, the girl appeared amused. She was wearing a narrow-waisted blouse, which hugged her figure without over-emphasising her bust, and a long blue skirt. The girl had the kind of beauty which could appeal to Sameer's Indian tastes. She was the first beautiful girl Sameer had seen in Athens. Both her cheeks dimpled at her amused smile as she spoke and Sameer fell for her smile.

"No, I'm staying at the Illyria," he blurted out.

"Then why do you want to go to Hilton?"

"I want to pick up an English newspaper there," explained Sameer.

The girl laughed when she heard Sameer's reply. It was a light-hearted amused laughter.

"And why do you want a newspaper at this time of the night?"

There was irony and mischief in her tone. For no apparent reason, Sameer found himself defending his nocturnal excursion.

"Oh, I have been out of touch with the world news for the last two days. I want to bring myself up to date."

Even to himself, the explanation sounded a bit pompous. He was so flustered that he could not think of a light-hearted reply.

"At ten o' clock on a Friday night? Don't you have anything better to do?" she asked. There was a hint of an invitation in that comment.

He hoped he was reading her right.

"By the way, I'm Maria and this is Corinna. We're friends," said the tall girl.

Corinna was a perfect foil to Maria. She was taller than Maria, almost as tall as Sameer himself. She was wearing a bright-coloured top that showed off her full bust with a display of cleavage which left Sameer breathless. Her leggings moulded her long slim legs.

"Hi!" said Sameer to Maria. "What do you think one could do better at this time of the night, Maria?"

"I could come to your room with you or, if you want, we can both come. We could have some fun together," said Maria.

It suddenly dawned on Sameer that he was being propositioned by two beautiful girls at the same time. In his wanderings around the world, Sameer had had some strange romantic experiences, but still it was a novel experience for him to be propositioned by two girls for an orgy. Maria was strikingly beautiful and Corinna posed a challenge. Sameer was sorely tempted.

"Two of you would be more than I can handle," said Sameer rather diplomatically. "And how much would it cost me?"

"A hundred dollars for me," said Maria, but seeing the look on his face, she hastily added, "and I will spend the whole night with you."

Sameer's Gujarati instinct for bargaining took over at this stage.

"Fifty dollars for the night, Maria," he offered. He could very well afford a day's allowance in dollars that the Reserve Bank of India allowed him in their effort to conserve foreign exchange. The ten thousand dollars were not in the reckoning. Theoretically, they were for business expenses.

Maria was offended. She became red in the face. "Then you'd better go to the Hilton and buy your one dollar worth of newspaper if that is all you can afford," she sneered. Both of them made as if to walk away. Sameer felt embarrassed. With a conscious effort, he suppressed his instinctive desire to conserve his cash. "Okay, a hundred it is," he said, before he could change his mind. The three of them started walking back to the Illyria.

"I will call a taxi for Corinna from the lobby," said Maria taking Sameer's arm.

It took almost ten minutes to reach the Illyria, but

they got a taxi just as they reached the drive. "Have a good time children," said Corinna as she got into the taxi. "Look after yourselves!"

Yannis was just closing the Reception Counter. Seeing Sameer with a beautiful girl, he gave him a broad wink and a thumbs-up. "Good night, Kapadia Sir," he said, with a conspiratorial wink. He was not surprised to see Sameer returning with a beautiful girl to the hotel. He must have seen such a scene many times before.

Sameer took Maria up to his room. "I'm really thirsty," she said, "let's see what your fridge holds." She threw off her high-heeled slippers and walked to the fridge. From the top of the TV cabinet, she picked up the room keys, opened the fridge and took out a bottle of ouzo.

"The very thing to quench your thirst," she exclaimed picking up two glasses from the shelf. She poured the liquor and added some water. As the liquid slowly clouded over, she relaxed on the sofa and put her feet up on the bed. "God, my feet hurt so. I've been dancing since seven this evening."

Sameer picked up his drink and went and sat by Maria. He put his arm around her waist which was narrow enough for his arm to encircle it fully.

"You are from India?" she asked.

"Yes, you know about India?" Sameer asked her.

"Yes, I have read some books. You have lots of tigers, elephants, snakes and yogis, no?"

Sameer wasn't sure whether she was serious or making fun of him, so he just laughed. "And also, many handsome men like me," he said squeezing her waist a bit.

"And what brings the handsome man from India to Athens?" Maria asked.

"I am here on a job," said Sameer, not wanting to waste time on talking about his business affairs.

But Maria would not let go. "What job is that? I thought the only business you had was being handsome." That was a mischievous dig.

They bantered inconsequentially and finished two bottles of ouzo. The ouzo and the banter helped Sameer unwind and he found himself telling Maria of the Nagpur Textile Company, the Spanish viscose fibre, the Greek tramp steamer and all his woes. Between sips of ouzo, the whole story came out. Between the ouzo and Maria, Sameer spent a very pleasant night and felt that the hundred dollars were well worth it.

Maria was up the next morning by six, and she woke Sameer up. She was already fully dressed and chirpy. "Get up lazy boy, don't you want to go sightseeing today? You have come all the way from the land of yogis and snakes to the land of Aphrodites and Dianas. They are all waiting for you round the corner. Don't disappoint them. Come on lazy boy, get ready. I will take you on a sightseeing tour." Maria was wearing his kurta which she had borrowed as she had brought no nightsuit with her.

Maria's offer to spend the day with him came as a pleasant surprise. Apparently, Maria too seemed to have enjoyed his company at night. And here she was, offering to save him from a lonely day around the city. So, he got ready quickly and took Maria down to the breakfast room.

Sameer told her of his experience of an attempted bus ride of the previous day.

Maria had a hearty laugh.

"You poor sod. All your reading has not acquainted you with the fact that the Greek Orthodox Church has prohibited all its acolytes from taking a bath all their lives. Once they are baptized at birth and immersed in the holy water of the font, that water should not be washed away. Next time you see a black cloak waiting in the queue, take the next bus!

After breakfast, Maria took him round to Sintagma Square to see the towering Mount Lykavittos which reared a thousand feet up in the centre of the city with gardens and parks at the top; the Acropolis which they entered through the huge Propylaea and the Erechtheum with the beautiful Caryatids holding the roof. Finally, they went to see the Parthenon, the magnificent temple of Athena.

"You know, Lord Elgin took away more than fifty of the best sculptures from the Parthenon?" Maria asked.

"Yes, I have seen them in the British Museum. They

are known as the Elgin Marbles there. Lord Elgin gifted them to the Museum."

"Lord Elgin, my foot! He was no nobleman, no lord or knight! He was a low-down petty thief," Maria cried in a bitter tone. "And you know how much he got for those priceless marbles from the British Museum?"

"No, I thought Elgin donated them to the Museum."

"Donated? No chance, not that mean robber. He sold them to the museum for a mere 35,000 dollars." Maria bristled with anger, recalling the ancient wrong. Sameer could sympathise with her, himself recalling the priceless Indian artefacts in the British Museum, which the British had robbed during the course of their occupation of India. And also, the priceless artefacts from Egypt, Syria, Turkey, China, Africa and the rest of the world that the British stole during their colonial dominance, and adorned their museums. Lord Elgin, of course, was a crook of the first water. He claimed that he had removed the marble friezes of the Parthenon and several other marble statues from other temples in Greece and transported them under permission (*firman*) from the Sultan of Turkey, who himself was in illegal occupation of Greece. The Sultans of Ottoman Empire rarely had any interest in the preservation of their own ancient heritage. The Sultan had no interest in preserving the ancient heritage of Greece; but Elgin never produced that *firman*. The rapacious government of England and the greedy British Museum too supported the robber baron. Naturally, they bought the marbles and turned a blind eye to the destruction wrought in Parthenon when those friezes were pulled out from the parent marble.

Sameer and Maria came down to the Agora, and had their lunch in a restaurant close by. The very look of the elegant restaurant frightened the Gujarati in Sameer, for it looked the five-star kind. As they took their seats, the steward brought the wine list. Maria ordered a champagne and Sameer's heart sank. He contented himself with a glass of water. From the hors d'oeuvre menu, Maria chose mussels cooked in a piquant sauce while Sameer confined himself to a salad. After all Gujaratis, at least most of them, are known to be vegetarians. For the main dish, she ordered courgettes stuffed with minced mutton flavoured with saffron and marjoram with artichokes on the side. Sameer contented himself with a dish of mixed vegetables. For dessert, she had kopanisti, the reputed Greek blue cheese with Muscat of Samos, a famous Greek wine to go with it. Sameer was happy with plain Turkish coffee which the locals called Greek coffee. He certainly did not look forward to the steward bringing the bill. All the while, Maria kept asking him what plans he had to obtain the photographs of the burnt-out ship.

"I will meet Spyro on Monday," said Sameer, "and I hope he will have some plan."

"Spyro is an old Greek idiot and you are an Indian

fool," said Maria. "If that dolt couldn't do it in six months, how do you think he is going to produce a plan over the weekend?"

"You have a point there," Sameer conceded. "But what can I do? Here I am in a city I don't know well. My only contact is Spyro. How do you expect me to come up with any plans, when such an experienced lawyer like Kazantzakis couldn't do it?"

"Let us go over to Piraeus tomorrow and have a look at the Knossos. May be the sight of the ship will suggest something," Maria said hopefully. "In any case, I am sure you would have had enough of Athenian architecture and Hellenic statuary before the day is out."

In the meantime, in response to some unseen signal from Maria, the steward brought the check. Before Sameer could even have a glance at it, Maria took out the hundred dollars which Sameer had given her in the morning and placed them in the folder. "Come, come, let me pay." Sameer made half-hearted noises.

"You will my dear, you will, at the proper time. But this one is on me," Maria interjected. Sameer was rather surprised. Maria had bargained hard for the hundred dollars last night, but was willing to splurge it on a single lunch.

After lunch, they saw the temple of the Olympian Zeus with its huge columns, some of them over seven feet in diameter. Around Monastiraki Square, Maria showed Sameer the old Greek quarters with houses with vine covered pergolas, narrow streets paved with dressed stones, taverns where you could drink the best local wines and listen to the plaintive music of the bouzuki, a kind of lute. Sameer bought a few elegant komboloi, the string of worry beads which was the legacy of the Turks to the Greeks.

There were a number of shops around the square selling typically touristy souvenirs. Practically every monument of Greece was reproduced in plaster of paris, plastic and copper. Sameer and Maria went window shopping arm in arm. Sameer spotted the Parthenon and Erychtheum in plaster, the Caryatids in copper, and several statues in plastic. There was a beautiful horse on four wheels in copper. Sameer could not recall having seen its original in any of the monuments.

"That is the Trojan Horse silly," laughed Maria. "You didn't see it because the original was made of wood, and wood does not last."

"Even if it had survived, it was too large for any museum." Sameer recalled Homer's *Iliad.* When the Greeks despaired of storming Troy, they resorted to a stratagem. Their carpenters had made a hollow wooden horse. Some elite Greek warriors had concealed themselves in the belly of the horse. After the Greeks pretended to sail away seemingly abandoning the siege of Troy, the jubilant Trojans opened the gates of the city and brought in the wooden horse as a spoil of war. Though many wise old warriors remonstrated against the sacrilegious act, the drunk citizenry paid no heed. When the victory-drunk Trojans had fallen asleep, the warriors descended from the belly and opened the city gates to the Greek army which had sailed back in the dead of night. Troy was taken unawares and sacked. All the pillage, rapes and massacres are detailed in *Iliad.* Nobody knows what happened to the Trojan horse. Actually, it should have been called the Greek horse; the Trojans were only the dupes. But the Greeks continued to make replicas of the horse, to celebrate the memory of their victory. Maria insisted on buying a copy for Sameer, much against his protests. While they waited at a bus stop late that night to catch a ride back to Illyria, Maria excused herself for a few minutes and vanished. Sameer waited for her for more than half an hour and was getting rather fidgety when she turned up with a small night bag. "You wanted me to stay over, didn't you?"

"You know I want nothing better," said Sameer, with unconcealed eagerness.

"So, I went over and packed a few clothes and the usual things a girl needs," she explained.

"You live somewhere close by? Why didn't you take me?" Sameer asked.

"Some other time, may be," she replied.

After dinner Maria took him to a disco. Corinna was

also there and Maria introduced Sameer to several young men. Sameer didn't understand much of the conversation as it was mostly conducted in Greek, but there was no difficulty in following the ear-splitting music, which was the same in the discos of Bombay and London, as were the flashing lights and skimpy dresses and the wild gyrations, twists and contortions.

That night, as he lay beside Maria in the hotel bedroom, Sameer wondered at his good luck in having found such a wonderful girl to give him company. And he did not even have to spend for that delightful company. That was some compensation, he thought, against the dismal prospect that awaited him on Monday in the lawyer's office. As he looked at her lying stretched on the bed in her flimsy night dress, he thought of Canova's *Psyche* and Goya's *La maja desnuda.* He had seen the one in Louvre and the other in Museo del Prado. Maria had a perfect but voluptuous figure. More than that, she had a lively and mischievous mind, and restless hands and hungry lips which made Sameer's night memorable.

Sunday morning found Sameer in bed, with a pleasant languorous feeling of satiated lethargy, but Maria would not permit him to wallow in the pleasant memories.

"Get up silly, and get ready. We are going to Piraeus to have a look at your burnt-out ship and get some ideas for your friend Spyro to try."

Sameer cursed himself for not having thought of it

himself. He should have done that himself yesterday. He thought he could at least report to his boss that he had visited the ship and confirm what Spyro had said.

Sameer found himself driven from bed to bathroom to the wardrobe, to the suitcase for taking out some cash and to the restaurant for a quick breakfast.

Maria put on a short colourful skirt and a halter top which showed her cleavage to great advantage. She looked bewitching in the ensemble. There were one or two wolf whistles from the local youth when they entered the restaurant.

Maria took Sameer to the Agora from where they took an electric train to the harbour of Piraeus. Piraeus, the port of Athens, happens to be the largest port in Greece and bustling with activity. All around the basin, there were tall buildings, chemical and engineering factories and shipyards. Maria seemed to know the place well. She took Sameer to the boatyard and they engaged a small motor boat. The Greek girl then made some enquires and used her charm to locate the derelict ship. From the photographs provided by Spyro, it was not difficult for Sameer to spot the hulk of the burnt-out ship which was anchored a couple of kms off-shore. The sea was calm and Maria steered the boat skillfully through the fleet of kayaks, row boats and paddle boats which seemed to be out on a Sunday picnic. As they approached the ship, Maria put on dark glasses, asked Sameer to take the wheel and stood up to hail the guard on the bridge. Her dark hair flew in the breeze raised by the speeding boat. A well-bronzed young man, in a T-shirt and jeans leaned over the railing and leered at Maria. There was a silly smile on his face. Sameer felt a sharp pang of jealousy as the young man's eyes literally devoured the luscious figure of the girl, but the conversation that followed was all Greek to him.

"What was that all about?" he asked Maria.

"I have asked him to allow me to come up on the bridge of the ship. He has invited me to come up," Maria said.

It was less the lure of entertaining a tourist than the halter top of Maria that persuaded the horny guard to permit them to go on board.

The youngster waved to them to approach, and Sameer steered the boat close to the bobbing steel ladder. Maria in a whisper told him to be alert. She had persuaded the guard, more with her figure than by words, that she was bringing an Indian tourist who wanted to see a ship. She would engage the guard in banter while Sameer could wander about and film the burnt-out hold. That was indeed a clever and bold stratagem. Sameer wondered at the hidden depths of Maria. She was not only beautiful and good in bed; she was possessed of a high intelligence too. That was perhaps her Greek heritage. As they climbed up the ladder, the young guard, whose name was Yorgos, held out his hand to help Maria climb across the railing, a courtesy which he did not see fit to extend to Sameer.

Yorgos took Maria's arm, and Sameer followed a few steps behind. The young Greek lad was apparently holding forth on the construction of the ship and its various parts in an obvious effort to show off and Maria displayed clear signs of being suitably impressed through well-timed giggles, laughs and smiles. Sameer took advantage of Yorgos' engrossment to quietly slip down the few steps to the hold where he took out his camera and clicked away. He moved around and took photos of the gutted bales of the Spanish viscose, some of which, half-burnt, showed the brand name and manufacturer's signs clearly. He had taken more than two rolls of film before he heard Maria's laughter coming his way. That was a signal to him to finish his clandestine photography. Quickly, he concealed the camera and went up. The guard appeared still engrossed in Maria's vivacious company, but started a little guiltily when he saw Sameer's lonely figure emerge from the hold. He invited them to have a beer in his guard room, which was actually the bridge and they accepted the offer.

When they reached the shore, Sameer was elated. He had hardly expected to get his problem solved so smoothly. He had gone along with Maria in the hope of getting ideas by looking at the ship, instead of which he had brought back two full rolls of valuable film. He knew Spyro Kazantzakis would be very happy, as he recalled his appointment with him at noon on Monday. For the return journey to Athens they took a taxi. Sameer felt that he could afford it now. He had not been looking forward to the prospect of staying on indefinitely in Athens, even in Maria's company, until the Commission of Enquiry submitted its report.

These photographs would not only help him get the insurance money released but take him home sooner than he had hoped. He could visualise the figure in rupees in his bank passbook after he had deposited the ten thousand dollars minus the expenses and the gift he proposed to give Maria. He knew that Maria had contributed a lot to his success and she deserved something. After long deliberation during the return, Sameer resolved that two hundred dollars would adequately compensate her for her efforts, or perhaps he would buy her an expensive present the next day. When they got down at the Illyria, Maria took him to the photography shop in the basement, where they delivered the rolls for developing and taking out prints. The shopkeeper promised to give them the prints at 9 am the next day.

To celebrate, Sameer took Maria out for dinner. This time he insisted on paying. They enjoyed an excellent Italian meal at an expensive restaurant and went to the disco afterwards. The third night with Maria proved to be the most ecstatic for Sameer. Maria's restless hands and hungry mouth kept Sameer awake till the small hours of the morning. When he woke up after a deep satisfied sleep, it was rather late. Maria wasn't by his side. The bed was empty. He thought she might have gone to the washroom. He waited for some time but did not hear the shower. He called out her name but got no reply. A little concerned, he got up to look for her, but found the washroom empty. Knowing that she was a working girl, he assumed that she must have left early, so he got ready and went down to have his breakfast

He found Yannis standing at the reception desk, twirling his fierce mustache. Seeing Sameer, he greeted him with a broad smile and wink.

"A remarkable girl you have found for yourself, Kapadia Sir."

"You know her?" Sameer asked.

"No, not very well. I have seen her a couple of times here when she had stayed overnight with her boyfriend."

"Where does she live?" Sameer asked hoping to find her address.

"I am sorry, I don't know," Yannis replied. Sameer finished his breakfast and went down to the basement to collect the photographs. He was told that Maria had already collected them at 9 am. "She paid the charges, Sir, but I have the negatives. I can make another set in a couple of hours, if you want." Sameer did not want another set, as Maria had collected a set and he was sure to get it; but he was puzzled. What could Maria want with those photographs? And where was she? he wondered. They were of no use to anyone except Sameer and Spyro. He spent the next hour wondering about Maria and the missing photographs and then left Illyria to keep his appointment with the lawyer. As soon as he entered the lawyer's chamber, Spyro came out of his chair with a loud "Congratulations! Wonderful, wonderful! Your girlfriend has done a marvellous job, Sameer. To get those photographs in a couple of hours was remarkable. She has solved our problem, my friend, though I believe you were a bit inconvenienced. I was sorry to hear that. But then, all's well that ends well."

Sameer sat down slowly in the chair. He did not understand a word of what Spyro had said. The words were there, but he missed the purport.

"What are you talking about? Who told you about the photographs? And where did you meet my girlfriend?" asked the bewildered Sameer.

"Oh, she didn't tell you when she got you released?"

"Released from what?" asked Sameer.

"From the jail."

"What jail Spyro? I haven't understood anything of what you've said; please explain the whole thing step by step."

"This morning I got a call from a girl who said her

name was Maria and who claimed to be your girlfriend. She said you had been arrested attempting to board a gutted ship in the harbour of Piraeus and she wanted to meet me urgently. I asked her to come along and she met me at ten. She told me the whole story of your escapade, your arrest and detention. She produced the photographs and asked for ten thousand dollars in cash to post bail for you. I gave her the money on the insurance company's account. In any case, she left the photographs with me. These photographs are worth more than ten thousand dollars to us, my friend. She said she would return with you after getting you released. So where is she?" Spyro asked.

"I think you have been taken for a ride Spyro; or rather we have been taken for a ride. I wasn't arrested nor was I in jail. She has taken $10,000 off us, that's all," Sameer said.

The lawyer leaned back in his chair with an amused look. He remained silent for a long time and then leaned forward with a sigh. "A remarkable girl, all the same," he said. "These photographs are worth more than that. I was willing to spend more than $30,000 to get the photographs. Your company stands to gain its full insurance money now."

The lawyer agreed to certify the photographs and send them to Spain and assured Sameer that the insurance money would be paid in full in a couple of weeks. He said he would charge the $10,000 as business expenses to the

Spanish Insurance Company which had engaged him.

Sameer was rather disappointed in Maria. He was shocked at her having cheated the lawyer out of 10,000 dollars. However, his job was done and the Nagpur Textile Company would be happy with the full payment. Maria had got her fee of $10,000 for helping him get the photographs. He had saved his own $10,000. He did not expect to meet her, so there could be no occasion now for him to buy her that expensive present. He decided to leave for India the next day. Spyro helped him get a reservation for Bombay on the next day's flight.

He took a taxi to return to the hotel to pick up his ticket and get his reservation confirmed. As he entered the lobby of the Illyria, he was greeted by Yannis in his booming voice. "Hello Kapadia Sir. I didn't expect you so early. I thought you were meeting Maria for lunch."

"Who told you that?" asked Sameer.

"She was here as soon as you left. She told me that you were meeting her for lunch at Sintagma. She picked up your keys and went to the room to pick up her purse."

"What purse?" Sameer asked with a sinking feeling.

"She said she had left her purse in your room when she had gone out in the morning." Sameer knew she had left no purse in the room; he would have seen it if she had.

Sameer grabbed the key and took the stairs two at a time to reach his room. When he opened it, the first thing he saw was his suitcase lying open. The folder that contained his passport, ticket and cash was on the table lying beside the copper Trojan horse. He picked up the folder and opened it. The passport and the ticket were there, but the cash, all ten thousand dollars, was missing. There was a piece of paper lying beneath the Trojan horse. Sameer picked it up. It read, "*Timeo Danaos, et dona ferentes.*"

He remembered the translation–"I fear the Greeks even when they bring gifts." It was signed 'Maria'.

For a few moments, only a few moments, Sameer felt a pang of regret at having lost all his savings from the trip, but it passed. He recalled his three nights with Maria and the words of Spyro and Yannis. A remarkable girl indeed! he thought.

The Runaway Bridegroom

The day Mushtaq ran away from Minambur had dawned like any other Friday. But for many years afterwards, Zain continued to hear the villagers date events from that momentous Friday. Much later, the Tuesday massacre of innocents in Minambur by the Customs Police replaced it.

"Kareema, the harelipped, was born six months before Mushtaq ran away," Nanijan would reminisce years after, as though Kareema's harelip had something to do with Mushtaq's running away.

"Why is Kareema harelipped?" Zain's seven years demanded to have mysteries cleared. He had seen the girl with her mother and had noticed the different way she looked and spoke; and differences to a seven-year-old were always disturbing.

"Shush," his grandmother had hushed him into a reluctant silence. "You are not to call her harelipped before others."

The admonition had stung Zain. It was all right for Nanijan to call Kareema harelipped, Khatoon hump-backed and Bijoo lame, but it was taboo for Zain to use such descriptive terms. These grown-ups were so confused and confusing, Zain had thought, and so unfair. Grown-ups never seemed to understand anything and it was too irritating for Zain to deal with their ignorance, but he kept his opinion to himself. His grandfather, Nanajan, had advised him not to find fault with elders, quoting the Persian couplet.

"Khata-e buzurgan giraftan khata ast"

(To seek the fault of the elders is itself a great fault)

Zain did not know Persian, but his grandfather spoke many languages. Whenever he wanted to shut up Nanijan's fulminations, he would resort to Persian. That would effectively shut her up. Like Zain, Nanijan too did not know Persian.

Mushtaq's running away from Minambur on Friday would not have occasioned such consternation, had it not been his wedding day. Running away from Minambur was a fairly common occurrence. Ibrahim, the tailor who used to pedal his Singer machines on Nanhe Sab's doorstep, had run away to Madras. Zain recalled him as a pint-sized, perpetually perspiring man, wearing a wet undervest and a dirty lungi, constantly drying his face with a tattered old towel draped over his left shoulder. It was rumoured that he was running a bakery in Madras and doing well. Akbarjan, who sold shrivelled stale vegetables from a basket at the street corner, had run away to Bombay. People who had visited that city gossiped that he sold second-hand bicycles there. Adi, the *padial*, the landless serf, whose young wife had started living with Bade Sab, the zamindar, had run away to even as far away as Rangoon. Since Adi worked as a labourer in the fields of Bade Sab, and moreover belonged to the adi-dravidar caste, news about him was of no interest to the zamindars. Rumours about what he was doing there had not managed to reach Minambur yet. Rangoon was darya-par, across the oceans. Rumours found it difficult to fly unaided across such vast distances.

People ran away from Minambur for a variety of reasons—to escape from the clutches of creditors, to avoid paying their debts to the Agriculture Cooperative Bank, or to join the madrasa in Umrabad which offered free education, free food, accommodation and so on.

Minambur, in any case, was the sort of place people generally ran away from. The village was full of navayatas, and navayatas, which in Arabic meant sailors, were fond of travelling and quarrelling. Nanajan believed that whenever two navayatas met, they were sure to find something to argue about. Even mere theoretic arguments led to disputes, and sometimes disputes led to physical fights and migration. He should know, for he was a navayata himself, of the purest pedigree. In Minambur, there were over a thousand of them, and for a long time the number remained stagnant. Nature, it appears, believed that a thousand Navayatas was close enough to a critical mass. Any addition beyond that would lead to instability and explosions. Hence, there were always people running away to Madras, Bombay, Rangoon, Singapore and such other far-off exotic places, to preserve the equilibrium.

It was a humid morning on that historical Friday. Zain's sleepy eyes flickered to the sound of Amanna, his aunt, churning the curd. Every morning, he had woken up to that purring sound, most irritating even on weekdays; but it was especially infuriating on a holiday, when there was no school. He tried to keep his eyes shut. Zain did not want to wake up on Fridays. He tried to ignore the sound; he had heard the reverberations of that noise a thousand times at dawn. Usually, his somnolent brain would absorb it and make it a part of his ongoing dream.

Zain's grandfather had persuaded his father and mother to leave Zain in Minambur when he was less than two years old. Nanajan wanted Zain, the first-born male child in his household to inherit his lands and his jagir, as he had no son of his own. By the time Zain was seven, he had understood that he had a younger sister who lived with his parents in Madras and another sibling was on the way. But Zain did not miss his parents; he had rarely lived with them. They came to Minambur once or twice a year and he looked forward to their short visits. They brought all sorts of goodies when they came, like almonds, walnuts, dried apricots, sugar candies, éclairs and so on, the goodies that were not available in Minambur or even at Gingee, the nearest town.

The house was always in turmoil when they came. Amanna would select the fattest chicken for the curry and rice dish on the day of their arrival. Even though the entrance had no door, to enable the cattle to come in and go out without any hindrance, no thief ever entered the house. Stealing was rare in the village, for if a thief was caught, he would be banished from the village and never allowed to return. Just after the entrance was a large courtyard with a *kotha*, a kind of shed with thatched roof, partitioned in two. The larger part was full of old discarded colonial furniture—teak chairs whose wooden canes had all sunken, their arm-rests broken, old couches with dust embedded, cracked planks gathering mites, British-type chaise lounges with broken, woven, reed backrests and long footboards that would open up and swallow Zain whenever he attempted to recline on them.

The other smaller part housed an enclosed kitchen with

dry fuel wood stacked in a corner. During rainy seasons, no one could get into the kitchen without getting wet, since one had to leave the shelter of the house. Sometimes, Bapu would go in carrying an umbrella as the dripping water from the eaves would not spare any sari or shirt. Once or twice already cobras had taken refuge in the stacked fuel-wood and had to be killed with great effort. Driving away the snakes was no option, for they would escape and then seek refuge in the main living quarters.

The courtyard had a large peepal tree which Zain loved. He always cried when just before the sowing season, the padials came and cut down all the leaves and flowers to use as mulch for the zeerak-samba rice field. That aromatic short-grained rice was the favourite for pulao, *baghar-e chaval* (ghee rice) and khichdi. You could smell the aroma a furlong away when it was being cooked.

There was a deep uncovered well in the corner of the yard. Both Amanna and Nanijan kept Zain frightened of the ghoul that lived in the well by saying if one approached too close to it, the ghoul pulled everyone in, especially children. Adults were immune to the ghoul's appetite for human flesh. Since the well was taboo for Zain, it held a strange fascination for him. When nobody was looking, he would go as close to the mouth of the well as he dared and peep into its dark depths, hoping yet fearing to catch a glimpse of that notorious ghoul. He would do it only when the sun was shining brightly.

Apparently, the ghoul would not show itself during the day. It would hide itself under the dark depths of the water. The padials and servant-maids like Mampeta and Kavaria constantly drew water from that well for household chores. The ghoul never harmed them.

The backyard which was much larger than the courtyard abutted on the yard. Part of it was used to stack the paddy-hay used as feed for the cattle, but most of it was used for growing vegetables, greens and aromatic herbs like mint and coriander. There were some orange, custard apple, pomegranate, jujube and wood apple trees, but most of the yard was covered by tall wild shrubs—home of insects, snakes, centipedes and such other frightening creatures. Zain rarely went into the backyard except when commanded by necessity.

At the back of Zain's mind, there was a vague feeling that today was a special day and his eyes reluctantly opened as though forced. With his half-opened eyes, he saw the central courtyard of the house through a foggy haze. The retreating night had left misty patches behind and Zain could barely discern the peepal tree through the fog. The green foliage of the heart-shaped leaves had all merged into an impression, but the golden yellow flowers glimmered like fading stars in the early dawn. As he sleepily rubbed his eyes, Amanna's presence took shape and registered itself more distinctly. She was sitting close by squatting on the chowki. Most of the day, Amanna sat on that rough-hewn unpainted plank with four midget legs, almost flush with the floor.

He noticed the work-worn wrinkled hands of his aunt moving to and fro to the sound of the wooden whisk, churning the frothy mixture of curd and water. She held one end of the rope in each hand. The rope was wound round the pillar before which she sat and pulled the rope in a to and fro motion that made the whisk to churn the curd. Small droplets of white whey shot out from the black mouth of the large earthen pot and settled on Amanna's dark hair. Her calloused hands busy with the rope, she made no effort to dry them. Every few minutes, she would stop churning, whisk the white frothy butter off the pot and pat it into an enamel plate.

Zain wished that Friday was like any other day. He had made that wish every Friday of his seven years, but an uncaring divinity refused to interfere with the laws of nature. Today, he had to go to his weekly Friday prayers at noon. That was a chore he was willing to live with, but before that would come the morning walk with his uncle, Bapu, to the large irrigation tank outside the village. On normal weekdays he would go to the tank with his school friends, but on Fridays he had to accompany his uncle. Going with Bapu to the well was as bad as going to school with the class teacher. Every step of the way, Bapu's do that, don't do that, would turn this otherwise pleasant outing into a bore.

The metallic pinging tones of a fluid jet striking an aluminium vessel made him turn his head towards the peepal tree. At the far edge of the courtyard, Bapu sat on his haunches under the tree, a *lagan*, an aluminium vessel, held between his two knees. His thick fingers were squeezing the mottled udders of the cow alternatively, first the right and then the left. Thin streams of milk squirted into the half-filled *lagan*, the sound of the frothy "*shurr shurr*" mixing with the "*slurrp slurrp*" of his aunt's churning. Bapu was wearing his usual short-sleeved thin cotton vest and his cotton dhoti was hitched up to his waist to prevent it getting soiled. When at home, Bapu never wore anything else.

From a corner of the *dalan*, the wide front verandah which ran the length of the village house, Zain heard his grandfather get up from his creaking bed. The village house in which Zain lived with his grandfather, grandmother, two aunts and an uncle, was built in the traditional village style. There was a wide *dalan*, with two bedrooms at each end.The dalan was separated from a narrower *osara* (lower verandah) with a row of tall teak pillars. At one end of the *osara* was another bedroom and the other end was left open, without a door, a kind of large alcove. That was where the parboiled rice was pounded in the mortar with a five-foot long pestle. Zain could see the tall *vara*, the silo in which unmilled grain was stored, and the smaller *ranjan*, the large earthen pot which stored the milled rice for daily use. Though the door of Nanajan's bedroom was ajar, it was still dark inside.

As long as Zain could remember, grandpa's room was always in darkness. He rarely ventured into that cave which had no windows. It had an aperture high up near the roof through which some light reluctantly trickled down when the sun was high up. Even when the courtyard dazzled in the midday glare, one could barely make out the hazy outlines of the high four-poster on which the old man slept. When he was up, he was usually perched four feet off the ground, like some ancient deity in a sanctum sanctorum glimpsed dimly through the portals of a ruined temple. Zain, lying on his bed, turned his head slowly to see if Nanajan was up but could feel no movement.

Nanijan never slept in the same bed with Nanajan. It was infra-dig for her. He knew that for grandpa the daily routine had not yet started. Usually, Nanajan would get up and shuffle along to the stone edge of the *osara,* put on the wooden pattens, pick up the copper tumbler of water and fade away with measured steps into the morning mist of the backyard. Long after he had vanished into the tall shrubbery, Zain would continue to hear the faint clip-clop of his wooden pattens until Nanajan reached the open enclosure in the distant corner of the backyard which served as the toilet for the household. Toilets in village houses were always located at the farthest corner of the backyard.

But today was Friday. On Friday, Nanajan's routine broke. As soon as he emerged from the grotto, Nanajan adjusted the folds of his lungi and instead of shuffling across the osara, walked to where Amanna was churning the curd.

"Will you take out my clean clothes and brush my cap, Maa?" he asked Amanna, who continued to churn. On Fridays, every devout Muslim wore his pill-box Turkish cap. It was also an index of his affluence. The poor could not afford to buy a maroon Turkish cap. Zain could not make out whether Nanajan's mumbled request had penetrated Amanna's ears through the noisy churning. Zain could never understand why Nanajan addressed Amanna as Maa, 'mother', considering that she was his daughter, but that seemed to be the common practice in the village. Every old man addressed his daughter as 'maa'. Zain's own mother lived in Madras, so he called his grandmother and his aunt Ammaju and Amanna—different forms of the word 'mother'.

Nanajan's mumbled request had apparently been swallowed up by the mixed sounds of the "slurrp slurrp" and "shurr shurr". By now, Zain was fully awake. He pushed himself up on his elbow to look at his grandfather standing patiently behind his squatting daughter busy with her work, waiting for an acknowledgement of his request. Nanajan must have been quite tall in his younger days, but age bends even the straightest shoulders and shortens the backbone. Nanajan's stoop, acquired after three score years, had taken off a few inches from his height. There was a six-day old scrub of grey growth on his round head and the unruly tufts on his jowls needed trimming. Zain recalled that today was the day when the village barber, Ratnam, would come with all his bag of tricks for his weekly ritual.

Nanajan would shuffle along to squat on a low stool, a chowki, placed on the flat stones near the *deori*, the main entrance to the house, under the shade of the thatched shed. Ratnam would flourish a soiled, grimy towel and tuck it in around Nanajan's neck. He would take a small aluminium bowl from a leather bag and ask Zain to fetch some hot water. Then he would wet Nanajan's head with the water, massaging it into the growth with his nimble fingers. As Nanajan sat with his head bowed, Ratnam would then take out from his bag a thick leather strap and a long vicious looking cut-throat blade. He would hold the strap with one end in his left fist and grip the other end between his chin and shoulder. With a deft flourish of his right wrist, he would flick open the razor and proceed to whet it on the strap. Occasionally, he would dip his fingers into the metal bowl and sprinkle a few drops of warm water on the strap.

By this time, Nanajan's bristling scalp would have become soft enough to be handled. Then starting from the back of the head, Ratnam would shave long furrows across the scalp to the front. In no time, Nanajan's scalp would look like a ploughed field. Ratnam would then pause, wipe the razor, and whet it again on the leather strap. All this while, Nanajan would sit with his head bowed before the barber. Then with a flourish, he would shave off the residual ridges, leaving behind a glistening pate. With a pair of large rusted scissors he would trim Nanajan's beard. Nanajan, who would normally roar whenever he perceived a slight to his dignity, behaved like a pliant child in Ratnam's hand.

Zain thought of all this while still in bed. Nanajan was still standing over Amanna's shoulder and Ratnam had not yet made his weekly appearance. Friday was still looming large and the threat of the long walk with uncle Bapu to the tank was still a hanging threat. Zain got out of his string-bed with a sigh and walked up to Amanna.

"Amanna, Amanna, Nanajan wants something," he drew her attention to grandpa's request. Amanna's moving hands came to an abrupt halt at Zain's intrusion. Some whey drops flew off the mouth of the vessel.

A few white whey drops settled on Zain's face too. His cheeks tingled. "What is it?" Amanna turned towards him, an annoyed frown on her otherwise serene face. She didn't like breaking the rhythm of her churning, though the pause gave her a chance to wipe her wet hair with the hem of her sari.

Amanna was in her childless thirties and had settled

down with her husband in her father's house. She was not childless by choice; it just happened. In fact, the cruel neighbouring ladies who had large broods would never refrain from commenting on her barren state—sometimes even to her face, but the comment would be couched in words that oozed false sympathy. Even complaints about being harassed by their brats were meant to bring to Amanna's mind that she had no harassing brats around her, because she had no children of her own. Amanna showered all her unfulfilled motherhood on her nephew Zain. She not only took care of him, but uncomplainingly suffered all his tantrums. It was she who managed the entire household too. She looked after Nanajan who was growing cantankerous as he advanced in age, Nanijan, Bapu, Bajijan and Zain, not to mention the numerous servants, the cattle, the poultry and the kitchen garden in the backyard. Anybody who ever needed anything in the house always shouted for Amanna.

"Will you take out a fresh pajama and shirt for me?" repeated Nanajan, this time in a rasping voice. "And brush my cap. After prayers I will call on Khasab. We have to go to Nollai Manaigar's son's wedding today." The last word was delivered as though it was the first time he was going to Khasab's house.

Zain was suddenly reminded of why this Friday was a special day. It was Mushtaq's wedding day. A wedding in Minambur was a glittering, gala affair. Whether the bride and the groom were excited or not, Zain and his friends enjoyed the occasion, what with the *shabgosht* (the procession in the night where half the village was in attendance), the fireworks, the groom all decked up in a glittering pugree, a bright coloured sherwani, his face and half his body hidden behind the *sehra* and garlands of flowers, perched on a half-emaciated horse (emaciated because since the groom had never ridden a horse in his life, a healthy and well-fed horse may start rearing when the firecrackers go off and throw off the groom, an event devoutly to be avoided). The grand feast that followed—the pulao, the roast chicken, the multi-coloured sweets, and the post-nikah looting of the almonds, the dried dates and the sugar candies, were added attractions.

Zain wondered why his grandfather went to call on Khasab every Friday after the prayers even on a special day. Of course, they were good friends, but Nanajan had many friends in the village. He rarely, if ever, called on any of them. Zain suspected that he had some special business relationship with Khasab. Khasab was the richest man in Minambur and his house was the largest in Big Street. Big Street was not much bigger than other streets in the village, but all the rich landlords lived there. The main mosque too was located there. Khasab was the most respected elder in the village. The lazy citizens of Minambur felt that his real name of Khan Saheb was too long so they called him Khasab. Every time Zain passed through Big Street, he had seen Khasab sitting on his chabootra with his turbaned cronies, gossiping. As a big landlord employing a platoon of servants, he had nothing else to engage him. He was always dressed immaculately with a white pugree round his head, long white shirt, and white tight trousers that hugged his thin calves and bunched up at the ankles. He was very fair complexioned, with a handsome visage distinguished by an aquiline nose and a white beard.

For Zain, however, Khasab held a special interest. He was the man who enjoyed eating those large lizards that occasionally strayed into village houses from the shrubbery that grew on the outskirts. They grew to a size of almost two feet and his young aunt, Bajijan, had told him that thieves used the clinging capacity of these lizards to climb walls. The moment a couple of these large agile reptiles were spotted scuttling across the backyard, there would be a hue and cry in Zain's household. Shouts of "*pakdo, pakdo*" would resound from all directions, but no one needed to be told to catch the poor creatures. Half a dozen semi-clad padials would abandon whatever chores they were doing and scatter around in obedience to the shouted command, and with loud cries and much scampering around, capture the scurrying creatures which had taken refuge in the hay-stacker or thorny scrub. Zain would watch with a mixture of excitement and apprehension as the wriggling lizards, all of two feet in length, would be forced into a gunny sack to be later delivered to Khasab's house, with the compliments of Nanajan. As a *shafii* Muslim, Khasab could enjoy the meat of these lizards, but as a *hanafi*, Nanijan would puke at the mention of the word 'ghorpad'. The very word evoked visions of dried dung and farmyard manure in her mind.

Bajijan, his younger aunt had told Zain the day before that he would be going along with his grandfather to attend the upcoming wedding. The whole village, it seemed to Zain, was waiting for this event with bated breath. The Muezzin Sab, the thin grey-bearded old man, whose plaintive voice called the devout villagers to prayer five times a day from the big mosque, had come calling at their house weeks earlier. He doubled up as the village announcer who broadcast news of all momentous events and delivered all invitations. He had taken position in the open entrance of the house behind the reed screen with a long sheet of paper held in his thin scrawny fingers. The screen protected the ladies of the house from the prying gaze of passing strangers. Few houses in the village had wooden doors that could be barred. It was an open society.

The Muezzin had called out, "Peace be upon you. Is Zakir Hussain Sab at home? Is Khalilullah Sab at home?" That formal service of notice to the household heralded that a message of some importance was about to be delivered. The Muezzin Sab maintained an updated list of all the households that mattered, the navayata households. His livelihood came from that list. When not engaged in calling the worshippers to the mosque, he went about delivering wedding invitations and death notices. For this service, he was paid with a bag of rice at harvest time by each of the households. Much as he would have liked, the Muezzin was not allowed to make commercial announcements, which were better paying. A muezzin's religious standing would be impaired if he were to do that. Once or twice, he had made some such announcement on behalf of some shopkeepers. For days after that, he was not allowed to make the call for prayers. Zain recalled that when Macchi Mehmood brought marine fish from Arkonam twice or thrice a month, it was not the Muezzin Sab but Ratnam, the barber or his assistant, who announced it by beat of the drum.

On hearing the Muezzin's well recognised voice, Nanajan had responded, "Peace be upon you too; yes Muezzin Sab, we are here." Sitting on the string cot in the osara, Nanajan's baritone was loud enough to be heard by the Muezzin Sab across the expanse of the courtyard. Nanajan, of course, knew very well what the Muezzin Sab had come for. For the past several weeks, nothing else but the wedding had been discussed at the *khoot*, the village square, and the whole village was well aware of it. But there was a time-honoured ritual to be observed on such occasions and protocol had to be followed.

"Janab Kazim Hussainsab Shakir presents his humble salaams to Janab Zakir Hussainsab Shakir. The auspicious nikah of his dutiful son, the light of his eyes, Mushtaq Hussain Shakir has been fixed with Kareema Begum, the lucky-starred daughter of Janab Sultansab Ambarkhani on Friday, the 7th of *Shawwal* (tenth month of the Islamic calendar), after the Friday prayers. You are respectfully entreated to join him with your household and other members of your family on this auspicious occasion, and put him under your eternal obligation by your presence and by partaking of the humble repast laid out thereafter." While the long and ornately-worded message was ponderously delivered in a monotone, specially reserved for marriage invitations, Zain had silently crept up on the Muezzin Sab and was looking up at him with an interested stare. The pinched face of the muezzin and his thin long beard which bobbed up and down as he intoned the invitation always fascinated Zain. It reminded him of the famished goats that browsed on the edge of the water hole, on the way to the bathing tank. The sight of the Muezzin's goatee was always a treat for Zain. He would have liked to give a gentle tug at that scant growth to see how the man would react. But Zain stood in awe of the august calling of the Muezzin and the consequences that would ensue if he indulged in such sacrilege, both in this and the next world.

Unmindful of Zain's stare, the Muezzin Sab delivered the invitation in full and then desired to be informed whether Khalilullah Sab was at home. When Bapu acknowledged his presence, the Muezzin repeated the message in the same sing-song monotone to the delight of Zain. According to protocol, invitations had to be extended individually even if all the invitees were present in the same house. A collective invitation was considered an insult. If you clubbed a grown-up married son living with the father, it implied that you did not recognise his independent status. "What! You expect me to tag along with my father to your marriage? I am not a child anymore. I am the father of four!" The son would exclaim to the host. Death messages, however, could be delivered jointly to the household, in a different tone. On the latter occasions, the Muezzin Sab managed to inject a melancholic note in his doleful voice.

Zain had asked Bajijan why the Muezzin Sab had said that it was the marriage of Kazim Hussain's son when everybody in the village talked about the wedding of Nollai Manaigar's son. Bajijan had explained to him that Kazim Hussain and Nollai Manaigar were one and the same person. Kazim Hussain was his real name and he was the village munsif, magistrate of Karmandi, a neighbouring village—an important official of the gora sarkar, the white man's government. He had only one eye; either he had been born so or had lost one at birth, or through small pox, Bajijan did not know which. Since then, he had been known as Nollai (one-eyed), highlighting his disability, and when he became the village magistrate, he was called Nollai Manaigar, the one-eyed village magistrate. People did not call him Nollai Manaigar to his face, of course, Bajijan explained. That would cause great umbrage with dire consequences for the foolish culprit; but no one called him anything else behind his back.

The whey drops settling on his forehead reminded Zain that like Nanajan, he too would have to bear the torture of wearing a Turkish cap today. That's what a fez was called in Minambur—a Turki topi. He hated wearing that rough-edged headgear made of maroon felt stiffened with inside hardboard support that had no air holes for ventilation. Wearing that felt pill-box even for a few minutes made his head hot and sweaty especially in the humid weather of Minambur. Besides, the constant swinging of the dangling black tassel as he walked distracted him from whatever he was doing. After a couple of hours, the edges of the fez would become damp and limp with perspiration and the cap would keep slipping off. Ever so often, he would have to free his hand to replace it on his head; but then wearing a Turkish cap was the distinct mark of a devout well-to-do Mussalman. It distinguished you from all others.

"Yes, yes, I have already taken out your clean shirt

and pajamas, Dadabhai," Amanna replied to Nanajan testily. "Zain go and pick up your towel, soap and your lungi. Go with your uncle to the well and, mind you, come back soon. Don't dawdle there." Then raising her voice to a higher pitch so that her husband milking the cow under the peepal tree could hear her, she said, "Aji listen, you have to go to Nollai Manaigar's son's wedding. You must hurry up and finish the milking. You have to take the boy for his bath; don't let Zain remain too long in the water." His aunt believed that when he went with his friends for the bath, he always dawdled too long. There was some truth in that.

Zain doubted whether that admonition to hurry up in his chore would have any effect on Bapu, for Bapu was never in a hurry. He would not get up until he had milked the cow dry. His answer was a grunt faintly heard from the vicinity of the peepal tree. Zain was not quite sure whether it was his uncle's response, or the cow's. That was the problem, Zain thought. He was never sure of anything with his uncle, and that made life complicated. His uncle changed words, changed meanings, changed styles and even changed character. One moment, he would be all softness, love and affection and the next, he would be indifferent, cruel or downright sadistic. Zain recalled the time when he had returned from school and had demanded a blue eraser with a pink tip. His classmate had one just like that. Bapu had promised to get it for him from Gingee the next day but Zain had wanted it the same day, so he had thrown a tantrum. He had to have it before he went to school the next morning, and he would not stop sulking until he had the eraser in hand. So, Bapu had laboured down on the creaking old bicycle to Gingee and back, a distance of over six broken-surfaced miles to satisfy Zain's whim.

On the other hand, Zain also recalled the day when Bapu had taken him to the tank for his first lesson in swimming. He was just four and the sight of so much water frightened him. He was mortally afraid that he would drown and die if he entered the water. He firmly believed that one should not enter the water until one had learnt to swim. As Bapu waded into the deep, Zain had clung to his neck with all the strength of his tiny arms. "Look, I am holding you; you won't drown. Let go of me. Trust me, I'll hold you up as you swim," Bapu had tried to reassure him. But the wet and dripping Zain was in the grip of panic. He was in no condition to trust himself, much less trust anyone else. Bapu's assurance had only resulted in a tighter grip around his neck. Then Bapu muttering something under his breath had come out of the water, carried Zain up the steps and dropped him on the parapet unceremoniously.

As the relieved Zain was thanking God for his narrow escape, Bapu had unravelled a rope that was wrapped around his waist and tied one end of it around the waist of the struggling Zain. Then as an exasperated fisherman would throw back an unwanted fish caught in his hook, Bapu had thrown Zain back into the water. Standing on the parapet, with a cruel smile on his lips, Bapu had held the other end of the rope. "Now, come on, swim for your life. If you don't, I will let go of the rope." That was Bapu's way of teaching a four-year-old how to swim. Zain spent the rest of his life trying to learn breast strokes and to persuade himself to forgive his uncle who only taught him frog-stroke.

As Zain watched, Bapu continued to engage himself with the cow. He was least concerned with his wife's urgings to hurry up. In this case, Zain empathised with his uncle. He could not appreciate what all the hurry was about. The wedding in any case was to take place after the Friday prayers; that could be any time until the prayers at sunset or even thereafter. Weddings in the village in any case never took place at the announced time. The Qazi could not start the rituals until everybody, especially the close relatives had assembled at the venue, and they always turned out to be the last ones to arrive on the scene. They often chose to rake up long-standing grouses at wedding time, throw tantrums and refuse to stir out of their houses, just to draw attention to their importance and to generally make life miserable for the hosts.

The younger ladies of the household would be sitting behind the purdah, all dressed up, knowing fully well that eventually they would all go to the wedding, but not until the hosts had grovelled before the invitees and personally come to smooth their ruffled feathers. This was an occasion to air all old grievances and show the hosts who was master. The hosts had to leave the marriage venue, walk over to the uncle or cousin's house, practically fall at their feet and beg them not to spoil the happy occasion by remaining absent. "My nose would be cut if you don't come," the host would plead. If your "nose is cut" you lose face in the community. After much pleading, the uncle or cousin would come down from his high horse and condescend to attend the nikah. Until then, all other guests just dawdled around at the wedding venue. But they never minded the wait; after all, this happened at every wedding and such occasions provided grist to the gossip mill. Bapu's indifference to calls for hurrying up was therefore understandable. But then, Zain knew that unlike Bapu, Amanna was always in a hurry. She rushed about her chores as though someone was after her with a broom. Sometimes, Zain believed, she even rushed through her thoughts, even when she was churning the curd. Often, the rhythm of the gentle *slurrp-slurrp* sound would suddenly accelerate into a fast *slrrp-slrrp*, as though keeping pace with her rushing thoughts.

Zain's train of thought was interrupted by the clip-clop of Nanajan's returning pattens. Nanajan left the dusty pattens on the stone steps, dipped his *tambalu* (small pot) into the large earthen pot, drew up sufficient water to wash the pattens and his feet and returned to his room.

Zain could hear his grandmother's gentle snores from the swing on which she slept in the *dalan*. She did not like the bedroom, hot and humid and stuffy in the summer and rains, and cold and clammy in winter. Nanijan always woke up before the others so it was unusual for her to be sleeping so late, he thought. Once up, she would lie awake in her swinging bed waiting for the others to get up. If they did not, her impatience at such lethargy would drive her to rouse them. The others, of course, didn't appreciate this. Every morning, Zain would hear the squeaks of the rusty chains that held up Nanijan's swing before he heard any other sound. As he was wondering why Nanijan had not woken up yet, Bapu finished milking the cow and Adi brought in the *lagan*. The swirling white froth splashed out of the vessel as Adi climbed the two stone steps and came into the *osara*.

"Put it by the hearth and then light the stove. Be quick about it Adi; Dadabhai will want his tea soon." Amanna always called her father Dadabhai; so did Bajijan and Nanijan. In fact, everybody in the village also addressed his grandfather as Dadabhai.

"Dadabhai is a term of respect; it means Brother Grandpa," Bajijan had once explained. "Your Nanajan is the munsif of two villages. He is the head of the villages and no one can commit any crime because he watches over them. If anyone does anything wrong, he will send the *toti* to fetch him and punish him." The *toti* was the lowest level village official and was attached to the village munsif. He ran all the errands, looked after the cattle-pound, carried the village records on his head when the land revenue clerk came to the munsif's house and implemented all his master's orders. Obviously Bajijan was very proud of Nanajan and his authority, but Zain had noticed during his rambles in the village that not everybody held Nanajan in the same awe as Bajijan. He had even heard some villagers call him Khar Dada behind his back. His friend Fazlu had irreverently explained what it meant. "Your grandfather snores the loudest in the village, and when he snores he makes the sound—*khar, khar, khar*. So, he is called Khar Dada."

"How do they know that?" Zain had protested.

"Because they have heard him in the mosque when he was snoozing after prayers," he had said. That didn't sound very respectful to Zain, but he hadn't said anything more to Fazlu, nor had he mentioned it to Bajijan. It had been constantly dinned into his young ears that nothing derogatory should ever be spoken of the elders, even behind their backs.

Every member of the household was in awe of Nanajan except, of course, Nanijan. She didn't hold him in any respect at all. Nanijan had always nagged Nanajan as long as Zain could remember, but ever since she had gone blind, she had become even more querulous. While her handicap had confined her to the swing most of the time, it had given greater freedom to her tongue. She took out the frustration of her blindness and her immobility on all and sundry, mostly on Nanajan. She would sit dangling her feet and her body movements would rock the swing. So long as she remained awake, it would be gently swaying to and fro. Even if she didn't open her mouth, you knew that Nanijan was up from the regular squeaks of its rusty chains. But whenever she was angry or agitated, or wanted something done in a hurry which was most of the time, the squeaks would grow louder and irregular.

"Mampeta, Mampeta," she would call out to the servant-maid who looked after her. The maid belonged to the neighbouring village of Mampet and, therefore, was called Mampeta. No one knew her real name; that was not important in any case. The landlords of Minambur were not interested in the actual names of their serfs. The serfs were there to till the land, sow the paddy, peanuts or sugarcane, collect the harvest, thresh the grain, pound the unmilled cereal and put it into those large silos. Their wives and daughters served in the household of the landlord for a lifetime. They grew old along with the wives and daughters of the house.

"Mampeta, today I am going to take a bath." Squeak, squeak. "Mind you, heat enough water this time." Squeak,

squeak, the swing would add its emphasis. "Akbari, what is your father doing? Is he still asleep? Wake him up." Squeak, squeak. "And Mampeta find out whether Adi has taken out the cattle." Squeak, squeak. "Akbari, Akbari (that was Amanna's name), where has Zain gone? I haven't heard the brat's voice since morning. That boy is being spoiled silly by his grandfather; keep an eye on him." Squeak, squeak. (She refused to acknowledge even to herself that in spoiling Zain she had a greater role than her husband). All her staccato orders were not necessary. Her daughter very well knew that the old lady took her regular full bath on Fridays and Mampeta knew how much water was needed to be heated and to what temperature, then mixed with the cold water to bring it to the right temperature.

But this Friday morning there was no squeak from the swing. She wouldn't have slept so soundly had she known that Mushtaq was planning to run away from the village that very moment, and in a few hours the whole village would be in turmoil.

"Come Zain, let us go to the well," Bapu called out to Zain picking up his lungi, towel and plastic soap box. At last the hour had struck. Going to the tank before the sun rose fully was always a pleasure, except on Fridays. It was still the hour when the first feeble rays of the rising sun had not yet fully cleared the wisps of the morning mist. The yellow bell-shaped flowers on the upper branches of the peepal tree were gleaming like gold in the pale sunshine, and every drop of dew on the heart-shaped leaves reflected the slanting rays, a myriad diamonds gifted by the departing night for Zain's pleasure.

As he came out from the house onto the unpaved street, Zain saw that the day had already begun in the village. A couple of mats flitted across the dusty street raising miniature dust storms in their wake. This was a regular sight but mostly to be seen in the afternoons when the menfolk took their siesta after the noon prayers and the village streets were deserted. But a marriage, a death, or a birth always disrupted the normal routine and one could see several mats flitting across the streets at all odd times of the day. Zain knew that behind every reed mat there was a woman, sometimes more than one, intent upon crossing the street unseen by male eyes. Using a mat to screen yourself from the curious male glances was a more convenient way of veiling yourself than wearing a hijab or a chadar. Moreover, if you were visiting a neighbour, a mat came in handy to sit on without putting your host to the inconvenience of finding one for you. In any case, few households in the village had chairs and tables.

Zain could see only the knuckles of a feminine hand holding up the mat high up above the head. Many of the mats were proceeding to Nollai Manaigar's house, ostensibly to lend a hand in the wedding chores but in reality to share in the gossip of the day. Some curious ladies stood behind half-open doors even at this early hour and peered out hoping perhaps to glean something of moment and build up a juicy scandal of it. Bapu, of course, kept his eyes lowered, as behoved a God-fearing Muslim. It was a sin to look at strange women, even if they were half-concealed in the shadows of a closed door.

As they turned left crossing the path that led past the Muddy Pool into the paddy fields, Zain's nose twitched. The odour told him they were approaching the pond where the goats were slaughtered daily. In the far distance, Zain spotted a butcher returning from the pond with the first carcass of the day. Though he could not make out his features from the distance, this early it could be none other than Pyare. Pyare took great pride in the fact that he was always the first butcher of the day to be on the street corner, and the first to carve a seer of meat from the goat's haunch at sunrise. Even before any of his competitors had rubbed the sleep out of their goat's eyes, Pyare, clad only in a lungi tucked up and tied at the waist, would be hefting his squealing animal by its hind legs and making it ready for slaughter at the edge of the village pond. Having slaughtered the goat, Pyare would have flayed the skin, removed the entrails but leaving the liver, lungs, the spleen and the 'white bread' in place, would bring it to the street shop.

As Pyare drew nearer, Zain could see the skinned goat slung across his left shoulder, the quivering flesh gleaming pink in the morning rays. Under his right arm, Pyare carried three long bamboo staves, tied with coir rope at the top. When opened, they would form the tripod from which the carcass would be hung at the street side shop. His right hand held a large chopping knife and under his armpit were several sharp carving knives rolled into a dirty bundle. Zain always wondered where he carried the snuff box, for Pyare's flaring nostrils were always shedding the stuff copiously.

"Aside, aside," Pyare shouted to the passers-by. He leaned on the balls of his feet as he trotted forward balancing the quivering carcass on his shoulder. Zain was fascinated by the sight of the sinewy biceps and the pink perspiring muscles of Pyare's chest rippling in the sunlight, and the goat's carcass bobbing up and down. As they moved forward together, Zain could hardly distinguish where the goat ended and Pyare began. As they crossed each other, Zain could smell the stench of fresh blood mixed with the pungent body odour of Pyare's sweat—an unpleasant mix.

By the time Bapu and Zain reached the pool, a stream of butchers had passed them, each with a flayed goat slung across his shoulder. There was Aziz, Nausho, Abdul Qadir, Hafez and the Ajasthis-Mahmud and Samad. The ajasthis were lower down in the hierarchy of butchers, being butchers merely by profession and not by heredity. Amongst them too was Saifu, from whom Bapu bought his daily meat, brain, liver or occasionally trotters and tripe. None of the others appeared as full of life to Zain as Pyare. He was the one who made the loudest noises, the most pungent comments, and chopped the fastest mince. Sometimes, Bapu was the target of his barbed tongue. That is why perhaps Bapu did not like Pyare and he never bought any meat from him. "He is too conceited and he doesn't keep his insolent tongue under check," Bapu would say. "One day he is going to meet a bad end," which, eventually, Pyare did, but not for his caustic tongue.

By now, uncle and nephew had reached the village pond where the goats were slaughtered. The pond could not be by-passed as that lay right on the route. When there was no special occasion demanding a wholesale slaughter, the good Muslims of Minambur consumed around a score of goats a day. Rich or poor, every navayata had to have meat at least in one meal of the day. The poorer a navayata, the larger the number of meat dishes on his *dastar* (tablecloth), Nanajan had once remarked. Even Abdullah the water-carrier would rather forego a pair of sandals than sit down to a meal without meat. But this Friday, there were easily twice the normal number of carcasses being flayed. The bleating goats waiting their turn and the clamorous butchers competing for the narrow space near the pond raised a huge racket. The sight of the spurting blood and the stink of the offal and droppings were overpowering. To add to the cacophony, a murder of crows was landing, taking off and pecking at the bones and the offal with loud cries. A few vultures too were hopping around a little away hoping for some overlooked morsels with the village mongrels chasing them off. A crimson film spread gently over the muddy waters of the pond.

"Why are so many goats being slaughtered today Bapu?" Zain asked of his uncle.

"That is for Nollai Manaigar's son's wedding. The Manaigar has invited the whole of Minambur to the feast you know," said his uncle. A large quantity of meat was used in cooking the pulao. No Muslim wedding was ever sanctified without serving that delicious rice and meat concoction, it being the main dish of the wedding feast. Though Nollai Manaigar would serve whole roast chicken, shami kebabs, samosas with minced meat filling, brinjal bharta and other dishes, the guests came mainly for the pulao, especially pulao cooked in the large copper pots. Pulao cooked by the village bawarchi, Noorjahan, had a different taste altogether from what one cooked at home. On wedding days in the village, brain, liver, trotters, and especially tripe would be sold for a song, Zain knew. There were few takers for such superfluous offal on auspicious occasions. The crows, vultures and dogs had a feast, too.

As they took a turn to cut across the lush green paddy fields to climb the broad bund that would lead them to their bathing tank, Zain saw Qadeer Ahmad returning from his morning swim. A thrill passed through Zain as he saw his uncle-to-be, for Qadeer Ahmed was betrothed to Bajijan, his young aunt. Qadeer was in his early twenties—a tall, handsome young man with a thick crop of black hair, a lock of it curling on his forehead. His sharp nose and firm chin, clean shaven, gave evidence of his pure bred navayata ancestry. His bronzed complexion, a result of his outdoor life, glistened with perspiration. On Fridays, he wore his maroon Turkish cap tilted at a rakish angle with the black tassel hanging free. He was Bajijan's first cousin, but marriage between first cousins was the order of the day among navayatas. He had been a regular visitor to Nanajan's household until the betrothal; since then Nanajan had prohibited his visits. Zain had asked Bajijan why Bhaiju, that is what he called Uncle Qadeer, came to the house no more. Qadeer and Baji were lucky. They had seen each other, met and talked, although in the presence of elders, but most Muslim weddings were between couples who had never met each other, much less talked with each other. That was never done. Marriages were always decided by the families; the bride and the groom had no say in it.

At first Bajijan had appeared too embarrassed to answer the question. Zain did not know that mention of her fiancé before a prospective bride was taboo. No village girl could talk of her own marriage without being called a brazen hussy. Such boldness would be frowned upon by the elders. But Zain's innocent persistence forced her to overcome her reticence in the privacy of the backyard. "You see, I am to be married to him. You remember the *mangni*?" She had confided when no one was around. Of course he remembered the betrothal. How could he forget all those lovely sweets—the egg halwa, the gourd lozenges, the almond filigree sweet and other navayata delicacies? He particularly liked the nan khatai. The small cakes made of ground semolina mixed with thickened cream, almond paste and sugar literally melted in his mouth. He liked to hog the sweet and sour amrit phal—balls of sweet thickened milk mixed with dry curds, fried in butter, and doused in sugar syrup.

"Since I am to be married to your Bhaiju, we are not supposed to see each other until the wedding. That is why he doesn't come home anymore."

"But why?" persisted Zain in his ignorance of Muslim traditions. After all, Bajijan was all of fifteen going on sixteen. She was grown up enough to answer his question.

"Because that is the custom. Those who are engaged should not see each other until after marriage," she explained.

Zain tried to understand this conundrum. If a man and a woman could live together after marriage, why should they not even see each other until their wedding? Another mystery beyond his comprehension.

"You have got ready very early today, Qadeer. The

wedding is after the Friday prayer, you know," Bapu ribbed Bhaiju.

"If at all it takes place," said Bhaiju with a frown on his handsome face. This ominous remark halted Bapu in his tracks. Even Zain felt there was mystery behind the 'if' in Qadeer's remark.

"Why do you say that?" Bapu's curiosity was aroused at the shocking implications of Bhaiju's words. Nobody had heard of a marriage being cancelled after the Muezzan Sab had extended the official invitations, much less on the very day of the wedding. The only reason such a dire event could happen would be if the father or mother of either the bride or the groom died suddenly; even then, the simple nikah would take place without the festivities.

"Mushtaq is having second thoughts. He doesn't want to get married. He has suddenly developed cold feet and wants to call off the wedding. He informed the Manaigar sab late last night of his misgivings, and then he called me and some of his friends. You know that Mushtaq and I were in school together; we have been close friends for years. Manaigar wanted us to persuade him to go through with the nikah ceremony. We sat through the whole night trying to convince him. I left him a couple of hours ago to have my bath."

That was in character for Uncle Qadeer, his being called in on such an assignment. Uncle Qadeer was a great one for managing the affairs of others. Even as a young man, he was exhibiting signs of a natural leader and was always seen surrounded by half-a-dozen youthful hangers-on. As he grew older, he would revel in being called the nadar, a title highlighting his diplomatic skills and his ability to settle disputes. Zain held him in great affection mixed with some awe. Bapu, he could take for granted, but Uncle Qadeer was someone you could not fool around with. Zain recalled many an occasion when he had been spanked by Uncle Qadeer. There was that time when the circus had come to the village. He had gone with Fazlu to their camping ground. It was early morning and the acrobats were busy in their tents and no one was around at the tall cross-bars pegged to the ground with steel ropes. While Fazlu stood watch, Zain had pulled himself up to the bar, hand over hand on the tethering cable. Just as he swung free from the bar, he heard Fazlu's warning—"Your uncle is coming." In panic Zain had jumped down at the imminent risk of breaking his limbs. Luckily, he had landed on the deep sand spread below, and had sprinted home in record time. Sure enough, Uncle Qadeer had seen his acrobatics and had followed him home. It was Amanna's intervention that had saved him from a sound thrashing that day.

"Why doesn't he want to marry the girl?" Bapu asked. "Something wrong with her?"

"Oh, it's nothing to do with the girl. Mushtaq just does not want to marry anyone. He says he isn't ready to marry yet; he wants more time."

"Then why had he agreed in the first place?"

"It was his father. He did not consult Mushtaq. You know Nollai Manaigar; he takes everyone for granted. He can be very obstinate when he makes up his mind."

"Mushtaq is not a child. If he didn't want to get married, he shouldn't have waited till the day of the wedding to announce it. So much preparation already done! And what about all the money already spent by Sultan sab for his daughter's wedding? Who is going to pay for it?" asked Bapu. Qadeer remained silent. Obviously, he had no answer.

"So, what's going to happen now? Will you persuade Mushtaq?" Bapu thought highly of Qadeer's persuasive skills.

"Well, I wouldn't say he has melted, but he sounded less obstinate. Perhaps another session with him will do the trick," said Bhaiju with a note of doubtful optimism in his voice.

"I hope you succeed," said Bapu as he took Zain's hand and walked on towards the bund. That was a hope shared by one and all in the village. The news of Mushtaq's misgiving and the late-night session with his friends had already gone round the village. If the wedding did not come off everybody would be disappointed, not least the butchers. They stood to lose the most. It was doubtful if Sultan sab would pay for the unconsumed meat.

By the time Zain reached the village well, a crowd of bathers ranging in age from six to sixty milled around in various stages of undress showing off their fair navayata skin. The diesel pump's *chug chug,* was muted by the sound of the water gushing out of the large pipe. Some of the older men, with their dhotis tucked up into their loins, jostled each other for space below the water stream and were getting pummelled by the force of the jet. Others with bare torsos sat washing their vests in the field channel that took the water to the paddies. The younger boys were climbing out of the steep well, some in their birthday suits, some in their shorts, to dive again from the high parapet.

A group of dark-skinned padial boys hovered in the background with hungry, longing looks, but they were never allowed to use the same well used by the navayatas.

"The water would be defiled if those pariahs touched it," said Machchar Masood. It was well known in the village that he kept two mistresses from that community and had fathered six children from them.

For Zain, the morning swim in the large deep tank was the high point of the day. He took off his banian and shed his lungi fast, and standing on the edge of the parapet in his briefs, he looked down into the green waters. He could see some heads bobbing up and down in the depths. It was his friends splashing around. Some adults had withdrawn to a corner and one of them was smoking a beedi as he trod water. Taking a deep breath, Zain dived feet first from the gravelly parapet. That was the only way he knew how to dive, feet first. As he took the twenty-foot fall, the wind rushed away on both sides and the sound of the pump and the water gushing out of the pipe faded away. He was plummeting into the silence of the well and he felt exhilarated. He hit the water with a splash and went down deep, until he could hardly bear the pressure on his ears before angling upwards. It seemed like ages before he broke surface, his chest heaving and his mouth spluttering, and water streaming down his hair into his eyes. As he trod water to keep himself afloat, he cleared his eyes with one hand and saw Fazlu swimming a couple of feet away.

"What took you so long?" Fazlu asked, "I have been here since the last half an hour."

"Well, we met Bhaiju on the way. Bapu stayed back to chat with him," Zain replied.

"Why do you have to come with Bapu on Fridays? Why don't you come by yourself as on other days?" Fazlu asked.

"That's Amanna's orders. On Friday, Amanna thinks that we should come back early and get ready quickly to go for prayers. She doesn't trust me to do that if I am alone. Besides, today is Nollai Manaigar's marriage," Zain said.

"His son's marriage," Fazlu corrected. But the correction was lost on Zain as he had dived back under water. He tried to reach the bottom and pick up a handful of gravel. He could do that in summer when the crops had sucked out much of the water, but it was too deep after the rains to touch bottom. The pressure pushed him upwards. As he came up spluttering, he found Bapu too had joined them.

"Finish your bath; we have to go back," Bapu admonished. After half a dozen laps, they decided to go up. Zain swam towards the row of stones projecting from the wall of the well to form steps. He trod on those jutting slippery slabs with caution. Years of wet feet had ensured that the slabs were mossy. Also the crevices between the stones sometimes harboured poisonous creatures—snakes and scorpions. Saifu the butcher had once been bitten by a lurking cobra as he was climbing up and was saved only by a miracle. *Andhe* Molisab, the blind preacher who lived in the mosque, was the only one in the village who knew the charm which could cure scorpion and snake bites. It was he who had saved Saifu's life. Saifu had kept the Molisab supplied with free meat for one whole year. For many days after Saifu's misadventure, no one went to the well. But since no other well had clearer and fresher water, gradually the fear faded and bathing was resumed. A cobra was never found again but people still took care to tread those steps gingerly.

As they were walking back, Zain saw that the slaughter-pond had now been deserted. The butchers had left it for the vultures and crows to take over. They were having a feast, all unconcerned with what was happening in Sultan sab's household, fighting the village dogs for the offal and other rejects. Skirting the bank and holding his nose, Zain turned towards home. He looked down the long vista of the street already lined by the butchers' shops. The word shop was a misnomer. They all sat on their dirty gunny sacks as seats. Pyare, of course, was sitting right at the *khoot*, the cross-roads where Pool Street cut across the Link Street. That was a prime location.

Pyare sat, tailor-fashion, on a tattered piece of the gunny sack, matted with pieces of dried meat and blood. Placed in front of him was a rough-hewn log of wood, a cross section of a large tree. The remains of the goat hung from a hook tied at the top of the bamboo tripod. Apparently, the sales had been brisk. Next to him sat Naska Chutka, similarly ensconced. Everyone knew why he was called a 'Pinch of Snuff' but no one knew what his real name was. Even his parents had forgotten it. Then came Nausho; few really knew why he was called that. Some said that his mother had lovingly named him the 'bridegroom' when he was a child, but the uncharitable said it was because he was permanently in search of a bride with no one willing to give him his daughter in marriage—a bridegroom in waiting.

"Khallu Sab, Khallu sab," Pyare shouted knowing full

well that Bapu would not respond. "I have some excellent kapoora for you today, very cheap. This goat was very virile. He has serviced many ewes. His kapooras are really large. They will be very useful to you." There was a burst of laughter from all the butchers at this sally. This was a gibe at Bapu because he was childless. Now, Zain was very fond of goats' testicles. When fried with a pinch of salt and red peppers, they were delicious. Though Bapu too would have bought the delicacy, he didn't like the way Pyare was trying to insult him. Bapu bristled at the way his name was shortened and shouted across the street. "No, no, I don't buy from you. If I want anything I will buy from Saifu," but his voice was drowned in the clamorous haggling between the butchers and their score of customers milling around the shops. Some were taking away goat's heads, holding them by the horns or ears; some were carrying away a whole assembly of liver, heart, lungs, spleen and kidneys, the dripping blood marking the route from the shop to the house.

Zain ran ahead and darted into his house allowing Bapu to follow him at his own pace. The swim and the morning walk had made him quite hungry. He wanted to have his breakfast before going out to play. Today, the school was closed and his friends would all gather near the mosque in the Big Street. The adjacent graveyard was used by the boys as a playground. This was no time to tarry in the house. He found Amanna sitting in the stone-paved kitchen on a low ground-hugging stool. Zain stood in the doorless opening staring at his aunt who appeared unconscious of his presence. She was totally absorbed in breathing life into the obstinate embers of half-dried wooden chips used as fuel. Her dark hair and grey sari were flecked with specks of ash that her breath had stirred up through the *phukni*. The short iron pipe used to blow air into the hearth also came in handy as a weapon, as many a servant had found to his cost.

Though Mampeta or Kavaria could very well have taken up the kitchen chores, the menfolk would not eat anything cooked by low-caste maids; so Amanna had to spend a lot of her time in the kitchen. As Zain watched, the flames shot up in the hearth and flared out through the three open sides. His mouth watered at the thought of what was cooking in that clay pot that rested so precariously on the three projecting knobs of the hearth. Amanna had fried two goat's brains for him in clarified butter with onions, garlic, turmeric and chilli powder, and she served them to him in his favourite enamel plate. He gobbled them up with rice string-hoppers. As he rose to wash his hands in the drain that took the water out to the street, Bapu came back, excitement writ large on his face.

"Did you hear, Akbari Begum? The bridegroom has run away," he announced, his voice crackling with excitement.

"Who has run away?" Nanijan asked from her swing,

to the accompaniment of a loud squeak from the rusty chains.

"Is it that butcher?" She had woken up and was sitting with her legs dangling below the swing. The sharp tone of Nanijan penetrated into the gloom of Nanajan's bedroom and into his ears.

"What happened?" His booming voice sounded louder than necessary. Like most deaf men, he compensated the deficiency by raising his voice to a high pitch. As he emerged from his lair, Zain noted that Nanajan's clean-shaven head had droplets of perspiration and the upper part of his body was still bare. Two old cicatrices, where perhaps the village doctor had excised large carbuncles, glared angrily on his back.

"Nollai Manaigar's son has run away. They discovered it when they went to fetch him for the ritual wedding bath. He was nowhere to be found. Qadeer and his friends are still looking for him everywhere in the village," Bapu explained. His tone seemed to say, Ah, what a juicy scandal there is going to be in the village now! In his excited desire to suck the marrow from the juicy bones of the scandal, Bapu obviously forgot that now there would be no pulao, no roast chicken and no sweets!

"Why would he do such a thing?" Nanijan wanted to know. There was a note of piqued curiosity in her voice. "And who would hide him in the village?"

"He didn't want to get married; perhaps he had heard

some rumours about the girl," Bapu ventured. Every time an engagement was broken off in the village, suspicion always fell on the character of the girl.

"Nothing like this has ever happened in Minambur before. What is the world coming to?" Nanajan's shocked voice demanded to know.

"And don't say anything about the girl; I know her and she is the most innocent and sweet girl," Nanijan admonished.

"Where could he have gone, if he is not in the village?" Amanna, practical as ever, homed in on the issue that really mattered. "Call Qadeer here, Zain. Go and fetch him." She knew that Qadeer would know more of the matter than anyone else.

The excitement in the house had affected Zain also. Amanna's order now made him a part of the adult games. He ran out of the house without waiting for a repeat command. He could see that everybody in the street had heard the news. People were huddled together in groups, at street corners and before shops, gossiping about the runaway bridegroom. All buying and selling had come to a standstill to the dismay of the butchers and other shopkeepers. Even the sound of the butchers sharpening their knives on the whetstones was muted. Half-chopped chunks of meat lay abandoned on the blocks, looking forlorn. The hungry street dogs crept up unnoticed closer to the unattended meat. Speculation was rife on every tongue. What could have made Mushtaq sneak off in the middle of the night? Zain wondered as he ran towards the khoot.

Zain knew Mushtaq well, as a close friend of his uncle Qadeer. Mushtaq was a handsome, shy young man, fair complexioned and soft-spoken. He usually avoided the rough and tumble of the village life. He was rarely seen at the khoot, or with the young men who played cards on the chabootra of Chhote sab's house. Even when he came to the bathing well, he was too shy to take off his shirt and dive into the water. He would always climb down into the well, never dive in, and he would be wearing his vest and shorts. Zain had never seen him go across the slaughter pond. He would always take a different route. "I can't stand the stench," he had once remarked. But Zain knew that more than the stench, it was the blood and gore that put him off. Mushtaq always got along well with the village kids; all Zain's friends liked him.

As Zain turned right at the khoot towards the Link Street, he wondered where his friends were. His own guess was that they must have gathered near the cemetery at the Big Mosque. They were sure to have seen Bhaiju around and he would find out from them where he was. Sure enough there was Fazlu, Raheem Basha, Nazir and Kauser, all leaning against the crumbling wall of the maqbara. The arched open enclosure that served as family mausoleum of Zain's ancestors was a favourite gathering place of the village boys.

The first thing Zain did when he reached the maqbara was to greet his dead ancestors with a 'salaam alaikum', as taught to him by his grandpa. It would never do to show disrespect to your ancestors, dead or alive.

"Have you seen Bhaiju anywhere?" he asked his friends.

"Sure, he is inside the mosque talking to his friends," Kauser said.

Zain darted into the mosque, climbing the rough stone slabs that formed the steps in a couple of strides. He noticed Bhaiju standing with Machchar Mahmood, Machi Nazir, Altaf and others near the ablution tank. A few worshippers were washing their feet in preparation for offering some supererogatory prayers. "Ah, here comes a summons from your sasural," Machchar Mahmood teased Qadeer Ahmed. "You better go when your mother-in-law calls." It was not for nothing that he was called the mosquito. With his piercing tongue, he could get under anybody's skin. On the other hand, Nazir had gained the title of 'fish' because he used to go to Marakkanam on his bicycle once a week to bring sea-fish and prawns for sale in the village. Sea-fish was a delicacy and highly priced. The villagers could get murrels, large and small eels, small catfish, silver backs, etc. from the lake and their own private tanks. Pomfrets, seer fish, bass, prawns and other salt-water fish had to be brought from the coastal towns, some distance from the village.

"Bhaiju, Amanna wants you to come home." Zain tugged his uncle's sleeve. Qadeer heard him but the mosquito's sting was still smarting. He had to show that he had more important things on his mind than to run home at the call of his prospective in-laws. He stood talking to his friends as though he didn't have to answer the call.

"Altaf, you get the bicycles ready. I think Mushtaq has left the village. We have to pursue him, find him and bring him back. This is a question of the honour of the village. We will never be able to live down this scandal. As it is, Minambur has been producing more scandals than we could consume. If we don't bring him back, our nose will be rubbed in the dust and we will be the laughing stock of Madras for years." And Bhaiju could never stand that. "I will be back in a few minutes. Ammabua has called me; I don't know what for." Zain knew, but he didn't want to enlighten his uncle.

When Bhaiju reached the house, Zain noted that the osara was now occupied by a number of middle-aged ladies, some of them hanging around with their mats rolled up under their arms. His Bajijan had taken refuge in the bedroom. There was Ghud ki Khatoon who lived by the manure yard, Khadde ki Batul who lived near the stagnant pool, Begum Jan whose house was just across and many others. It was apparent they had come in response to summons from Amanna. Similar gatherings must be taking place in the neighbouring houses, Zain surmised. The village ladies had rarely come across such a juicy event before and they were flocking together hungrily to get every bit of malicious pleasure out of the scandal.

"Mushtaq is too soft for Kareema; she has always been a handful for Sultan Sab," said Ghud ki Khatoon.

"Perhaps, that is why he chose Mushtaq for a son-in-law. He wanted someone who would be under his daughter's thumb," said Begum Jan, taking out a paan leaf from the silver box kept in the centre of the receptacle. She dried it of the adhering moisture with the soiled hem of her sari, took out some scented lime, applied it to the leaf, put in a pinch of betel-nut, rolled it into a cylinder and carefully placed it in her mouth.

"But Samdani would not have let that happen. She makes up for all the softness of her son. You know how she treats Nollai Manaigar's mother. The old lady dare not open her mouth before her daughter-in-law. Most of the time, she is exiled to the dark alcove of the osara. That nollai never says a word. He just sits and listens when his wife is tearing into his mother," contributed Rahima Bi. She was in a position to know for her backyard adjoined Nollai Manaigar's.

"She doesn't even spare her husband, I believe. One day I heard she took a broomstick to him," came from Begum Jan.

"No, it was the *phukni*," said Ghud ki Khatoon, correcting Begum Jan as though it was of vital importance to distinguish between a broomstick and a blower pipe.

"Do you think Mushtaq ran away from the marriage because of that," asked Amanna. "After all, Samdani and Kareema in the same house would have made life hell for him."

And so the gossip went on.

It was approaching noon. The midday sun had driven away most of the butchers from the street. Even the dogs that were fighting over the bones and offal strewn around the stony street had abandoned their fight and were sitting around listlessly panting with their tongues lolling out. Bhaiju pulled out the towel that every man of Minambur carried flung on his left shoulder, and wiped the perspiration from his forehead. Nanajan had already got ready for the mosque. He had put on his fresh shirt, the rolled gold buttons in his collar reflecting his pride in being well dressed. He had not worn the Turkish cap. Perhaps Amanna had forgotten to brush it in all the excitement. His shaven head was instead covered by a large white pugree. Bapu also had changed into a fresh shirt, with his cap set at a rakish angle, gold buttons gleaming at the collar and gold cufflinks flashing in the sunlight. Even though pious Muslims were not supposed to use gold in rings and cufflinks, vanity often overcame the dictates of religion.

"So where is Mushtaq? Did you find him?" Bapu asked Bhaiju, as he got ready to go for prayers.

"No, he is not in the village; I think he has run away to Tindivanam. He will try to take the train from there to go to Madras; he has his uncles living there. He may go and hide with them. Tindivanam is five hours by bicycle. If we start now, and if he has stopped anywhere on the way to rest we can still get him before he reaches Tindivanam."

For Bhaiju and his friends, bringing back Mushtaq to the wedding hall was more imperative than attending Friday prayers. After all there were many Fridays in a year, but a bridegroom ran away but once.

"Why do you want to bring him back, the poor fellow?" Amanna said. "If the wretch doesn't want to marry, why force him? Why don't you let him be?"

"We can't do that; Mushtaq has to be brought back. Nollai Manaigar has threatened to kill himself if the marriage doesn't take place. Samdani Begum has shut herself up in her room and is refusing to come out. And what about all the meat and masalas rotting in the yard? Sultan sab will be ruined with having to pay for the feast which will be cancelled. Do you see the vultures hovering around in the skies? We can't have the marriage cancelled; we have to find Mushtaq," Bhaiju pleaded. He was always a stickler for honour and propriety. "I don't want to force him for he is my friend, but it is a question of our collective reputation." The reputation of the village and saving face all round was of great concern to all navayatas at all times.

After Bhaiju had left, Bapu, Nanajan and Zain proceeded to the Big Mosque in the High Street. The Big Mosque was called big, not because of its size alone, but because it was located in upper Minambur. Upper Minambur was where the navayatas lived. They claimed that they were the direct descendants of the Arab clan which migrated to India in the 8th century from Iraq. Lower Minambur which started from below the Pool Street was not even acknowledged to be a part of the village by the navayatas. They called it Palliampet, as though it was a separate village which had nothing to do with Minambur. Those who lived in Palliampet were not navayatas. They were darker in complexion and observed different cultural practices. They too must have come from somewhere, but no one in Minambur knew or cared; and no one talked of them either. There was hardly any social intercourse between Minambur and Palliampet.

The Palliampetans had a mosque of their own. It was located at the end of the Link Street and was called *Phadyan ki Masjid* (the Palm Leaf Mosque), for it was roofed with palmyra leaves. It had no dome or minarets like the Big Mosque. No navayata except one ever went to pray there, but then Hujjat al Kekdi was not a true navayata; at least Nanajan said so. Some even doubted his pedigree. Salvation for navayatas was to be found only in the Big Mosque. Let the hoi polloi and the dakhnis find God in the Palm Leaf Mosque if God were to be found there!

The Big Mosque was crowded this Friday. Everybody from upper Minambur was there—every navayata from the age of six up. Many of the worshippers had come not so much to pray but to see whether Sultan Sab and Nollai Manaigar would be brazen enough to show their faces to the congregation. Would they show any signs of shock or sorrow? Most had come to learn what would happen to the evening feast. Even Hujjat al Kekdi had abandoned the Palm Leaf Mosque and for once had decided to stand with his tribe, and add to the confusion and consternation with his convoluted arguments. Hujjat claimed he was a navayata, though his crazy actions belied that claim or rather affirmed it. He took malicious pleasure in scandalising the navayatas by praying in the Palm Leaf Mosque and consorting with the Palliampetans. He attended their social gatherings and he had even sent his son to Umrabad for education, an act which no self-respecting navayata could countenance.

No dyed-in-the-wool Navayata wanted to have an Umrabadi molvi in his household, for many of those who returned from the seminary kept mistresses from the villages of Kavarai, Shittampundi, Mampet, etc. The navayatas called them the quibbling crabs for they held many radical views and rarely kept them to themselves. Hujjat al Kekdi enjoyed relaxing on the chabootra of his house and airing his views to anyone willing to listen and argue with him; and there were always some who did. He once raised the hackles of the whole village by claiming that it was actually better to join the congregational prayers late than come in time. He argued that one earned greater merit by performing the additional obeisance prescribed as penalty for late comings. At the height of this controversy, Nanajan, who was an active participant, had said, "This man is impossible. Once he gets his verbal claws into a piece of rotting argument, he never lets go. He is a quibbling crab." The name stuck. Thereafter, he was called Hujjat-al-Kekdi.

The Imam Sahib conducted the prayers in a sombre, subdued mood. He, too, seemed affected by the events of the day. For once he breezed through the qutbas and recited the shortest suras from the Quran. His short prayer invoked Allah's help for Kazim Hussain Shakir and Sultan sahib Amberkhani and their families in this hour of trial. As Zain came out of the mosque, he saw the curious congregate in the street and on the chabootras. They sat there patiently talking in low tones, waiting for something to happen.

As the day wore on, a certain listlessness set in. Even the mats stopped flitting across the streets. The village was in suspended animation.

It was late afternoon when a triumphant Bhaiju and his jubilant friends returned from their successful foray. They had the fugitive Mushtaq in tow. They had found him fourteen miles away on the bank of a wayside lake. He had parked his bicycle on the shoulder of the highway, and tired out by his night vigil and long drive, had gone to sleep under a tamarind tree. That was his undoing. Perhaps he had not anticipated that a village posse would come after him in hot pursuit, otherwise he would not have parked his bicycle in full view of the road and gone to sleep. The whole village had turned up to see the return of the reluctant bridegroom.

Most heaved a sigh of relief. All that meat and those sweetmeats going waste would have been such a shame! They were sure that the wedding would now take place even if Mushtaq had to be brought to the *masnad* in chains. The two families of the bride and the groom were bent upon it, and the whole village supported them. After all, everyone was looking forward to the feast of pulao and roast chicken with the zarda to follow—so what if a reluctant bridegroom was being compelled to marry! Hadn't many a reluctant and unwilling bride been beaten by her parents to acquiesce in marrying a widower or a divorcee or even a disease-afflicted groom? He had no business being reluctant in the first place. Did he not owe a duty to his parents to honour their choice? Did he not owe any responsibility to the village to "uphold its honour?" And what about all those poor butchers, whose meat would have had to be fed to the dogs? As Mushtaq was being led to his house, Zain observed that his clothes were covered in dust and he looked tired and haggard. He had the look of a shackled slave, recaptured after a failed attempt to escape, being led to a severe flogging.

That afternoon, Amanna made Zain wear a new shirt and the Turkish cap which he hated so much. Nanajan and Bapu took him by a hand each and marched him to the wedding venue, as though he was the one who had run away in the first place. Zain was unhappy; he wanted to go with his friends and not be frog-marched between Nanajan and Bapu.

The enormous house of the Manaigar was overflowing with men, women and children, all in their best clothes. The women were, of course, segregated in a different part of the house, and they were all hidden behind screens. The bride was sitting in their midst, heavily bedecked in gold jewellery and tonnes of jasmine flower garlands. Her cheeks were glowing with *rez* (powdered gold leaf), and her teeth were blackened with *missi*, the powdered organic dye with which all brides had to be adorned. Many of the men were squatting on cotton durries spread out in the street, with eager looks. The village *Qazi*, in his white pugree and black cloak had already arrived and was occupying centre stage.

As Zain and his guardians took seats, the bridegroom

was led in by his friends. They looked more like jailors than his well-wishers. He came shuffling in, held up by the sturdy hands of his brothers-in-law. He was wearing tight white trousers and a long brown coat, the traditional attire of the bridegroom, but the heavy and closely-woven sehra, made of roses, jasmine and silver filigree veiled his face and chest Those curious to see his looks, and to gauge his feelings from his expression were disappointed. He was helped to sit down by the side of the Qazi. Manaigar flanked him on the other side. After a short Arabic prayer, the Qazi Sab raised his voice and hushed the audience into silence. All ears were eager to hear the proposal and its acceptance—the central ritual of the marriage. The Qazi Sab intoned the formal offer for acceptance by the bridegroom. "Kareema Begum, the virgin daughter of Janab Sultan Sab Ambarkhani is being given to you in marriage with the consent of her vakil Janab Abdur Qadir Sayeed and witnessed by Janab Abdul Rahman Sayeed and Aslam Hussain Aglay, for a dower of thirty-nine tolas of gold and eleven thousand rupees to be paid to the bride on demand after consummation. Do you Mushtaq Hussain Shakir, son of Janab Kazim Hussain Shakir, accept her in wedlock?" The Qazi Sab's soft voice ended on a questioning note. Every ear strained to hear Mushtaq's "I accept" but instead, it was his father's loud voice that proclaimed that he had accepted.

The vakil and the witnesses had earlier waded into the

packed concourse of ladies and obtained the consent of the bride. So, they informed the Qazi. The acclamations of "mubarak mubarak" from the relatives and friends that sat close to the bridegroom broke the hush and drowned out the rest of what the Qazi sab had to say. Even his prayers for the long and happy married life of the couple, as happy as that of Adam and Eve, Abraham and Sarah, Moses and Zipporah, Yusuf and Zulaikha, Ali and Fatima and the Holy Prophet and Khadija, could not be heard in the din. The ritual was over and all the guests lifted their hands and joined in the unheard prayer.

The moment it was over, several relatives of the groom brought out trays filled with dry dates, walnuts and sugar candies. These were flung by the handful amongst the guests. For Zain and his friends this was the high point of the wedding ceremony—the scramble for the dates and walnuts, catching them in mid-air, snatching them from the laps of the neighbours and treading on the toes of friends and strangers to grab as many as one could. Later they would compare who had got the largest number, date for date, walnut for walnut. The excitement of those five minutes would last till the next wedding.

The dinner was served on fresh clay plates. Every household maintained a couple of hundred of them stored in the loft high up above the dalan. Whenever there was a wedding in the village, servants would be sent around to borrow them from all the neighbours. The village potter was kept busy firing his kiln to mass produce these plates. So, any shortfall could always be supplemented by new ones from the kiln. Zain never liked to eat in the clay plates even after they were washed. A peculiar odour overpowered the aroma of pulao—the smell of baked earth and of wet new bricks after the first rains put him off. He ate little. All the evening's excitement had tired him out and he was feeling drowsy.

Saturday morning, Zain woke up to the sound of the churning curd. His eyes reluctantly opened to absorb the rays of the morning sun. He must have overslept, he thought, for Amanna already had two large dripping mounds of butter by her side. She had almost finished her morning's work. Bapu had already milked a cow whose dry udders were being unsuccessfully sucked by her calf. Zain sat up and glanced at the wooden pattens. They were wet, so his grandfather had already been to the toilet and back. Nanijan was sitting on the swing which was squeaking wildly. She was obviously quite agitated about something.

I have to go to school today, Zain thought with dismay. I won't have time to go for my bath to the tank.

"You don't have to go to school today," Amanna said, as though reading his mind. She had an uncanny ability to know when he was awake, and when he was pretending to be asleep.

"Why not?" Zain asked, a note of relief in his voice.

"Because the school will be closed today," she said. The school closed only on Fridays or when there was a special occurrence like the visit of the Sub-Collector or the Inspector of Schools. So why was the school closed on a Saturday?

Just then he heard the Muezzin-Sab's voice at the entrance.

"Are Janab Zakir Hussain Shakir Saab and Janab Khalilullah Saab at home?" The Muezzin Sab paused. No one from the house answered; they all perhaps knew the message he was about to deliver. Some news travelled very fast by word of mouth even before the Muezzin Sab came to announce it formally. The Muezzin Sab too did not wait for a response. In his doleful voice, reserved for such occasions, he intoned the short and succinct notice, with no ornate adjectives. "Janab Kazim Hussain Saab sends his salaams. His son, Janab Mushtaq Hussain Shakir left for his heavenly abode last night. The funeral will take place after the noon prayers and he will be buried in the Maqbara."

It was years later that Zain learnt how Mushtaq had died, and more importantly why? Mushtaq had left a note behind him. He was impotent.

******

For many days after Mushtaq's funeral, his tragic death

continued to haunt the village memory, but nobody ever took his name in private or public. They were all suffering from a deep sense of unacknowledged guilt.

Had Mushtaq died a natural death, the Manaigar would have held a *fatiha* ceremony at his house on the fortieth day of his death, with the whole village invited to a repast of pulao and lentil gravy. But since Mushtaq had died in such tragic circumstances, Zain never learnt how for a long, long time, the Manaigar only invited some of the elders (men and women), to come and recite the Quran at his house. Of course, the pulao had to be prepared and distributed to the poor and the near and dear.

"It's horrible," exclaimed Nanijan when a servant brought a large bowl of pulao to the house, "as though we are going to eat the pulao of that poor boy's *chehlum* (fortieth day ceremony)."

"They actually killed him," said Amanna, and quoted a popular saying—'*Jiye pe jalaye, mare pe palaye*' (torturing him when alive and lamenting him when dead).

It took many days for the death of Mushtaq to fade from Zain's memory, as he had felt a special affinity to Mushtaq, the shy and reclusive young man.